DESERT HEAT

Janice Sims

ARABESQUE

★BET BOOKS™

BET Publications, LLC
http://www.bet.com
http://www.arabesquebooks.com

ARABESQUE BOOKS are published by

BET Publications, LLC
c/o BET BOOKS
One BET Plaza
1900 W Place NE
Washington, D.C. 20018-1211

All Kensington Titles, Imprints, and Distributed Lines are available at special quantity discounts for bulk purchases for sales promotion, premiums, fund-raising, and educational or institutional use. Special book excerpts or customized printings can also be created to fit specific needs. For details, write or phone the office of the Kensington special sales manager: Kensington Publishing Corp., 850 Third Avenue, New York, NY 10022, attn: Special Sales Department, Phone: 1-800-221-2647.

First Printing: September 2003
10 9 8 7 6 5 4 3 2 1

Printed in the United States of America

This book is dedicated to the teachers and the scientists who have inspired me all my life. Educators like Dr. G. W. Mingo of the University of Florida. Scientists like Dr. Sylvester J. Gates, and Dr. Shirley Ann Jackson. It's also dedicated to the memory of Dr. Warren Elliot Henry who has been called the greatest African-American physicist. To the memory of Willie Hobbs Moore, the first African-American woman physicist. Also to Drs. Arlie Petters, Cynthia R. McIntyre, and Valerie Bennett. I would never have been able to dream up the characters in this story if I hadn't first known of your existence. Bravo!

ACKNOWLEDGMENTS

To my editor at Kensington Publishing, Chandra Sparks Taylor, thank you for letting me be myself! A big thank-you to Karen Thomas who really cares about her authors. Also to the editorial staff at Kensington Publishing: You guys have seen me through twelve projects. I'm truly grateful for your expertise.

Before I get too mushy, let me say how much I appreciate Kicheko Driggins at BET Books. She works hard for the Arabesque authors.

Whenever science makes a discovery, the devil grabs it while the angels are debating the best way to use it.

—Alan Valentine

When you are courting a nice girl an hour seems like a second. When you sit on a red-hot cinder a second seems like an hour. That's relativity.

—Albert Einstein

These are the reasons
I love you, she said:

Warm skin on warm skin.
Clean breath tickling the back of my neck.
Muscular thighs rubbing against mine.
Urgent, passion-filled words whispered in my ear.

You listen to me, even though you're
tired and want to tell me about *your* day.
When you ask, "How are you?"
you really want to know.

You check the oil in my car without being asked
because you want me to be safe.
The way you hold me: Your hands on my hips.
Hard body pressed firmly to my soft curves.

You look up and smile at me whenever I enter a
room,
and it makes me feel like I've been missed.
You touch me every chance you get because,
Heaven knows, you can never touch me enough.

In reply, he said:
You are my lover, my friend, my *life*.
You're the reason I will boldly dare to try anything,
believe everything is possible.

The day you walked into my life,
doubt left by the back door.
I can face *anything* this world throws at me,
as long as I can come home to you.

Should the gates of hell
imprison you, I would storm the ramparts
of the Dark Kingdom to rescue you.
There is *nothing* I would not do for your love.

—*The Book of Counted Joys*

One

"Miss Matthews!"

Katharine Matthews spun around to see Dr. William Allen smiling at her. He must have followed her from the ballroom where the award ceremony for the Twenty-second Annual Nuclear and Particle Physics Conference had been held. Kate felt slightly irritated because she had hoped she would be able to avoid any uncomfortable questions about her father's condition. She was at the conference only as a stand-in for him. Her father, Dr. David Matthews, had been honored for making The Discovery of the Year, but due to poor health had not been able to attend the ceremony tonight.

Kate squinted at Dr. Allen, trying to remember what his specialty was. She *knew* she had read several of his scientific papers. She tossed her heavy fall of blue-black hair behind her with a quick flick of a finger, and returned his smile.

By now Dr. Allen, grinning even wider, was directly in front of her.

He was around her height, five-eight. He appeared to be in his mid-thirties, had medium brown skin and a receding hairline. "Dr. Allen, hello," Kate said. Then, she remembered. "I've read several of your excellent papers on strings and singularities."

Dr. Allen's eyebrows arched in surprise. In his opinion,

beautiful women were rarely interested in science. At any rate, he saw no reason for chitchat, when it was information he was after, and the sooner he got it, the better. "Is it true your father's research has been put on hold indefinitely?"

Kate felt her stomach muscles clench. Not only did she find his closeness offensive, but his question had been put to her rather bluntly. Besides, she saw no concern for her father in his keen brown eyes. What she saw was morbid curiosity.

He must have read her annoyance in her gaze because he smiled again, and said, "I mean, it would be a pity for your father to have come so far with his research and then fail to see his theories proven."

"That's the chance all scientists take, isn't it?" Kate said, smiling too. "But, I can assure you, Dr. Allen, my father is recovering nicely, and he'll be back to work very soon."

That was the pat answer she'd been told to give to all inquisitive parties.

"Now, if you'll excuse me, I have a plane to catch."

To her absolute astonishment, Dr. Allen reached out and grasped her upper arm. For a scientist, he had a strong grip. "Your father would do well to turn over his research to an able-bodied scientist who can complete his work. The world does not stop spinning just because one man falls ill. His discovery is too important to be put on the back burner out of sheer egotism. Tell him that for me. He knows me well. Even if he doesn't *like* me, he must respect my work and realize that if anyone can bring his theories to fruition, I can."

With that, he released her. "You may go now," he said smugly.

Why did he have to touch her? Kate was many things, a loyal daughter, and sister. A competent science writer who had a doctorate in physics but had eschewed the life of a scientist in favor of a more free-spirited existence.

What she *wasn't* was someone who could be pushed around.

Dr. Allen had turned his back on her, preparing to walk away.

Kate went to stand in front of him. Nailing him with a cold stare, she said as she repeatedly stabbed her index finger into his chest, "I don't care who you are. Do not *ever* put your hands on me. And don't hold your breath waiting on my father to hand over his hard-earned research to you. If you want to be the first to make 'teleportation' a household word, then get off your butt and do the work!"

Dr. Allen trembled with outrage. His nostrils flared. His eyes narrowed.

Kate was not concerned until she saw his right hand raised in a fist, and swiftly coming toward her face. *Ah, you can never judge a book by its cover,* she thought. Dr. Allen looked like a pacifist, but apparently had a hair-trigger temper.

Kate stepped back, automatically assuming a fighter's stance for maximum equilibrium. However, before Dr. Allen could throw a punch, someone caught his arm by the wrist and said in a thick Boston accent, "I wouldn't do that if I were you, old man. Kate here might look harmless, but she has a black belt in karate and can kick your hindquarters up and down this lobby."

It was her father's best friend, and her godfather, Dr. Jason Edmonton. She thought she'd left him at their table deep in conversation with an attractive calculus instructor from Howard University. Jason was a confirmed bachelor at fifty-two, claiming that his work was his mistress.

"Dr. Edmonton, I assure you I was not about to strike

this young woman," Dr. Allen denied, embarrassed. He wrenched his arm free of Jason's grasp, and gingerly rubbed his wrist. Anyone looking on would have assumed he was the wounded party.

Jason shot Kate a questioning look.

"I was preparing to defend myself," she said by way of an explanation. "Dr. Allen didn't like the fact that I had a problem with his manhandling me."

"I did no such thing," Dr. Allen denied vehemently. "I only suggested that her father should do the altruistic thing and turn over his research to someone who can complete his work. Then, she turned on me!"

Kate slung her shoulder bag farther up on her shoulder and raised the sleeve of her blouse, showing Jason the imprint of Dr. Allen's fingers on her copper-colored skin.

Jason glared at Dr. Allen. "She didn't do that to herself!"

"Well, I most certainly didn't do it to her. However, I'm positive my chest will be bruised black and blue from her poking me in it with those bony fingers of hers."

Kate narrowed her eyes at him. Then she turned her gaze on Jason.

"I'm leaving now, Jason. Like I told this fruitcake before he grabbed my arm to detain me, I have a plane to catch."

"Oh, that's right, you're returning to Tucson tonight," Jason said. He moved closer and bent to place a kiss on her temple. "Have a safe trip. And no more fights, all right?"

Kate aimed another poisonous glance at William Allen, which he returned; then she left the two of them standing where they were. If her mother had witnessed the scene, she would have told Kate she should have popped the uppity Dr. Allen at least once.

Kate smiled at the notion as she hurried toward the

bank of elevators that would take her upstairs to her room where she could collect her already-packed bags. Her mother, Carolina Huerta Matthews, was a Pascua Yaqui Indian. Her mother didn't like using the term "Native American." In her opinion, she'd been an Indian long before the politically correct term ever surfaced. Besides, "Native American" could apply to any number of American Indian tribes. Though she embraced all of her Indian brethren, she was uniquely Pascua Yaqui Indian.

Carolina believed in knowing who your people were, and being proud of where you came from. That's why she and David had immersed their four children in both African-American culture and Pascua Yaqui Indian culture.

The reason Kate knew her mother would have advocated physically assaulting Dr. Allen was that Carolina was a staunch feminist. She would probably have thought giving Dr. Allen a black eye would make him think twice before putting his hands on another woman without her permission.

Kate, however, wasn't the martial arts dynamo that Jason had made her out to be. Her godfather had been pulling Dr. Allen's leg. Jason had a wicked sense of humor. Kate was tough, though. Years of being taunted by bullies in school had made her that way. Her high school years had been the worst. There was no crueler human being than a teenaged girl who felt threatened by you because of some imagined infraction of the "rules teenagers live by." Kate was picked on because she was smart. She was picked on because she refused to join the "cool girls" clique she'd been invited into. The date of her ten-year high school reunion was coming up soon. She wasn't going to attend.

* * *

"Are you serious?" Rafael Grant grumbled.

He was on the phone, hunched over his desk in the offices of the U.S. Marshals Service in Tucson. "Make up your mind, Jenny. Either you're coming this weekend, or you're not. I don't have time for your usual flighty behavior."

"Flighty!" Jenny, his younger sister by seven years, yelled. "You're still miffed because I chose to become an actor rather than use my college degree for something that brings in a steady paycheck, like you wanted me to. Controlling, that's what you are, big brother. Hey, at least I'm using my journalism degree."

"Writing scripts," Rafe said, not convinced she was putting her degree to good use. "Scripts that never get read by anyone, except you."

"One day I'm going to send one of them to a major honcho at a major studio, and then you'll see I haven't been wasting my time."

"Let's not get off the subject," Rafe said, aware of the fact that Jenny changed the subject whenever she felt as if she were on the hot seat. "Are you coming, or not?"

"I'll be there," Jenny hedged. "If I can finish shooting my scenes in time to make my flight, that is."

"I see," Rafe said. He really didn't see, he was just rolling with the flow, which was the best thing to do when dealing with Jenny, who was not one to stick to schedules.

"I *will* be there," Jenny said, sounding confident. "If I can't make it, I'll be sure to give you a call on your cell phone."

"Okay," Rafe said. "I've gotta go now. Duty calls."

"Wait!" Jenny said, remembering something she had wanted to tell him. "I'm almost finished with another screenplay, and in it you're a cold-blooded terrorist."

"A vicious killer, huh?" Rafe said, laughing. "What did I do to deserve that?"

"You forgot my birthday," Jenny said, reminding him.

"I apologized for that."

"Too little, too late," Jenny said. "I'd already made you the villain. I'll make it up to you, though. In my next script you'll be the Bruce Willis type of hero who saves the world from nuclear annihilation."

"The nuclear threat scenario. Have you ever thought of writing a good love story? Terrorist acts and the threat of nuclear annihilation are in the news every day. I, for one, would like to see a well-written drama up on the silver screen."

"Rafe?" Jenny asked quietly.

"Yeah?" His tone was serious to match hers. He'd heard the plaintive quality in her voice. Was there something wrong?

"Do you ever wish you could have had more of a chance to live it up instead of being saddled with a snot-nose kid sister?"

Rafe sighed on his end. "Have I ever given you that impression, Jen? When Mama and Daddy drowned, you and I became joined at the hip. I wasn't about to let you go into the foster care system. We were lucky Great-Aunt Delilah could take you in."

"Yeah, but it was your monthly checks that paid for my upkeep," Jenny said, sorry for his lost childhood even if he wasn't. "You were too young for such responsibility."

"It made me stronger," Rafe told her. He meant it. "And it made you self-sufficient. Even though I sometimes complain . . ."

"*Sometimes?*" Jenny said.

"Okay, even though I complain about your being an actor *most* of the time," Rafe said, correcting himself, "I'm also proud of you. Now, stop thinking you've somehow ruined my life and go to work so you can get on that plane on time tonight."

Jenny laughed. "All right. Love you, bruh."

"Love you," Rafe said, and hung up.

Shaking his head, he put the receiver back on its cradle and got to his feet. He stretched and surveyed the large area in which he worked. Cubicles separated one worker's space from another. The color scheme was gray and light purple. He wondered if the decorator had given much thought to the combination. After a while the two colors started appearing monochromatic and your brain begged for more color. You couldn't get it by looking out of the window, because the cubicles didn't have windows. That was one of the reasons he enjoyed being in the field, or out of the office on a case, so much. Another reason was that he enjoyed protecting people.

He was a deputy marshal with seven years of service. Before becoming a deputy marshal he had served in the navy, enlisting at seventeen shortly after his parents' deaths while Jenny moved in with Great-Aunt Delilah. After six years in the navy, Rafe was honorably discharged and then decided to go to college. He earned his bachelor's degree in criminal justice and, due to a random meeting with another deputy marshal, applied for the service. He'd never regretted his decision.

The offices of the U.S. Marshal and Deputy Marshals had been set up more than two hundred years ago by the first Congress in the Judiciary Act of 1789. Then, the marshals had full authority to uphold the ruling of the federal courts, which they still support today. U.S. Marshals serve as courtroom security. They transport prisoners from one trial location to the next. They also run the Witness Protection Program.

And when a prisoner escapes while justice is being dispensed, it is the duty of the U.S. Marshals Service to track him down and bring him back to face trial.

Rafe loved his job.

That didn't mean he wasn't going to enjoy his week's vacation beginning promptly at the stroke of five P.M., because he most definitely was. He glanced up at the large clock on the west wall: four fifty-eight.

"Stop watching the clock, you lucky dog!" Chad Roundtree, one of the members of Rafe's team, said as he came to stand at the entrance to Rafe's cubicle. "Tell the truth, what are you going to do with a whole week away from here?" Chad's blue eyes fairly danced as he added, "Got a woman you've been hiding from us? You've been here six months and you've never mentioned a woman. I'm beginning to wonder about you, Grant."

"Well, keep wondering," Rafe said, not moved by Chad's curiosity. It was true, he'd been assigned to the Tucson office more than six months ago, and in that time he hadn't gotten close enough to anyone to disclose his personal life to them. He was, by nature, slow to trust. As long as he did his job he didn't figure it was anyone else's business what he did on his off hours. Chad seemed like a nice enough fellow, but Rafe would wait and see how they all meshed as a team before letting down his guard.

It wasn't his wish to rebuff Chad's attempts at friendly overtures, though, so he laughed shortly, and said, "I've seen some pretty ladies in your fair city. Maybe I'll meet someone this weekend."

Chad had something to work with now. He came to sit on the corner of Rafe's desk and, peering up at Rafe with a contemplative expression on his face, said, "If you really want to meet someone, I have a friend who has this sister who is drop-dead gorgeous. She's around thirty, I think, and she used to be a Las Vegas showgirl. Man, she has legs that go on forever!"

"Oh, no," Rafe said, his hands up as if he were warding off Chad's attempt at matchmaking. "Huh-huh. The last time somebody set me up the woman was certifiable. She went nuts on me when I told her, on the first date, that I didn't think there could ever be anything between us."

Chad moaned loudly. "You're one of *those,*" he accused. "You don't play by the rules. You should never tell a woman things aren't going to work out on the first date. You tell her you're gonna phone her, but you never do. That's the proper way of letting a woman down easy."

"That's the coward's way out," Rafe said.

"Dear God in heaven," Chad exclaimed. "You're never gonna get laid thinking like that!"

Kate's plane landed close to the time it was scheduled to arrive at Tucson International Airport. She hadn't arranged for anyone to pick her up because it was after eleven P.M., and she, frankly, didn't want her mother to have to do it. She needed her rest.

Her best friend, Sophie, would gladly have come for her, but Kate didn't want Sophie to have to bundle up Renata, her eighteen-month-old daughter, and drive half an hour to get there. Sophie had recently lost her husband, Jessie, in a construction accident. She was a widow at twenty-eight.

Kate hurried toward the telephone booths near the exit. The terminal wasn't very busy tonight, not nearly as crowded as it was during the height of tourist season. There were plenty of unoccupied booths.

She went to one and deposited some coins into the pay phone. She knew the number by heart for the cab company she used on a fairly regular basis. However, just as she was about to dial the number, she heard a man's

voice say in threatening tones, "I'm a cold-blooded terrorist, remember? Your apologies mean nothing to me.
By the time I'm finished wreaking havoc in your little
scenario, nuclear annihilation will look *good* to you!"

Kate heard a phone being slammed down. She held
her breath as she peered around the wall of her booth
into the booth next to hers. His back was to her, but she
could see him well enough to tell he was black. That
didn't mean he wasn't a terrorist. Not anymore. The
field had become an equal opportunity killing ground.

She moved back fully into her own booth, her mind
racing. What if he really *was* a terrorist and he was planning to plant a bomb, or something, at the airport? Even
though the terminal wasn't very busy at this hour, people could still get hurt or, worse, killed. Kate stuck her
head out the other direction. Where was airport security
when you needed them, somewhere wolfing down
donuts and coffee?

She risked another look at the "terrorist." He was still
there, looking madder than a wet hen. In fact, he was
talking to himself and pounding his left palm with his
right fist in a fit of anger. Yikes! He was really screwy in
the head!

Kate had already replaced the receiver. She'd have to
worry about getting a cab later. Now she put her huge
bag on the shelf next to the phone and began rummag-
ing in it for a weapon, something, *anything!* Why
couldn't she be a hair spray user? A good shot of that in
the eyes could incapacitate a man for critical minutes
during which she could yell for help and pound his head
with her heavy shoulder bag. Which had nothing but
harmless items in it: a cell phone too tiny to wield. A six-
teen-ounce bottle of water, half empty. A rolled-up copy
of *New Scientist*.

She kept digging.

The most lethal object she could find was an old Snickers bar. It would probably give him a stomachache if she could force it down his throat. Yeah, right!

Her ears perked up.

He'd gone silent over there.

Kate peered at him again.

He'd raised his right hand to smooth the hair on his closely shorn head and when he did, she saw a gun in a shoulder holster beneath his jacket. Shocked, she wondered how he'd gotten into the building with a handgun. Was airport security that lax? Not after the recent terrorist attacks on this country's soil! What if he hadn't sneaked in, but had shown security personnel bogus ID in order to enter the terminal? Should she ignore her gut instincts and simply walk away, get a cab, and go home? If he turned out to be the terrorist she thought he was she'd be morally responsible for not doing everything within her power to stop him.

Frowning, she continued to watch him without his knowledge. What a waste, she thought, taking in his utterly masculine build. He had a hard body that was unmistakable even hidden under his jeans and jacket.

He suddenly turned, looked her straight in the eyes, and smiled.

Nice smile, too.

Calling forth all her feminine wiles, Kate gave him a seductive grin.

He showed her some teeth, which were strong and white for a bloodthirsty terrorist.

I may live to regret this, Kate thought as she purposefully walked over to him.

He was in full flirt-mode now. In her opinion he looked like the proverbial cat about to eat the canary for a midnight snack.

There was no mistaking the lascivious bent his mind

was on when his gaze scanned her figure in those jeans and rested, momentarily, on her shapely hips before moving up again to meet her eyes.

Kate moistened her lips for effect, and parted them to say something.

He absently chewed on his bottom lip in expectation of what she was about to say.

However, before either of them could make the next move, their tableau was interrupted by an ear splitting "Katie, Katie bo Batie, banana nana fo fana, Katie!"

Kate turned at the sound of that irritating voice. Not her nutty cousin, Vance! She changed her tone when she laid eyes on him, though. Vance Huerta was decked out in an airport security officer's uniform. She'd never been happier to see anyone.

She quickly spun away from the terrorist and ran, slid, *glided* (the floor was slippery) right into Vance's open arms.

"Vance, thank God, you've got to arrest that man," she said in hushed tones.

Vance grinned at her. He hadn't seen his cousin in a while. But apparently she still enjoyed playing practical jokes on hapless victims.

Kate had his arm in a steel vise and was pushing him toward the stranger, who had a bemused expression on his face. "He's got a gun," she said in equally low tones. "And I heard him talking to someone over the phone about nuclear annihilation."

Vance, thirty-two, five-ten, and of slight build, looked at the big stranger, then back at Kate, confused. "Kate, it's late. Don't be pullin' my leg. I'm on duty, and even though you don't take my position seriously, I most certainly do. Just because you've got a big, fancy degree in physics doesn't mean the rest of us aren't making a contribution to society, too. Hey, you aren't even working in your field. All those years of education, and you're not even using all that learning—"

"Will you shut up and arrest him!" Kate shouted.

This time, the stranger heard her.

He looked behind him as if she might be referring to someone else. Then he observed the woman and the security guard staring at him, and he realized she was talking about him. He placed his hand on his chest as if to say, "Me?"

"Do your job, Vance!" Kate cried, pushing her cousin forward.

The stranger stood there frowning at the both of them. "What is going on here?"

Vance walked up to him. "Look, man," he said in conciliatory tones. "I'm gonna have to ask to see some ID."

Kate stood next to Vance, her eyes peeled for any sudden movements from the terrorist. When he went to go into his inside jacket pocket, she thought he was going for his gun and that's when she slugged him in the nose.

"What the *hell!*" Vance exclaimed, rushing forward to catch the felled man whose legs had buckled under the onslaught. Kate had given it all she had.

When Vance grabbed the stranger about the waist in an effort to support him he felt the gun in its holster. He quickly switched movements and pushed the stranger to the floor with both his hands behind his back, and slapped handcuffs on him.

Kate triumphantly danced up and down upon seeing this. "All right, Vance! You've got him now. Didn't I tell you he had a gun?"

"Are you people insane!" the stranger accused them. His speech was garbled due to blood gushing from his nose, into his mouth.

Vance was on his radio. "Pete, get down to sector four, near the entrance. I need backup, pronto."

"I'd just gotten off the plane from San Francisco," Kate explained. She was really hyper now. "I went to a pay phone to call a cab because, you know, I didn't want to bother Mom to come pick me up."

"How are your folks?" Vance asked.

"I'm a deputy marshal with the U.S. Marshals Service," the stranger said from his uncomfortable position on the floor.

They ignored him.

"They're both fine," Kate said. "Dad is doing a lot better. He's walking almost as well as he did before the stroke now, but his speech still needs a lot of work."

"I was heartbroken when I heard," Vance sympathized.

"My badge and ID are in my left jacket pocket," the stranger offered hopefully.

"We all were," Kate told Vance about her father's condition. "We're lucky we still have him with us."

Pete Washburn, one of the other security guards on duty, arrived. He was the senior officer. He was in his mid-fifties with a heavy build, gray-blond hair, and green eyes.

He took one look at the fellow on the floor and said, "What is Deputy Marshal Grant doing all trussed up like a Thanksgiving turkey?"

Kate and Vance looked at each other. Then they peered down at Deputy Marshal Grant. Kate's face twisted in a grimace.

Vance had the presence of mind to rush to Grant and remove the handcuffs. He helped the poor man up. "I'm really sorry, sir," he said.

Vance skewered Kate with an angry stare.

Kate started talking fast. "He was on the phone talking about being a terrorist and he angrily told the person on the phone that when he was done we would all wish for nuclear annihilation, or something to that effect . . ." She trailed off and looked apologetically at Deputy Marshal Grant. "I thought I was stopping a terrorist before he struck. You've got to admit, the media has all of us spooked."

She moved toward him, trying to get a better look at the bloody mess she'd made of his nose.

Rafe cautiously took a step backward.

Tears sat in Kate's eyes, she was so sorry for what she'd done.

"Look, man, if you want to press charges, I can call the police for you," Vance told Rafe.

Kate gave her cousin a sharp look. *Traitor!* she thought.

Kate had gone into her shoulder bag for tissues. "At least let me help stop the bleeding," she said, offering him the tissues.

Rafe accepted the tissues but he didn't let her touch him again. He tilted his head back and pinched his nose closed with the tissues. "I would like to see some ID, miss," he said.

Kate retrieved her wallet and tiptoed to show him her driver's license while he continued to tilt his head back.

Rafe took it from her and took his time reading the information.

Feeling contrite, Kate stood to the side, ready to accept her punishment.

"So," Pete Washburn said, "Deputy Marshal Grant, do you want me to call the paramedics? You gonna be all right?"

"She didn't hit me that hard," Rafe said. "I'll be fine, thanks."

Vance and Pete took that as their cue to leave.

"How do you know him?" Vance asked Pete as they walked away.

"He's been through here several times, transporting prisoners," Pete informed Vance.

Alone with Rafe now, Kate pursed her lips, blew air between them, and awaited her fate. What kind of a nut went around punching out innocent people in public places anyway? She was in need of extensive therapy.

Stress. That was the culprit.

Months of worrying about her father, whether he'd ever fully recover his usual physical capabilities. Worrying about the effects of the stroke on his mental acuity. He'd been a brilliant man prior to the stroke and on the cusp of making his theories about teleportation of physical objects bear fruit.

Kate would have liked it, right now, if a teleportation machine would whisk her back home, safely to her bed, and out of the presence of this fierce-eyed deputy marshal.

"I really *am* sorry," she said again.

Rafe handed her the wallet. He lowered his head to test whether the bleeding had slowed down or not. It hadn't. Tilting his head back again, he said, "Regardless of what I said to those fellas a minute ago, I think I should go to the emergency room and have this checked out."

He fished in his pocket for his car keys. "Here, you're driving."

Kate grasped the keys, managed to shoulder both her carry-on bag and her shoulder bag on one side, and took his left arm, directing him with her other hand toward the exit while he still had his head tilted.

Outside, she helped him onto the passenger seat of his late-model Ford Expedition, firmly closed the door, and hurried around to the driver's side.

"Pima County's closest," she said as she got behind the wheel. "We'll go there if you have no objections."

"That's fine," Rafe said, trying not to bleed on his car seats.

Kate reached over and helped him buckle up, and then she buckled up herself. Starting the car and putting it in gear, she backed out of the parking space and followed the curved path out of the parking garage.

"I've never hit anyone before," she said as she pulled out of the garage onto the street. "I mean, yes, as a kid I got into shoving matches with other kids, but I've never drawn blood before. I feel sick."

"You're not going to faint or anything, are you?" Rafe asked. "Because getting into a car crash on top of having my nose broken does not a good Friday night make."

"Do you think it's broken?" Kate asked, worried.

"No," Rafe said truthfully. "But it sure hurts like hell. For someone who has never actually hit anyone, you did a damn good job."

"I could cry!" Kate exclaimed.

"Not right now," Rafe said. "First, get us safely to Pima County Hospital. After that, you can let loose with the guilty tears."

Kate sighed. "This has been some day. First some nuclear physicist accosts me at a physics conference, and then I crazily think I'm saving the world and punch you in the nose. All I want to do is go home and climb in my bed, and hide from the world for a while."

"All I want to do is be able to breathe through my nose," Rafe said. If she thought he was going to let her off the hook any time soon, she could think again.

There he was, minding his own business, having a mild temper tantrum over Jenny's not phoning to tell him he didn't have to come all the way to the airport to pick her up because she was held up in Los Angeles, and he looks up, sees a beautiful woman, and the next thing he knows, he's seeing stars and being shoved to the floor by an airport security officer. He had the right to be upset!

"I'm really not as crazy as I seem," Kate told him. "I'm a science writer. I work mainly for national magazines, but

I've written two books, one a college physics textbook for first-year students, and the other an introduction to quantum physics that was picked up by a commercial publisher."

"Then you're a rocket scientist," Rafe joked.

"Actually, yes, but by the time I'd earned my degree I'd decided there were enough rocket scientists in the world. What we needed were more people to explain how science works. I've always found that more fascinating than figuring out how to build a better nuclear bomb."

Rafe just stared at her. "You're serious, aren't you?"

"Yes," Kate said, almost apologetically.

"No, no, never be sorry for what you've worked so hard to achieve," Rafe told her, momentarily forgetting he was mad at her. "Wow. I don't think, no, I *know,* I've never met an African-American woman who was a physicist. That's deep."

Kate briefly glanced at him before adhering to safe-driving rules again, and keeping her eyes on the road. "Thank you, Deputy Marshal Grant."

Two

"Did you get the number of the bus that hit you?" the young woman doctor joked with Rafe as she deftly ran her fingers over his nose.

"No, but I memorized her driver's license number," Rafe said, his nose in the air.

Kate stood in the corner of the examination room with her arms folded across her chest, observing everything. She winced every time Rafe's nose was touched.

"It doesn't appear to be broken, just badly bruised. You can expect some swelling though."

"More than it already is?" Rafe asked.

"Count yourself lucky," the doctor said.

She stepped over to the counter and scribbled on a prescription pad. Ripping the top sheet off, she handed it to Rafe. "Use ice for the swelling. Take Tylenol if you have any soreness. And just for tonight, see if someone can stay with you while you're sleeping. It doesn't happen often, but sometimes it can start bleeding again in the middle of the night and choke you. Of course, most people tend to wake themselves up when that happens, but better safe than sorry, right?"

Rafe stood as he accepted the slip of paper with her suggestions written on it. "Okay, thanks, Doctor."

"It was my pleasure," she said, and smiled at him before leaving the exam room.

In the doctor's absence, Kate gave a relieved sigh. "Thank God it wasn't broken."

Rafe smiled at her. "Yeah, I should be back to my devastatingly handsome self again in a few days."

"Let's not get crazy," Kate joked. "I mean, you're good-looking, but who's to say my handiwork isn't going to be an improvement on the original?"

"We'll just have to wait and see," Rafe said, moving closer to her as she backed out of the room. He held out his right hand. "My car keys if you please?"

"What for?" Kate asked, all innocence. "I know the way to my place."

Rafe regarded her with narrowed eyes. "Your place?"

Kate turned and began walking down the corridor.

Rafe had to admit, he liked the view from behind. Those jeans were hitting on every curve of her lower body. And there was something about all that hair she had falling down her back. He'd never really cared if a woman had short hair or long hair. But he liked the way her wavy hair suited the rest of her.

"Woman, if you don't give me my car keys I really *will* have you jailed," he said menacingly.

Kate hummed a cheerful ditty as she continued toward the exit. When she'd reached the double electric doors that served as the entrance/exit to the emergency room, she turned to look back at him. "It's late, Deputy Marshal Grant. I need a ride home, and you need someone to watch you sleep tonight. I'm volunteering for the job."

Rafe shook his head in the negative. "No. I'll drive you home, then go home myself. I'll be fine tonight. This isn't the first bloody nose I've gotten in the course of doing my job."

Kate walked through the exit in a huff. "If you aren't an alpha male, I don't know one when I see one," she said. "Macho, stubborn, think you know the best course of action for any given situation. Oh, yeah, you fit the description all right."

The October night air was chilly, as it usually is in the desert. Kate wasted no time getting to the parked car only a few yards from the entrance. While Rafe took his time.

Having dealt with a father and two brothers all her life, Kate knew she had to use what her mother referred to as her superior female reasoning to get through to Rafe. Her mother's premise was this: the easiest way for a woman to get a man to do something she wanted him to do was by making him think the whole idea was his in the first place!

In this way, the male sense of his far superior logic would be satisfied. And, of course, the woman would get her way. And all would be right with the universe.

Therefore, Kate stood at the driver's-side door with his car keys in the palm of her hand and sweetly said, "All right, it's your car. And a lovely vehicle it is. You know that they say a hit on the head is equivalent to being legally intoxicated. But, if you insist on driving . . ."

Rafe looked at the keys in her palm, then back up at her. "Okay, you can drive."

They got in, buckled up. Kate started the car and pulled out of the parking lot. Once they were on the street, she calmly said, "May I ask why you were at the airport tonight?"

"I was there to pick up my sister, or so I thought. That was her I was yelling at over the phone."

"I see. She was supposed to come for a visit, didn't make the plane, and forgot to inform you," Kate surmised.

"Exactly," Rafe said. He was no longer upset by Jenny's absentminded behavior. He knew she would have come if she could have. But like most big brothers, he had to let her have it with both barrels just to give her something to think about should she ever think of treating him that way again. He'd phone and apologize when he got home. "And you were returning from San Francisco, after attending a physics conference."

"Great deductive reasoning," Kate congratulated him, buttering him up.

"Nah," he said. "I heard you telling the security guard you'd recently arrived from San Francisco, and you told me about being accosted by a physicist at a physics conference."

"Yeah, but, see, I would have forgotten all that by now," Kate said.

"You knew him."

"The security guard? Yes. He's my cousin, Vance Huerta."

"Your cousin?" He turned toward her. "If I'm not mistaken he was Native American."

"Yeah, well, so am I. Half of me anyway. My mom's Pascua Yaqui Indian. They compose the largest Indian tribe in this area. They've been here hundreds of years. My dad's African-American. He's originally from Florida. But when he was in high school he won a scholarship to attend the University of Arizona. Good thing, too, because he met Mom here in Tucson."

"So, they got married and produced you."

"And three others. I have two brothers and a sister, all younger than I am."

Rafe didn't want her to feel self-conscious, so he turned his attention back to the road. "What was it like growing up around here?" he asked, changing the subject. "I've never lived in the desert before. My folks were from Raleigh, North Carolina. They drowned when I was seventeen and my sister was eleven. There were only two of us kids."

"I'm sorry about your parents," Kate said, her tone soft and sympathetic.

"It was a long time ago," Rafe said. "My great-grandfather passed away three years ago, and Grandma still talks to him every day as if he never left her. I thought she might be having a nervous breakdown so I went to her one day and had a long talk with her. She told me she was not losing her mind, she was holding on to him as long as she could. When she stopped talking to him, *then* we could start worrying about her mental health. We all mourn in our own way. I think that's a nice way of remembering him," he added.

Kate smiled. "I think so, too."

Looking out the window, Rafe said, "I noticed we're leaving Tucson." He said this calmly as if it were a passing thought, when he was actually a bit more perturbed than that. "Where are you taking me?"

"My place," Kate told him. "I live on a ranch just outside of Tucson."

"A ranch?"

"Uh-huh."

"With cows and horses?"

"No cows, but lots of horses. We raise them."

Rafe turned to glare at her. "This is going from bad to worse. You mean you're taking me to your parents' house?" he asked, incredulous.

"That's where I've been staying for the past four months, yes. Although, technically, I don't live in the same building. I live in the guest house. I'm not going to introduce you to my parents tonight, if that's what you're afraid of."

"Under different circumstances, I wouldn't mind meeting your parents. But given the way I look right now, my nose swollen and my clothes covered with blood, I'd prefer not to meet anyone."

"You won't, I promise," Kate assured him.

She slowed the car to turn left onto a country road. "We're almost there. Listen, Deputy Marshal Grant—"

"Would you please drop the Deputy Marshal Grant and simply call me Rafe? It's short for Rafael."

"Thanks. Deputy Marshal Grant was a mouthful," Kate said. "As I was about to say, I feel guilty enough attacking you the way I did. If you should leave tonight and drive all the way back to Tucson by yourself I would worry about you all night long. Please, just relax and let me take care of you for the next few hours. I'd be very grateful for your cooperation."

Rafe was silent for a couple of minutes, weighing her request against his common sense. As far as he was concerned, the moment he'd met this woman his IQ had gone down a few points. He allowed himself to be caught off guard by her left hook because he'd been so busy salivating over her. If he was completely honest with himself he would admit that he'd made her drive him to the hospital because he'd wanted to stretch out the time they spent together. He wasn't a wuss, he could have driven himself to the hospital if, indeed, he would have bothered going. No, there was something about *Katie*, her cousin Vance had called her. What was her last name anyway?

"If we're going to be spending the night together, I should at least know your last name, Katie," Rafe said quietly, looking at her profile. His heart did a little somersault when he saw her grin with pleasure.

"Wonderful!" Kate said. She briefly met his eyes. "My name's Katharine Matthews, but everybody calls me Kate. Except Vance, who's inordinately fond of the name game."

"Katie, Katie bo Batie." Rafe mimicked Vance.

"Vance and I were close as kids," Kate told him. "He and

I sort of banded together because it was the consensus of the family that we were both either nuts or missing the much-needed 'caution' gene in our genetic makeup. You see, there was nothing we wouldn't try at least once. Trick riding? No challenge whatsoever. Rattlesnake wrangling? Piece of cake. I loved that boy!"

"Rattlesnake wrangling?" Rafe said, seeking elucidation on the unfamiliar practice.

"That's when you find a nest of rattlers and catch as many as you can. We'd take them to the university. A zoologist there would extract their venom for use in making snakebite serum."

Rafe laughed. "Good Lord, that's what you did in the desert for fun when you were a kid? Where were your parents when this was going on?"

"My parents never found out about it," Kate told him. "They would have tanned my hide good if they had."

Rafe blew air between his lips. "That makes me feel a lot better. You had parents who were normal, even if you weren't."

Kate laughed. "Being normal is no fun."

What he'd said gave her pause, though. She had done outrageous things as a kid, especially around other kids, because she didn't want to be considered abnormal. Her father was internationally recognized as a physicist to be watched even back then. Her mother was a local activist who was on TV quite often speaking on behalf of the various Indian tribes in Arizona, or championing the cause of illegal immigrants. Tucson had a large immigrant population, mostly Mexican. So many Mexicans had been in and out of the Matthews home that all of the Matthews children grew up speaking Spanish. To this day some of Kate's closest friends were Mexican-American.

Rafe saw lights in the distance. When they got closer he could make out a white fence around a large property.

Kate drove through an open arched gate. Rafe wasn't able to make out the words carved into the arch but he'd recognized an M as the first letter.

"Welcome to the Circle M Ranch," Kate said.

As she drove past the big adobe house, around back, they saw a light go on in the big house. Kate was certain her mother was up and had heard the car's motor.

"I'll have to phone them once we get inside," Kate said. "They expected me about an hour ago."

The guest house was also constructed of adobe. Desert dwellers had been using the material for hundreds of years because of the all-weather insulation it provided. Bricks made from straw and earth and then sun-dried blended well into the local environment.

The moment Kate unlocked the back door that led into the kitchen, The Puma launched himself from atop the refrigerator onto her. Ready for his antics, she caught the fat tabby in her arms and hugged him to her chest. Laughing, she turned and motioned a half-startled Rafe inside.

"Don't worry, he only does it to me," Kate told him.

When Rafe was inside the warm kitchen Kate switched on the overhead light. The kitchen, though relatively small, had the latest appliances and was spotless. Turning to Rafe, she said, pointing to the left, "The living room's that way. Go make yourself at home while I put The Puma out. He has his own house on the verandah. He must have slipped inside when Mom came in here for something in my absence. I love him, but I'm slightly allergic to cat hair."

Banishing the cat was all right with Rafe. He had nothing against cats, but he didn't want The Puma to suddenly get it into his feline brain that Rafe was fair game for that kamikaze act he'd just pulled on Kate, and jump on *his* head.

"Thanks," he said, and began walking in the direction of the living room.

Kate turned on her heels and went back through the back door with The Puma.

She made sure he had fresh food and water in his house out back before returning to the guest house, where she paused long enough in the kitchen to dial her parents' number.

As she knew she would, her mother picked up immediately. "Kate, I thought that had to be you returning home. What was the delay? We were worried."

"Hi, Mom," Kate said. "The plane arrived on time, it's what happened once I was in the terminal that delayed me." She quickly related the events of the last ninety minutes of her life.

Her mother was laughing when she'd finished. "Your dad is gonna bust a gut when I tell him," she said. "Okay, sweetie. I'll let you and Deputy Marshal Grant get some rest. Bring him to breakfast in the morning."

"That may prove difficult, he's a little shy."

"Invite him to your dad's birthday party, then," Carolina suggested. "I've got to meet him."

Kate had forgotten that next Saturday was her father's fifty-fifth birthday.

"Okay, I will," Kate said easily. "Good night, Ma."

"Night, baby," Carolina said, and hung up.

Her duty done, Kate strolled into the living room where Rafe was sitting on the sofa with the remote control in his hand, switching through the channels on the tube. *Leave it to a man to find the remote in no time,* Kate thought with a smile.

"I'm back," she needlessly announced. "I'm gonna go find you a pair of pajamas."

"You have men's pajamas on hand?"

"That's the only kind I wear," Kate told him. "Who gave

you men the right to corner the market on comfort? I buy them extra large, too, so they should fit."

Rising, Rafe said, "I'm not wearing your pajamas."

"Why?" Kate asked, looking innocent. "Do you prefer sleeping in the nude?"

"In what state I sleep is no concern of yours," Rafe said. What had he gotten himself into? He must not be thinking straight after that hit to his noggin. He'd let himself be driven out in the middle of nowhere by a woman he was physically attracted to.

Now, she wanted to know whether he slept in the nude or not.

Kate looked him up and down. "Well, I'm sure you look great in the nude, Rafe. But seeing as how we've just met, I'd prefer you to wear pajamas when we go to bed. If you would be so kind."

"What do you mean, when 'we' go to bed?"

Kate sighed. "I can't possibly watch you sleep from the other bedroom!"

Rafe sat back down. "You really are the most exasperating woman I've ever met."

Kate joined him on the sofa and placed her hand on his arm. Peering up at him, she softly said, "I can see you're having problems with this, Rafe. Is it because you have a jealous girlfriend who wouldn't understand your sleeping in the same bed as another woman?"

"My last relationship ended more than eight months ago," he archly informed her.

"Good," Kate said. "I mean, okay. That's good to know. I'm not seeing anybody right now either." She cocked her head so that she could look him in the eyes. "So, are you going to tell me the real reason you object to sleeping in the same bed as I?"

Rafe narrowed his eyes at her. "Isn't it obvious,

woman? I'm a man. You're a woman. When you put that combination together, things happen."

Kate smiled warmly. "You mean the normal chemical reactions?"

"Yes!" Rafe said, his brown eyes flashing indignantly. "Do I have to spell it out for you? I'm attracted to you. You wouldn't have gotten the drop on me back there if not for that reason. I don't believe I can sleep with you without certain bodily 'changes' taking place in me. I'm not a clinical-rocket-scientist type. I'm just your average Joe."

"You're attracted to me?" Kate said, all dreamy.

Shaking his head, Rafe gave up. There was no fighting this woman. If she was willing to sleep in the same bed as he, it wasn't up to him to lodge a complaint. Let nature take its course. Besides, he wanted to see if she really was a clinical-rocket-scientist type, or a smoldering volcano underneath that cool facade of hers.

"Would I be here if I weren't?" he answered.

"I'm attracted to you, too," Kate told him. "In fact, when I assumed you were a terrorist I thought, 'What a waste of a good-looking male.' But," she quickly added, "the difference between animals and us is our ability to control our impulses."

"So, you want to try this," Rafe concluded from her comments.

"I intend to see you through the night." Kate was adamant.

"All right," Rafe said, resigned. "Do you have an extra toothbrush?"

"Of course," Kate said, removing her hand from his thigh. How had it gotten there? She didn't recall placing her hand on anything but his arm.

She rose and hurried out of the room, her face hot with embarrassment. She hoped he hadn't noticed how intimately she'd been touching him.

In her absence, Rafe tried to control the tightness in his groin that was rapidly rendering the crotch of his pants too tight for comfort.

In her bedroom, Kate closed the door behind her and stood there with her back pressed against it for a while, trying to slow the rhythm of her swiftly beating heart. Something had occurred to her when she was speaking with her mom a few minutes ago. Could she have attacked Rafe because, subconsciously, she was attracted to him? All her life she'd been told the story of how her parents had met. Carolina had been riding in the desert and had almost run David down with her spirited mount. David had been so startled by the reckless Carolina that he'd lost his balance, fallen, and hit his head on a rock, knocking himself out. Carolina had brought him around and helped him onto the sorrel she'd been riding, and they had ridden double to the Triple H, which was the name of the ranch when Carolina's family had owned it. As an only child Carolina had inherited the ranch upon her parents' deaths.

Had Kate taken one look at Rafe, who was extremely good to look at, and completely sold herself on the terrorist angle because subconsciously she'd wanted to meet him? Or could she blame it on stress and fatigue? Admittedly she had heard him saying some very suspicious things to his sister over the phone.

Did I go cave woman on the poor man and hit him in order to drag him back to my cave? she wondered. She walked over to the chest of drawers and pulled open the top drawer. As she pulled out a pair of freshly laundered pajamas the honeysuckle fragrance of the sachet assailed her nostrils. She realized that all of the clothing in the drawers smelled like wildflowers. She guessed Rafe wasn't going to be happy about that.

She closed the drawer and went into the adjacent

bathroom to get a new toothbrush, still in its wrapper, from the medicine cabinet.

Rafe paced the floor.

He didn't do things like this. The truth was he was normally the soul of reason. Like Jenny had said, he'd always been the responsible one. Dependable to a fault. He treated women with respect. Never once had he suggested he spend the night when he took a date home on the first date. In fact, when in a relationship he always waited for the woman to bring up the subject of making love for the first time.

He reminded himself that this was a unique situation. Kate wasn't a date. They were not going to make love, they were simply going to be sleeping in the same bed. At the same time. He would smell her skin all night long. Feel her body heat.

Hopefully, she would snore. Loudly.

"Here you are," Kate said, reentering the room and handing him the pajamas and the toothbrush. Smiling at him, she said, "Are you hungry? I am. I think there's some grilled chicken in the fridge. I could make us some grilled chicken tortillas. Sound good?"

Rafe took the bundle from her. Her enthusiasm was contagious. "I could eat," he said with a smile.

They sort of gazed at each other for a long moment, seemingly coming to an understanding at last, and Kate was the first one to break the connection, once again pointing in the direction he needed to go. "The bathroom's down the hall. Fresh towels and washclothes are on the shelf. The shower massage is pretty powerful so watch out for it. And the hot water is very, very hot."

"If you hear me screaming, you'll know the shower massage got away from me," Rafe joked. What did she think he was, an idiot? A child could figure out a shower massage.

"All rightie, then," Kate said, and hummed her way into the kitchen.

Rafe noticed she liked to hum.

In the bathroom, Rafe took a moment to study the lump that used to be his nose.

It was not bruised black and blue yet, but it was definitely swollen. He rubbed his jaw. By tomorrow morning he'd have a pretty good beard started. He was thinking about not shaving during his vacation. See how long his beard would get before he had to go back to work.

As he began removing his clothes he realized he was thinking of mundane things to take his mind off the woman in the kitchen. Was she as odd as she came across? No matter how guilty she might feel about injuring him, what woman in her right mind would bring a stranger into her home and suggest sleeping in the same bed with him?

There was responsibility, and then there was *responsibility*. At the first opportunity he was going to have a talk with Jenny and tell her to never do anything like this. She might bring home a real nut!

He knew he was harmless, but had Kate ever done anything like this before? She certainly didn't seem like that sort of woman. She'd admitted that she was attracted to him, but except for innocently putting her hand on his thigh she hadn't made any overt moves on him.

Squinting at his reflection, he allowed that he was a fine specimen of an adult male but he was not possessed of movie star looks or the kind of confidence it took to be a player. He was still trying to figure out the real reason Kate had brought him home with her. He was enough of a dreamer to hope it was for carnal reasons, even if because he was a gentleman he would not take her up on her offer. He'd sincerely like to get the offer though.

"You are a lucky dog," he said aloud, recalling Chad Roundtree's comment earlier that day. "Just relax and enjoy it."

In the kitchen Kate was pulling containers out of the refrigerator and the freezer.

Because her mother and her grandmother had taken the time to teach all four Matthews children how to cook at early ages, she could whip up a meal in a matter of minutes.

After placing several containers on the countertop she glanced up at the wall clock: twelve forty-five A.M. Just the right time of day for her grilled chicken tortillas. She giggled shortly. Her body clock had always been screwy. Her mind was sharpest in the wee hours of the morning. She'd probably programmed it that way while she was in college and burning the midnight oil. Then, too, she was the type of physicist who became obsessed with problem solving. One time she'd stayed up fifty hours straight while trying to find a solution to a quantum physics problem. She'd slept nearly twenty hours once she came up with the answer. However, her behavior made her come to the conclusion that unlike her father, who had always been able to marry his profession as a physicist with his life as a husband and father, she was an obsessive-compulsive who could not. In her estimation it was her worst failing. She loved the discipline of physics but she would not allow it to take over her life. The biggest lesson she'd ever learned from her parents was that people were more important than any career. Where was the satisfaction in winning the Noble prize in physics when you had no one in your life who loved and cherished you? What was even more important was to love someone with all your heart.

So she'd turned her back on physics for the time being. She had hopes that one day she would be able to balance the discipline and a "real" life.

She washed her hands at the sink, dried them, and began chopping fresh onions and tomatoes. This done, she cut the grilled chicken breasts into strips. The day before yesterday she'd made some herbed brown rice and thought that would go nicely with the black beans in the flour tortilla.

Kate softly sang Norah Jones's "Come Away With Me," as she placed the chicken strips in a skillet to warm them before warming the flour tortillas on the stove-top griddle. She was flipping the tortillas with her fingers when she heard the masculine howl from her bathroom.

The shower massage strikes again, she thought as she hurriedly removed the flour tortilla she'd been flipping from the griddle and turned off the gas stove. She sprinted down the hallway, stopping only when she reached the bathroom door.

"Rafe, are you all right?"

"No, I'm not all right. This damned thing nearly scalded me!"

"That's why I warned you to watch out for it," she said sympathetically.

"You didn't tell me it was possessed!" But she heard laughter in his tone, and smiled with relief. He had a sense of humor.

"It's not possessed," she said. "It's been somewhat modified."

"Let me guess," Rafe said. "You invent gadgets too."

"I did a little something to it, yes. But you can adjust it to your liking. Fiddle with it a bit," she said. "Are you all right now? I need to get back to my cooking."

"Yeah, I'll live," Rafe said.

"I'm glad to hear it. Oh, what kind of cheese do you like in your tortillas? I have sharp cheddar and feta."

"Cheddar, please," was his reply. "Thanks for coming to check on me." There was a husky quality to his voice.

"It was my pleasure," Kate said, and turned away, her face growing hot once more.

When she got to the kitchen she went to the sink, splashed cold water on her face, and dried it with a paper towel. Then she resumed cooking.

A man in the house. A man in the house who wasn't related to her. A man in the house who wasn't related to her *and* who was attracted to her to boot! She'd hit the jackpot.

She was singing "A Sunday Kind of Love" when Rafe came into the kitchen barefoot and attired in navy blue pajamas. When Kate turned around and saw him her breath caught in her throat. If anything, he was even more magnificent. Gone were the blood-splattered denim shirt, jeans, leather jacket, and leather boots.

He stood there with his washables in his hands. "Do you have a washer and dryer?"

"Yes," Kate managed. She came forward and took the clothing. "I'll go put them in the wash now. I also have some oxidizing cleanser that should get those bloodstains out." She sighed contentedly as she turned to leave the room. "Have a seat at the table while I'm gone."

In the laundry room, she lifted the lid of the washer, removed the basket, and put his clothes in the drum. He was a Hanes man. Kate never thought she'd actually be doing a man's laundry. She had never done it for any of the guys she'd dated in college. As for the ones she'd seen in the past four years after receiving her doctorate, none of those had gotten laundry privileges. Yet, here she was getting some kind of sensual jolt out of touching a stranger's clothing, and desiring to do such a spectacular job of cleaning them that he'd surely reward her with a kiss.

A kiss?

Where had that come from?

Get real, girl. You've been thinking about kissing him ever since you learned he wasn't really a cold-blooded killer.

She started the water running and began adding the laundry detergent and a scoop of the oxidizing cleanser that promised to lift any stain known to man. She then replaced the basket and closed the lid of the washer.

She took a deep breath before reentering the kitchen.

Rafe was standing next to the stove looking at her. His dark eyes lowered to her feet. She'd taken off her shoes too. She had beautiful feet. He wondered what her legs looked like under those jeans. "I don't mind waiting if you'd like to shower before we eat," he offered.

"That would be nice," Kate said, wanting an excuse to get her mind together before sitting across the table from this unnerving man. She told herself all she needed was a few minutes to use self-hypnosis to convince herself she was immune to his masculine beauty. She had an IQ of 155, after all. What good was being smart if you couldn't use that to your advantage?

Rafe watched her leave the room. He never missed the opportunity to catch that hip action. It was better than watching a Victoria's Secret fashion show. It was better than the latest edition of the *Sports Illustrated* swimsuit issue. Kate Matthews was the embodiment of sexiness. And she wasn't even aware of it. Somewhere between his shower and his returning to the kitchen he'd decided that she was not putting on an act. She really was shy and inept, and rather inexperienced when it came to the opposite sex. Maybe it was because of all the years she'd put into her education. She couldn't have had much time for a social life.

That's why he'd made up his mind not to touch her. Even if she made the first move and assured him there would be no strings attached should something happen between them. He would not "rise" to the occasion.

He felt himself stir now just thinking about Kate re-moving her clothing in preparation for that hot shower she was undoubtedly looking forward to.

Tonight was going to be very interesting.

Three

"Black beans and red onions," Rafe observed as they sat down to enjoy their after-midnight repast. "You really *aren't* interested in trying to have your way with me, are you?"

Kate laughed and reached for the platter of flour tortillas. "Are you familiar with southwestern cooking? Or do I need to instruct you on how to build a tortilla?"

Rafe's teeth flashed white. "Get real, Einstein, I was eating these things before you were a twinkle in your daddy's eyes."

"What's that supposed to mean?" Kate said as she expertly piled strips of grilled chicken, herbed rice, chopped tomatoes, black beans, and cheddar cheese atop a huge flour tortilla. She met his eyes across the table. "You don't look that much older than I am." She noticed that he'd passed on the chopped onions, too.

"Are we telling our ages now?"

"I'll tell if you'll tell."

"Thirty-four."

"You *are* much older than I am!" Kate cried, grinning impishly when she saw the frown creasing his forehead. "Just kidding. I'm twenty-eight."

"I would've guessed around twenty-five," he told her. "But that could be because you have such an energetic personality."

"Is that what I have, an energetic personality?" Kate

asked. She bit into her tortilla and her eyes nearly rolled back in her head with ecstasy.

Watching her, Rafe had to smile. He wondered if she was that responsive to stimuli in other areas of her life.

He bit into his tortilla. She was right, it was delicious!

Kate had almost forgotten what they were talking about, but sufficiently recalled the thread after taking two more bites of her tortilla. "About an hour ago I'm sure you wouldn't have been so kind when describing my personality. You thought I was a worthy candidate for a rubber room."

"Who wouldn't?" Rafe said honestly. "But after some consideration I came to the conclusion that you're 'good people.'"

"Well, thank you," she said, her gaze dipping to his mouth. *How does he manage to look that damned sexy while eating a big ole sloppy tortilla?* she wondered. Her hormones must be in overdrive.

They ate in silence for a few minutes, each of them relishing the spicy mixture of southwestern herbs and spices. Rafe marveled at the sister's ability to make a great meal out of what she had in her refrigerator.

Kate only managed to consume one of the big tortillas, but Rafe put away two.

Afterward, Kate rose and began clearing the table. Rafe joined her, and when she started to protest he shot her a sharp look. "Don't even try it. My parents raised me right. I'm not gonna sit at your table, eat food you prepared, and then sit while you clean up the mess."

Kate went and ran water in the sink while Rafe finished clearing the table.

"How are you holding up?" Kate asked as she squirted dish detergent into the rapidly filling sink. "Are you sore? Need some Tylenol? I heard the doctor tell you to use that if you experienced any soreness."

"Maybe later," Rafe said, coming to place the leftovers on the countertop next to the sink. "Since you know where everything is, why don't you put the food away and I'll wash?" he suggested.

Kate thought that made perfect sense and relinquished the red-checkered dishcloth.

A little nervous in his presence, she chattered away while transferring the leftovers to plastic containers. "Earlier, you said you'd never lived in the desert before. Where did you live before moving here?"

"Philly," Rafe told her.

"Do you miss it?"

"Yeah, a little. I miss my friends. Didn't have any relatives there, but the job and my friends kept me pretty busy. And the bike trails were excellent."

"Oh, you cycle," Kate said. No wonder his thigh muscles were so fabulous. "Tucson has some good trails, too."

"Do you bike?" Rafe asked, and she could hear the excitement in his voice.

She had to disappoint him, though. "No, I ride another kind of beast."

Rafe laughed. "Oh, yeah, horses."

"Uh-huh. Been riding since I was five. Do you ride?"

"No," Rafe said with a grimace. "Where I'm from we didn't get much of a chance to do that sort of thing. That was for the rich kids."

"That's what they used to say about golf and tennis," Kate said. "Until Tiger Woods and Venus and Serena Williams proved they were anybody's games. At any rate, I can teach you to ride in an afternoon, if you're interested." She was standing next to him at the sink.

Rafe wished she wouldn't stand so close. She'd put her hair up and a tendril had fallen down and had snaked its way down into her royal-blue pajama top where the swell

of her lush breasts was noticeable even beneath her masculine attire. On top of that, God help him, she smelled
good enough to eat for dessert. She was wearing a light,
flowery scent that stole into his nasal passages and made
him want to inhale deeply. He had no intention of doing
that. He'd already let this woman worm her way into his
senses quite enough for one night.

Kate stood with her back to the sink so she could look
him in the eyes. His eyes were the color of brandy, a
medium golden brown brandy that was rich and intoxi-
cating. "Are you interested?" she asked huskily.

Rafe tried to concentrate on washing the few dishes
left in the sink. *What the hell did she ask me a couple of minutes ago?* he thought. *Oh, yeah, riding lessons.*

"What?" he joked. "You didn't succeed in doing me in
at the airport so you want another crack at me?"

Kate laughed, turned around, bumped his hip with
her own, denoting she wanted room at the sink, and
began rinsing the dishes he'd washed. "I think you're
chicken," she said, not looking at him. "Mr. big, bad
Deputy Marshal Grant is afraid of horses. That's it, isn't
it?"

"Damn right," Rafe said, unashamed. "I don't get on
anything that has a brain of its own. Which means it has
a *mind* of its own. I could want to go left, and it decides
it would rather go right. I could end up somewhere in
Mexico."

"Lost in the Catalinas," Kate said, laughing. "After the
horse threw you and returned to the ranch, they'd find
your dried-up bones twenty years from now, and next to
them you would have scrawled a message in the dirt,
'Kate made me do it!'"

She rinsed the last dish and placed it with the rest to
drain in the dish rack. Rafe dried his hands on a paper
towel, and regarded her with clear eyes. "You have a very

vivid imagination. But, yes, I'd probably blame you for my untimely death."

"I'm willing to take that risk," Kate told him, looking deeply into his eyes. "Come on, one lesson and I'll never bug you again."

"You promise?"

"On my honor."

"I want to kiss you, Kate."

She hadn't seen that one coming.

Nor, apparently, had he. Wasn't he the one who'd resolved not to touch her tonight?

His hands were at his sides. They were standing about three feet apart, and their gazes were locked. Kate let out a soft sigh, and sucked the air back in. She moistened her lips with the tip of her tongue. Rafe waited. He knew the ball was in her court, and whatever happened in the next few seconds would determine the course of their relationship. If, indeed, they would ever have a relationship.

"Is this a date?" Kate said softly as she moved closer to him.

"An unorthodox date but, yes, it feels like a date," Rafe offered hopefully.

"I don't kiss on the first date," Kate replied. Her gaze fell on his mouth. "What time is it?"

Rafe glanced at the wall clock. "It's after two."

"Then, technically, it's the next day. I kiss on the second date," she told him, and placed her right hand on his chest, which was as hard as she'd imagined it would be. Rafe bent his head, and Kate rose up on her toes to meet him halfway.

The hand that had been on his chest was now on the side of his powerful neck. She could feel his pulse there. His left hand was on her back while his right was at the back of her neck. It was a warm, strong hand, and Kate felt secure in his embrace.

Unlike some men who went for the mouth right away, afraid the offer of a kiss would expire before they got to the good stuff, Rafe was in no rush. He cupped her face in his hands and looked deeply in her eyes; then he bent down and planted a soft kiss on her right cheek. He was breathing in her scent, enjoying the texture of her skin.

While he had her face in his hands, he ran the pads of both thumbs over her cheekbones, then traced the outline of her lips with deliberate slowness.

"Your parents did good," he murmured.

To which Kate smiled. "So did yours. Except for that nose. That nose could use some work."

Rafe's smile was crooked as his lips descended upon hers. "Maybe you can kiss me and make it better."

"It's worth a try," said Kate just before her mouth was firmly covered by his.

Kate gasped with her lips parted. Their breath mingled. Rafe turned his head slightly to the right and deepened the kiss. He'd never been as curious about how a woman tasted in his entire life. But he'd had to find out how Kate felt on his tongue. She was sweet, and the feel of her in his arms set his nerve endings on fire. Why had he known it would be like this from the moment he set eyes on her in the airport terminal? It was as if a spark of electricity had come down from heaven and struck him squarely in the heart. No wonder he hadn't seen that left hook coming.

Kate tried to hang on to a sense of balance. This couldn't be happening to her. She'd gone through high school and seven years of college without this happening to her. Whenever another man had kissed her she'd always been the one in control. Able to pull back when she thought things were progressing too swiftly.

She hadn't been prepared for the way Rafe kissed. He was methodical. Slow and intensely sensual. His tongue was igniting other pleasure points on her body that she'd rather not have awakened right now. Her nipples were pressing against the material of her pajama top, and Rafe was equally aroused. She felt his erection on her thigh. Even that didn't send warning signals to her brain.

On the contrary, all she wanted to do was fall deeper into Rafe's kiss, press closer to him, and lose herself in him. Her female center began to throb with a pulse all its own. A beacon that called for satisfaction.

Rafe moaned deep in his throat and abruptly broke off the kiss.

Kate was unsteady on her feet so he held her in his arms a few moments longer.

"I think I should go home," he said softly in her ear.

Kate raised her eyes to his. "Why?" She was still breathless.

"Because you're so damned sweet there is no way in hell I can sleep in the same bed with you and not want to make love to you, Kate. Besides, the only reason I let you lead me around by the nose is that I liked being led around by the nose by you. Am I making any sense?"

"Plenty," Kate said. She smiled at him. "You had no intentions of following the doctor's orders by the letter. You were humoring me because you think I'm cute."

"No, darlin', I think you're beautiful. And *way* out of my league."

He bent and kissed the tip of her nose. "Thanks for that great meal, the shower, and a very interesting evening. But I know when to make an exit, and that time has come."

Kate didn't like the sound of that, but she stood there while he turned and went in search of his clothes, which were in the dryer by now because Kate had put them in there shortly before they'd sat down to eat. As she watched him go she selfishly wished she would've forgotten to put them in the dryer.

A few seconds later, though, she cheered up and realized he was probably right to leave. She was twenty-eight, and had never had a one-night stand. No use spoiling her record now. Though she was tempted.

Rafe was pulling on his jeans when she knocked at the entrance of the laundry room.

"Are you decent?"

"In more ways than one," Rafe said.

Kate strolled in. She had to remind herself to breathe normally when she got a load of his broad-shouldered torso, sculpted pectorals and arm muscles, and a washboard stomach. Cycling definitely did a body good!

"Was everything dry?"

"The jeans were a little damp, but they'll do in a pinch."

Kate felt something shift between them. She wanted to ask him if this was it. Would she ever see him again after tonight? She could not form the words. She wanted to tell him she was going to worry about him all night long. And if he never brightened her door again, she'd always remember tonight. But that sounded too pathetic even as the sentiment came to her.

"Good," was all she said.

"And I don't know how you did it, but you got the stains out. Thank you, Kate."

"It was the least I could do after causing them."

Rafe was buttoning his denim shirt now. His golden brown eyes raked over her face. "Let's not start that up again. You've apologized enough. I forgive you."

At any other time hearing him say he had forgiven her would have made Kate's heart sing with relief. But his tone had such a final ring to it that she was filled with sadness instead.

"Thanks," she said.

"I left my boots and jacket in the living room, I think," Rafe said, moving past her.

Kate followed. "The boots are in the bathroom. The jacket's in the living room."

Rafe laughed shortly. "I promise you, Kate, I don't normally leave my shoes in the bathroom."

Kate perked up when he said that. Why would he care about her opinion of him if he were never going to see her again?

"Yeah, tell me anything. Next you'll be telling me you don't watch Monday night football, or leave nail clippings on the carpet."

Rafe paused long enough to meet her eyes as he turned the corner. "I do watch Monday night football, but I never leave nail clippings on the carpet. Too dangerous."

He then went and collected his boots, carried them out to the living room, and sat on the sofa to pull them on. Kate noticed they were low-heeled leather cowboy boots. *He wears cowboy boots but he doesn't ride,* she thought with a smile.

She helped him on with his jacket.

Rafe put one arm in, then the other, and as soon as that arm was enclosed in the leather sleeve he slipped it around her waist and pulled her to him. Kate was caught off guard by the move, but welcomed another chance to feel his arms around her.

Rafe bent his head and placed a kiss on the side of her neck. "Do you want to see me again, Kate? Because if you'd rather not, tell me now so I won't do something stupid like get my hopes up."

Kate was stunned. She blinked. She had to bite her tongue to keep from shouting with joy. She grinned like an idiot instead. "Yes, I definitely want to see you again."

Rafe smiled his pleasure. He reached into his left jacket pocket and produced a card. "May I borrow a pen?"

"There should be one in my bag, it's in the kitchen."

Rafe went with her, figuring he'd come into the house by the kitchen door and he could leave by it as well. In the kitchen, Kate retrieved the pen and handed it to him.

He wrote his home phone number on the back of a business card and handed it to her. "Now, yours."

Kate gave him her number and watched closely as he wrote it down on the back of another card. She didn't want him to accidentally transpose the numbers, or something!

At the door, Rafe took her hand and peered into her eyes. "Are you free for dinner next Friday night?"

Why so far away, why not tomorrow night? Kate thought. "Yes, I am," she said.

Rafe grinned. "All right. Around seven-thirty?"

"Sounds good," Kate said calmly.

"Great. Then, kiss me, Kate."

Kate laid one on him that had him light-headed as he walked through the door.

Kate thought it peculiar that he was having trouble getting his key in the lock. He waved to her before pulling out of the guest house's yard.

Kate stood at the door and watched until she could no longer see the red taillights of his SUV. Then, she went to bed.

Going to bed was one thing. Going to sleep was quite another.

Kate's mind was racing at the speed of light. Not only were her thoughts consumed with Rafe, but they kept going back to the strange behavior of Dr. William Allen earlier in the evening. She wondered what could have possessed him to send such an incendiary message to her father through her, of all people!

Physics was a competitive field, like any other scientific discipline. Physicists vied for choice positions at major universities. They competed for scientific grants and awards. That was all common. However, to suggest that one scientist turn over his hard-earned research, data that he could very well have spent the better part of his life compiling, to another scientist, except upon his *death*, was preposterous!

Lying in bed now, she wished she did have a black belt in karate and *had* kicked Dr. William Allen's butt for saying such a thing. She would tell her mother about the incident and, together, they would decide whether or not to tell her father.

Her father didn't need the added stress.

Kate rolled over for a better view of the alarm clock: three-thirteen A.M.

Just like a man, she thought. *No consideration for a woman's feelings. Didn't I tell him I would worry about him if he didn't spend the night so that I could keep an eye on that schnozzle of his? Is his arm out of commission? He can't dial a phone? He has my number, for God's sake!*

She fell asleep mentally blessing him out.

Sometime after five, the phone rang.

Kate didn't bother opening her eyes as she felt around on the nightstand for the phone.

Bringing the receiver to her ear, she sleepily said, "Yeah?"

"Kate, are you awake?"

"Barely."

"Would it help if I sang 'The Star-Spangled Banner' to you?"

"Wouldn't hurt."

"'Oh, say can you see . . .'"

"I take that back, it did hurt," Kate said, laughing and quite awake now.

"Don't like my singing, huh?"

"No, but I like the way you kiss."

"I like the way you kiss, too. Listen, Kate, I can't possibly wait nearly a week to see you again. I foolishly set the date that far away because of vanity. I was hoping against hope that my nose would be sufficiently healed by then. But, let's face it, you've seen me at my worst. If tonight didn't turn you off, I guess seeing me again . . . tomorrow night? . . . won't faze you. Please tell me you're free tomorrow night."

"No, I'm not free. It's gonna cost you."

"What? You've already collected a pint of my blood!"

"The whole family is going to the festival tomorrow night."

"What festival?"

"You do live in Tucson, don't you? Signs about the festival are plastered all over the place, and they've been talking about it on every radio and TV station in town for several weeks now. It's the biggest party of the year, the Tucson Meet Yourself Multicultural Festival. It's been a mainstay in southern Arizona for over twenty-five years. I promised my grandmother, she's really my great-grandma, that I'd help her set up her paper flowers booth. I've been helping her for years, so she's come to expect me to be there. She says I'm her good luck charm. You can either come early and help, or I can meet you afterward. You should know, though, Gram will talk your ears off. She's partial to handsome men. All of her cronies are, too. They run in packs."

"Sounds like fun. I'll come early and help set up," Rafe said, laughing softly.

"You're a brave, brave man," Kate told him.

"Not brave," Rafe corrected her, "greedy. For every hour we spend at the festival you have to pay me with a kiss."

"Baby, that's just more incentive to keep you there longer," Kate fired back.

"Uh-oh," Rafe groaned.

Kate awoke the next morning to the sound of someone knocking on the kitchen door. Rolling over, she pried her eyes open. Sunlight glinted through the slit in the curtains. Reluctantly sitting up in bed, she felt around for her slippers.

She rose and trudged through the house to the kitchen, yawning all the way.

Pulling back the curtains that adorned the top half of the kitchen door, she peered into the smiling face of her younger sister, Davida. Everybody called her Little David because she resembled their father, David, so much.

"Let me in," Davida cried, pounding harder on the door.

"Go away, Little David, I'm not done sleeping."

"Is he still here?"

Laughing, Kate unlocked the door, pulled it open, and stood there, not allowing Davida to even peer around her into the kitchen. "So that's why you're here so bright and early. You want a look at my houseguest."

Davida, fifteen years old, five-five, and slender, craned her neck. "Nobody wants a look at your houseguest. I just came over to extend an invitation. Mom wants to know if you two will come to breakfast. And for your information, it's after ten. You're usually up way before now. You must have had a rough night."

"What my night was like is none of your business, short stuff."

Kate stepped aside and allowed Davida to enter.

Davida shot past her and headed straight for Kate's bedroom.

Kate couldn't help laughing at her baby sister's eagerness.

She allowed Davida to determine for herself that there was no one there except her and Kate.

Davida came back into the kitchen at a much slower pace. "Dang! Where'd he go?"

"He left very early this morning," Kate said truthfully. She got a clean glass from the dish rack, walked over to the refrigerator, and poured orange juice into the glass. "Want some?" she asked Davida.

"No, I don't want any orange juice," Davida emphatically stated. "I want to meet the guy you slugged at the airport."

"That can be arranged," Kate told her with a smile.

Davida eyed her sister suspiciously. As the baby of the family, she knew she always had to be wary of favors from her siblings. Especially favors that she hadn't coerced out of them.

"What do I have to do?" Davida asked, dark brown eyes narrowed at her sister.

"Help Gram with her flower booth. You can be Gram's bait tonight. What do you say?" Kate was aware that her grandmother, cagey woman that she was, used *her* to get males to buy flowers supposedly for their girlfriends and wives. "There are gonna be a lot of young, handsome males there tonight."

"You don't have to bribe me, I'll do it," Davida answered immediately. "I was wondering when Gram was going to ask me. You're getting way too old to draw much of a crowd."

Kate placed her glass of orange juice on the counter, and playfully lunged for her sister's throat. Davida squealed and ran through the kitchen door.

"I'm not so old that I can't still beat your little butt,"

Kate told her, hot on her heels. "You've been asking for this for a long time."

A good fifty yards separated the back door of the guest house from the back door of the big house. Davida screamed for her mother at the top of her lungs the entire way.

Carolina was at the sink washing the skillet she'd scrambled eggs in when she heard the commotion. Her ears were attuned to all manner of mayhem produced by her children, and she instinctively knew Davida wasn't in any real trouble.

She went to the back door, anyway, to watch.

Kate was gaining on Davida. Davida knew it and yelled louder. "Mommy!"

David was at the kitchen table trying to read the morning paper. He'd heard Davida's screams, too, and the sound made him smile. Kate and Davida were more apt to roughhouse than their brothers had ever been. David Jr. and Kent were at college now but they had been studious boys and had become even more serious men. Like their father. The girls apparently took after their mother when it came to unadulterated fun.

Carolina got out of the line of fire precisely as Davida flew through the doorway. Just as Davida shot past her, Kate slowed down long enough to give her mother a peck on the cheek. "Morning, Mom."

"Morning, Katharine," said Carolina. "Where is your Cary Grant?"

Davida was standing behind her father's chair, safely out of Kate's reach. She stuck her tongue out at her sister. Kate frowned. "As I was telling my nosy sister, he left early this morning."

"I stated a simple fact, that she's older than I am, and she got all upset," Davida said.

Ignoring her sister for the time being, Kate addressed her father. "Good morning, Daddy. How are you today?"

"Good morning, sweetheart," David said. He spoke haltingly, sounding almost like a foreign-born person learning English. Kate knew her father's progress was quite good according to his doctor, and that his thought processes were much swifter than his ability to translate them into the spoken word. As much as her father used to like to talk about his work, and everything else under the sun, she knew he must feel frustrated sometimes.

Kate walked across the room and spontaneously threw her arms around his neck, and kissed his stubble-covered cheek. "Physicist of the year!"

David shook his head in the negative. "It would mean more to me if it were you they were honoring. But since you have taken yourself out of the running, where is it?"

"Believe it or not, no one actually got to take an award home last night. The award is handmade by African artisans, and it will be a few weeks before it can be shipped to you. I saw it, though. It's a figure of a nude male with the earth in the palm of his right hand. It's formed out of crystal, sitting on a base carved out of mahogany. It's really stunning."

"Did Jason make the conference?"

"Yes, he was there. We shared a table at the awards ceremony. He spent most of his time flirting with an attractive calculus instructor from Howard University."

"Aha!" said Carolina, accusingly. "You told me those conferences were boring, and you couldn't wait to get back home to me."

"They are boring," David said, smiling at her show of jealousy. He loved it when she fussed over him. "One of these days you're going to have to attend one and see for yourself."

"I don't want to break up your orgy," Carolina teased him.

"Perhaps there would actually be one if you went with me," David said.

"Hello!" Kate said. "Children present." Meaning both Davida and herself. She was only joking. It made her very happy that her parents still adored each other. It gave her hope that one day she'd meet her match, and live happily ever after too.

The warning was a little too late, though, because Carolina was leaning over the table and David was about to plant a kiss on his wife's lips.

Kate stood and gestured for Davida to follow her. "Come on, let's give them some privacy."

Davida, unlike her sister, was appalled by her parents' behavior. She didn't want them to *divorce* but their being demonstrative in public seared her teenage sensibilities. No self-respecting fifteen-year-old girl wanted to imagine her parents actually making out!

When they were out of earshot, Kate joked, "From the looks of them, you may not be the baby of the family for long."

Davida's eyes grew wide with horror. "You can't mean that. Mom is forty-eight, and Dad's gonna be fifty-five next Saturday! They're too old to have any more kids."

"Oh, please," Kate said. "It's not uncommon for a woman in her late forties to have a healthy child. Think of it, you would be sixteen when he or she arrived. You could be put on diaper detail. I changed your diapers. What goes around, comes around."

Davida bit her lip, thinking. Then she spun on her heels and headed back to the kitchen. "I've got to break them up while there's still time to prevent a catastrophe!"

Four

"Jenny, will you please stop laughing? My ears are ring-ing from the volume," Rafe complained. It was around noon, and he'd phoned to apologize for snapping at her last night. Then he'd made the mistake of telling her about his encounter with Kate.

"I can't help it," Jenny told him, sniffling. She was laughing and crying simultaneously. "Your story sounds like one of those romantic comedies that I never tire of. Rafe, I've got to meet her."

"No, you don't. It's too early for a family get-together."

"You're meeting her grandmother tonight," Jenny re-minded him.

"That's just her grandmother. Besides, I would've walked over hot coals just to see her again."

"Wow!" said Jenny, her tone awe-filled. "This may be something! Okay, I'll back off for the time being. But you've got to promise me that if you two reach the six-month mark, I'll get to meet her."

"All right," Rafe said. "Now, tell me about this new film you have four lines in."

Jenny sighed contentedly. "It's an independent film. The director is Scott McManus. He's young but well re-spected. And he specially asked for me, Rafe! He'd seen me in a local play. He told me he thinks I'm unique. I have presence."

"Are you certain he isn't coming on to you?" Rafe asked, being the big brother.

"I don't think his boyfriend would allow it," Jenny said, laughing softly. "Yes, I'm pretty certain he hired me because he thinks I'm talented."

"That's great, Jenny. I'm happy for you," Rafe said.

"Even if your worst nightmare may be coming true, and I may actually be able to make a living in this business from now on?"

"All I've ever wanted was for you to be safe and happy," Rafe said truthfully.

Jenny sniffed again. "I know. I've always known that. But it does my heart good to hear you say it."

"Ouch!" Kate exclaimed as Sophie pulled a wide-toothed comb through her wet tresses. "If you'd cut it off, we wouldn't go through this every time I come in here."

Sophie frowned deeply as she concentrated on getting the inevitable knots out of Kate's hair. "Don't start. You know I'm not going to cut your hair. I don't have a death wish. I don't want the entire Huerta clan after me. Huerta women don't cut their hair. That's final. I've heard that speech from Mama Carolina and Grandma Josefina. Both of whom pretended I had no clue that they were subtly threatening me not to cut your hair, since I'm your hairstylist of choice."

"How is Renata?" Kate asked, changing the subject because she knew she wasn't going to convince Sophie to cut her hair. Sophie truly had been spooked by her mother and her grandmother.

"She's doing great," Sophie said. "She still looks for Jess every afternoon when she gets home from the babysitter's, though. It breaks my heart every time."

Kate didn't know what to say. She'd never been in Sophie's shoes.

Eight months ago her husband, Jessie, left the house for his construction job and never came home again. He'd been killed in a freak accident when the stone he was breaking apart with a jackhammer suddenly splintered and a piece shot up and pierced his chest three inches deep. No one had ever seen or heard of anything like it.

The story ran on the local news for weeks afterward. The company didn't want to admit to liability for the accident because of the fact that it had never happened before. They called it an act of God. The courts decided differently. They said since Jessie was on the company's time clock when the accident occurred, it was responsible for making sure his widow and child would be taken care of at least as well as they would be if Jessie were still alive. When the company balked at that decision, the case went to trial, and the jurors awarded Sophie three times the amount the company would have paid if they'd agreed to the initial court ruling.

"You know I'd do anything for you and Renata, Sophie. All you have to do is ask," Kate said. "Do you think it would help if she stayed with me a few days? You know, to take her out of her normal environment?"

"I tried that," Sophie said. Finished getting the tangles out of Kate's hair, she began blow-drying it section by section. "I sent her to Phoenix with my parents. Renata cried until Mama and Daddy drove her home. Talk about a nerve-racking experience. By the time Mama and Daddy got here from Phoenix they were both ready for stiff drinks, and Mama doesn't drink."

"It's only a thirty-minute drive from my place," Kate said.

"To tell the truth," Sophie said, meeting Kate's eyes in the big mirror Kate was sitting in front of as she styled her hair, "I don't think I'm ready to be left alone in that big house. I depend on her for comfort as much as she depends on me."

Kate reached up and squeezed her hand. "Take your time, sweetie. Take your time."

Fighting back tears, Sophie said, "Can we talk about that fine deputy marshal you just met? You haven't described him yet. You just said he was good-looking."

Kate was happy to oblige. "He's around six feet tall. He's not bulky. He's muscular. He has the best leg and thigh muscles I've seen on a man since my college days at UC, and I was surrounded by athletes."

"I don't want to just hear about his physical assets. I want you to describe how he makes you *feel*," Sophie said. Her brown eyes in her pretty cocoa-colored face had a faraway look in them. "With Jessie, the first time we met, I swear, I was so smitten I wasn't sure what he actually looked like, except that his eyes were a *beautiful* shade of brown. But I remembered every emotion he evoked in me. He made me laugh. He made my heart beat double time. He made me feel so . . ."

"Alive," Kate said.

"Yeah, that's it!" Sophie said excitedly.

"As if electricity were coursing through your veins."

"Exactly!"

"And you're having trouble keeping your head from flying off and floating up somewhere in the clouds."

"Now, I wouldn't go that far," Sophie said, laughing.

Kate laughed, too. "Well, you asked how he makes me feel. He makes me lose my head."

"You can't take Church Avenue," Estrella Lopez said from the backseat. "Access from that street will be closed off all three days of the festival."

"I know, Auntie Estrella," Kate said from behind the wheel of the Jeep Cherokee.

Not only did she have her grandmother sitting in front with her, but three of her grandmother's friends were sharing the backseat.

"You ought to sell in the daytime, too, Josefina," Gloria Johnson said. "You're losing money by setting up only during the evening hours."

"I've been doing this for nearly twenty-five years, Gloria," said Josefina. "You get the best customers at night. Boys trying to impress their girlfriends, husbands doing penance for some wrong done to their wives. Besides, I'm too old to put in twelve hours. Six is long enough."

"You're not old!" her chorus said in unison from the backseat.

"Oh, I'm old all right," Josefina said. "I'm twenty years older than you are, Gloria; seventeen years older than you are, Estrella; and thirteen older than you are, Vera. Don't tell me eighty-eight isn't old, because it is. Tell me I still look good; then you'd be telling the truth."

Kate cast a sidelong glance at her feisty grandmother. Indeed, Josefina Huerta was a handsome woman with café au lait skin, sparkling black eyes, and thick white hair that she wore in a single plait down her back.

"'Vanity, thy name is woman,'" Kate said, quoting William Shakespeare.

"No, dear, it's Josefina Elena Margaret Huerta," Josefina said with a hearty laugh. "Just thank God you've got my genes. You, too, will look this good at eighty-eight."

Kate laughed uproariously. "Pay no attention to her, ladies. I suspect she had a glass of sherry before she left home."

"That shows how much you know," Josefina said. "I had *two* glasses of sherry before I left home. It's going to be cool tonight."

"Good thing I brought this," Estrella said, and Kate heard the rustle of a paper bag being opened. She didn't have to look in the backseat to know that Estrella was holding a bottle of some kind of spirits.

"That's my girl," said Josefina.

"Wait a minute," Kate put in. "Who is going to drive you drunks home tonight? I told you, Gram, I have a date. Estrella, I'm driving *your* Jeep to the festival. I was under the impression you were going to drive the other ladies back home."

Gloria spoke up. "Don't worry, Kate, I'm the designated driver tonight. We're doing girls' night. After the festival we're having a pajama party at my house. We're gonna watch old movies, eat popcorn, and talk all night."

"Whew!" said Kate. "All right. You gals had me worried there for a minute."

Josefina laughed. "What you need to be worried about is how we're gonna behave when your sweetheart shows up."

"Kate has a sweetheart?" Estrella asked, pleased.

Kate corrected Josefina. "I have a date. Not a sweetheart."

"Sweetheart? Date? What's the difference nowadays?" Vera Molina said. She was the quietest of the foursome but even she couldn't stay out of this impromptu questioning of Kate. "It used to be that a sweetheart was a serious suitor. But today the courtship stage is whittled down to nearly nothing, and as soon as you meet it's kiss, kiss, cuddle, cuddle, and into the sack. Don't you do that, Kate. Make sure he knows that you're worth waiting for. Get the ring on your finger first."

"That's a bit much, isn't it, Vera?" Gloria objected. "I see nothing wrong with sex before marriage as long as it's between two people who love each other, and who intend to marry each other."

"Why buy the cow when you can get the milk for free?" Vera said calmly.

"Raymond and I were intimate before marriage and we've been married for more than forty years," Estrella said as an example. "We were discreet, of course. Our parents would have killed us if they'd known. But such was the way of many couples. Sex simply wasn't talked about. It was definitely done. Just not talked about."

"That's right," Josefina said. "Even when I was a young girl, I knew of girls who did it and went on to have very happy marriages. Of course they had to be circumspect. They couldn't give it away to every Tom, Dick, and Harry who asked nicely. The key was to wait for someone who believed in the sanctity of marriage but who was simply too hot-blooded to wait for the wedding night. Of course the seduction progressed by degrees. First you indulged in meaningful looks for weeks on end."

"Yes," said Vera. "I remember when a glance from the right man could make me swoon. A smoldering look goes a long way."

"Then comes the touch," Josefina continued. "He might sidle up to you in church, and 'accidentally' touch your arm in passing. Oh, that sent your pulse racing. Or you might drop your handkerchief and he would pick it up for you, and when you took it, your hands would touch. Ah, bliss! There would be months of longing to be alone with each other. Then, finally, when you got the chance to be alone somewhere, your passion would ignite and making love would seem the right thing to do, the only thing."

"You sound like you're speaking from experience," Kate said. She had to admit, her eighty-eight-year-old grandmother had her full attention.

"I am, dear," Josefina told her with a mysterious smile.

"Can we change the subject now?" Kate sincerely asked, to which the foursome broke into laughter.

"Look at her, behaving as if she doesn't know one end of a man from the other," Josefina said. "You're twenty-eight, Katharine Josefina Matthews, and as far as I know, you've never been in love. Don't you think you're overdue?"

"Love is not something you take lightly. When have I had time for love?" Kate began in earnest.

"Time?" Josefina nearly shouted. "Who do you suppose schedules the time to fall in love? Do you think your mother was thinking like that when she nearly ran down your father in the desert? No. She took one look at him, and she *knew* he was the man she was supposed to spend the rest of her life with. It wasn't convenient for either of them. Her father was opposed to the marriage because of the color of your dad's skin. Edward even had the nerve to bring up the subject of Buffalo Soldiers: how the U.S. Army enlisted black men to hunt down and kill Indians in the West. I told him, 'What has that got to do with a hill of beans? The girl's in love!'"

Josefina sat with her hands folded on her lap, a contented smile on her face. "Two weeks later, your mother and father eloped. Edward disinherited your mother, but Consuelo, my dear daughter-in-law, God rest her soul, could not turn her back on your mother. She stood up to Edward and told him unless he welcomed David into the family, she would go live with her mother. Edward caved in, and the rest is history. Now, I have four great-grandchildren to cherish."

"And who cherish you," Kate told her.

"So don't tell me about time," Josefina said with a note of finality. "I'm telling you not to waste it. Because one day you're going to be as old as I am. Are you going to have memories of good sex with your man to look back on, or are you going to have an empty memory bank? Take it from your gram, and start making deposits in your bank."

They were in El Presidio Park by now. Kate found a parking space as close to the entrance as possible. "Okay, here we are. May I reiterate, ladies? Don't embarrass me in front of Rafe. He's not used to your brand of honesty. Let him get to know you slowly," she said as they all got out of the car.

She walked around to the back and unlocked the hatch where they'd stored all of the clear plastic bags in which Josefina kept her crepe paper flowers.

The ladies knew the drill, and each of them came around for their fair share of the bags. Each of the ladies also grabbed a folding chair, while Kate, being the strongest of the group, carried the folding card table. They were off to the festival!

The air was getting brisk already at nearly five o'clock. The main entertainment on Saturday night didn't get started until six. However, El Presidio Park was teeming with people, some of whom were dressed for the Costume Paseo or a demonstration of native ethnic dress. Tucson boasted ethnic groups from all over the world as represented in the folk arts that were being offered at the festival. There were booths that demonstrated the making of African-American quilts, Apache violin making, Chinese traditional art, Japanese origami, Lao weaving, piñata making, Ukrainian wood carving, Yaqui paper flowers (Josefina's booth), Riata rawhide braiding, and many, many more arts and crafts too numerous for Kate to recall.

Inside, Josefina found her spot between a woman demonstrating the art of Indian hand-painting, and a man who specialized in peach-pit carving. Josefina made a point of going over and introducing herself and her friends to both of them.

Kate kept busy by putting up the card table.

"It's about time you got here," said a masculine voice behind her.

Kate had unfolded three legs of the table, and was in the midst of unfolding the fourth. She leaned the table against her thigh and grinned up at Rafe. He was wearing jeans and brown leather boots, a pale blue western-style shirt, and a brown leather jacket. The bridge of his nose was covered with a small white bandage. There was some bruising there but it didn't look as bad as Kate had imagined it would the next day.

"You're a sight for sore eyes," Kate said. Her heart thudded in her chest, and she suddenly wanted to be rid of the pesky table leaning against her thigh.

Rafe came over and took the table from her, straightened out the final leg, and set it on its legs. They stood there gazing into each other's eyes while the rest of the world seemed to disappear.

"I like your hair," Rafe said.

Sophie had curled it so that it fell about her shoulders in a dark, wild mass. Kate had had to wear a headband in an attempt to tame it. Sophie called it "hair that drives a man crazy with desire."

"I'm glad you like it," Kate said, making small talk when all she wanted to do was throw herself into his arms and kiss him. "You look very handsome tonight."

Handsome? More like good enough to eat! she thought.

They moved closer. Rafe held out his hand. Kate placed her hand in his and something electric passed between them. It was just as Josefina had described a few minutes ago.

Rafe leaned in. Kate rose up on her toes. Their mouths were mere inches apart. Kate inhaled his scent, a combination of spicy aftershave and his own skin. She swallowed. Her lips parted a minuscule amount. Rafe's mouth glanced over hers, and then someone screamed behind them, "There she is!"

Kate groaned softly when she recognized Davida's

voice. She and Rafe quickly parted, turned, and painted welcoming smiles on their faces.

"You're going to meet more than my grandmother tonight, after all," Kate said for his ears only. She took his hand and squeezed it reassuringly.

"Relax," Rafe said. "We're gonna love each other, I'm sure."

While Davida and her parents were still a few yards away Kate took the opportunity to say, "Sorry. I had no idea Davida would be here this early. She was supposed to show up at around seven. She'll be helping Gram with the booth tonight."

"Maybe that means we can steal away earlier," Rafe said, trying to put a positive spin on the situation.

Kate met his eyes. He was smiling so warmly at her that the pit of her stomach felt woozy. Whenever he smiled, the nicest crinkles appeared at the corners of his eyes. "You can bet on it," Kate said with a saucy smile of her own. "Did you dream about me last night?"

"You know I did," Rafe said. He hadn't blushed in a long time, but he felt one coming on now. Could it be because her parents were only six feet away while he was imagining their daughter in compromising positions? Why had Kate said that, knowing that he was about to meet her parents for the first time?

He got his answer when he looked into her mischievous brown eyes. She *liked* shaking him up. He'd have to stay on his guard around her.

By the time Davida, David, and Carolina reached Kate and Rafe, Josefina and her crew had finished socializing with their booth neighbors. Kate and Rafe found themselves sandwiched between seven people who were all itching to learn more about the mysterious man Kate had dragged home with her last night.

As was a common occurrence in her family, everyone started talking at once:

"So this is Deputy Marshal Grant," Carolina said. "He's every bit as handsome as you said he was, Kate."

"Good going, Granddaughter," Josefina said enthusiastically. "You don't want to throw *him* back!"

"*Ay, caramba!*" said Estrella. "If I were only fifty years younger."

"You still wouldn't have a chance," Gloria told her. "Not if I saw him first."

"You two are embarrassing me," complained Vera.

"We're always embarrassing you, Vera," Estrella replied. "So, what's new?"

"Mommy, why can't *I* date?" moaned Davida. It was a question she'd asked her parents practically every day since her fifteenth birthday when she was told she would have to wait until she turned sixteen to date.

"Would you hens stop cackling?" David said. "Give the boy a chance to breathe."

"Thanks, Daddy," Kate said gratefully. "Now, if you all would stop talking long enough, I'd like to introduce you." She paused, waiting. "Okay, Rafael Grant, I'd like you to meet my mother, Carolina Huerta Matthews."

Carolina, five feet three and slender with coppery brown skin and salt-and-pepper hair that was as wavy and long as Kate's, stepped forward and shook his hand, holding on to it as she peered up at him with eyes dark as obsidian, but infinitely friendly. Rafe liked her at once. "Hello, Rafael."

"And this is my father, Professor David Matthews," Kate said.

David smiled at him. "You're new to Tucson, son?" he asked as they shook.

"I've been here about six months."

"You have to be careful or you'll wind up staying forever," David said with a meaningful glance in his wife's direction.

Carolina didn't miss a thing. "As if you've suffered any during your thirty-two-year stay here!"

Laughing, Kate continued with the introductions. She went to her grandmother and placed an arm about her shoulders. "This outspoken lady is my great-grandmother, Josefina."

Rafe felt as if he should bow in Josefina's presence. She stood with her back straight, and her black eyes looking directly into his. "It's a pleasure, young man," she said in imperious tones. Her grip was firm and no-nonsense.

"The pleasure's all mine," Rafe said respectfully.

"And these ladies are close friends of the family," Kate continued. In turn she introduced him to Estrella, a Mexican-American, Vera, a Pascua Yaqui Indian, and Gloria, an African-American.

Davida noisily cleared her throat when Kate was finished. "What about me?"

Kate went over and mussed Davida's cornrows. "And, finally, this is the baby of the family, Davida."

"Hello, Rafael," Davida said dreamily.

Rafe smiled at her. "Hi, Davida. Good to meet you."

Davida squinted at his nose. "Oh, she got you good, didn't she?" she said, frowning and shaking her head in sympathy.

Rafe touched his nose. "Yeah, she got me good."

"Okay, okay," said Josefina. "It's time to get down to business. We've got to get the flowers on display before six. That leaves us half an hour."

"David and I are going to get out of your hair," Carolina said, clasping David's hand in hers. She gave Davida a stern look. "We'll be back for you at ten o'clock. Be here. I don't want you gallivanting all over the place with those friends of yours. Help your Grandma like you promised to do."

"Can't I go get something to eat with Sherry and Kyle at eight? They said they'd be by around then so we could hang."

"Only if your Grandma says it's all right," David told her firmly. "Do not leave the grounds, and be back here by ten. If we have to go looking for you, it's your hide."

"Oh, ease up on her, she's a teenager," Josefina said in Davida's defense.

"That's why we're so tough on her," Carolina said. She went to plant a kiss on her grandmother's silken cheek. "And don't let my child flirt too outrageously with male customers. I know you've been using Kate as bait for years, you old fox."

"And I've been selling out every year," Josefina said with a chuckle.

Carolina turned away, laughing too. "Okay, everyone, David and I are off. Have fun, ladies. Rafe, it was good to meet you. Don't keep Kate out too late tonight."

"Mother!" said Kate.

"I was just kidding. Take her to Mexico if you want to," Carolina said as she and David strolled off, both of them laughing.

When they were out of earshot, David said, "Nice boy."

"Yeah, cute, too," said Carolina.

"Is that all you Huerta women think about, a man's sex appeal?"

"Wait until I get you alone in the theater, and I'll show you."

Kate and Rafe rolled up their sleeves and were preparing to pitch in and help remove the paper flowers from the plastic bags and put them on display when Josefina pulled Kate aside. "Would you and Rafael get out of here! I have enough help. Go make some memories."

Kate didn't have to be told twice. She hugged Josefina. "We're going."

"Take him riding in the moonlight. That's how I snagged your grandpa."

"It's too cold for that," Kate said.

"Improvise," said Josefina.

Kate walked over to Rafe, who was surrounded by Gloria, Estrella, and Vera. "Gram told us to get lost."

"So soon?" said Vera.

"Why don't you run along and leave him here, Kate?" Estrella proposed.

"Yeah, we haven't had the chance to ask him if he has an older brother yet," Gloria, who had lost her husband many years ago, said.

"No brothers, sorry," Rafe said, backing away from the three of them.

Kate grabbed him by the hand. "Good night, Aunties!"

Estrella, Vera, and Gloria laughed heartily as they watched Kate and Rafe hightail it for the exit. Josefina clapped her hands sharply, getting her crew's attention. "Okay, you've flirted enough for one night, let's hustle!" She looked around them. "Where is Davida? That little devil has slipped off already!"

Kate and Rafe wound their way through the burgeoning crowd, heading for the exit.

They were walking with their arms about each other's waists, and Kate could not help noticing how right it felt being this close to him.

"Your family is as nutty as you are," Rafe said. "I liked them very much."

"Good, because they liked you, too," Kate told him, pleased.

She grinned at him, displaying short, white teeth in her golden brown face. "So, Mr. Grant, where are you taking me tonight? Am I dressed appropriately?"

She was wearing a short long-sleeve dress in autumn red with a brown leather jacket over it. On her feet were half-calf boots also in brown leather.

"You look beautiful, no matter where I'm taking you," Rafe said. He wanted her to walk ahead of him so he could get his fill of her long, shapely legs, which he was seeing for the first time tonight. She wore everything with gusto. Be it pajamas or dresses.

"You're being evasive," Kate said of his reply to her question about whether her manner of dress was appropriate for where he was taking her.

"It's a surprise," said Rafe.

"Kate!"

Kate and Rafe stopped and turned.

Vance Huerta was strolling toward them with a date in tow. The young woman was dark-haired and very pretty. She cast a not-too-friendly glance at Kate. Kate figured Vance hadn't told her that she was his cousin and not an ex-girlfriend.

"Hey, Kate, I thought that was you," Vance said. "Hey, man, didn't you get enough of her last night? You should know that Huerta women are hell on wheels."

Kate saw his date visibly relax. She even smiled at Kate.

"Hello, Vance," Rafe said. "You should know that Huerta women are also hard to resist."

"I have to agree with you on that one," Vance said. "There sure are enough Huertas around to vouch for that." Remembering his manners, he said to Kate, "Kate, you remember Trudy Rodriguez from school, don't you?"

Kate peered a little closer. She hadn't even recognized Trudy. They'd graduated from Tucson High School the same year. Trudy had been a cheerleader. In fact, she'd been one of the girls who had relentlessly tormented Kate when Kate had told them she didn't want to become a cheerleader and join their clique. Kate felt more at home with the so-called nerds. High school could be pure hell for anyone singled out by people like Trudy Rodriguez.

Of course Trudy wouldn't associate Kate with Vance. Kate had gone by the name Matthews in high school, not Huerta.

"Hey, Trudy," Kate said pleasantly. "It's been a long time."

"It sure has," Trudy said, beaming. "You look good, Kate."

"So do you."

"You know they're having the reunion in December, don't you?" Trudy said. "I guess they figure lots of us will be home for Christmas and it would be a good time to have it. I hope you'll be there. Vance and I are going."

Vance looked uncomfortable when she said that. But he quickly smiled down into her upturned face before she noticed. He regarded Kate. "Well, cousin, I'm sure you and Deputy Marshal Grant have places to go. So we'll see you later."

"All right," said Kate. "Bye, Trudy. Good seeing you again."

"It was good seeing you, too," said Trudy. "Hope you make the reunion." The two couples separated and went in opposite directions. Kate quickened her pace. Rafe pulled her closer to his side as they walked. "I take it she isn't a friend of yours."

"She, along with several of her friends, made my life a living hell in high school," Kate told him. She was amazed at how strongly those feelings of being ridiculed had returned upon recognizing Trudy Rodriguez. It had happened ten years ago. She wasn't that insecure girl anymore. *No one can make you feel insecure unless you give them permission to do so.* That was her mantra today.

"You want to tell me about it?"

"There isn't that much to tell, Rafe. I'm a woman now. I don't let that sort of thing steal my peace of mind. I did, however, have a physical reaction to her when I remembered her. My stomach muscles clenched painfully when I recalled how truly cruel she, and others, had been. I know now that they'd attacked me because *they* were so insecure themselves. But back then I didn't have that figured out, and it just hurt."

"It's hard to imagine anyone picking on you, Kate. You would have beaten them senseless."

Kate laughed. "I wasn't always as confident as I am now. Back then, I was just a girl in love with science and horses. I wanted to be left alone to study and ride horses, that was all. However, like it often is in high school, others sought to dictate my life. Trudy and the other girls in her group figured I looked like them, so I should be one of them. What's more, I should be grateful they chose me, because, after all, I was a half-breed."

They were near the exit now, and Kate was pleased, because she didn't want to run into anyone else she knew. All she wanted to do was go somewhere to be alone with Rafe and talk all night long.

"They knew my mother was an Indian because she volunteered at the school. They saw her on a fairly regular basis. And Dad was very well known around here because of his work in quantum physics and because he taught at the university. Everyone knew he was black. Whenever the local news reported anything about him they made a point of mentioning his heritage."

"Yeah, I know how that is," Rafe put in. "It's as if the media are always amazed that a black person can be accomplished at something, and has to mention it as though the person is unique and a credit to his race."

"Exactly," Kate said. "That really upsets Dad. Anyway

when I refused to be bullied into becoming a cheerleader they started calling me half-breed and accusing me of thinking I was better than they were. When the truth was I didn't think of them at all. They singled *me* out! All I wanted—"

"Was to be left alone to study science and ride your horses," Rafe finished for her.

"Amen!" said Kate.

They were through the exit and walking across the street to where Rafe had parked his car when Kate spotted Jason Edmonton making his way across the street, heading toward the festival's entrance.

Jason looked up and grinned at her. Kate always marveled at how good-looking Jason was. He was African-American, in his early fifties, six-two, in great shape, and had that "distinguished gentleman" thing going on with gray at his temples. Kate had had a huge crush on him when she was a teenager. Now she simply loved him for who he was, her father's best friend, and her godfather.

Jason gave her a bear hug there in the middle of the street while Rafe looked on.

"Hey, sugar," said Jason. He eyed Rafe. "Who is this?"

Kate swiftly made the introductions. "Dr. Jason Edmonton, Rafael Grant." She looked up at Rafe. "Jason is my godfather." She looked up at Jason. "Rafe is my date."

The men shook hands.

"A pleasure," said Jason.

"Same here," Rafe assured him.

Jason met Kate's gaze. "I assume your gram has her regular booth this year?"

"Like clockwork," Kate said.

"And the rest of the family?"

"Davida's helping Gram, and Mom and Dad are taking in a movie," Kate told him.

"Ah," said Jason. "I was hoping I'd catch your parents. I wanted to talk to your dad about something."

"Not work?" Kate was quick to ask. Jason and her father were colleagues at the university. Jason was her father's department head. Before her father's stroke they had been a real team. Jason enjoyed the recognition David's work brought to the department. Not only that, but because the university had David they were also first on the list when grants were being given out. The physics department had been in the black for years because of David. His illness could have a negative effect on the financial health of the physics department. That's why Kate was so protective of her father where Jason was concerned. Jason was her father's friend, but he was also his boss. He wanted his cash cow back working for the university as soon as possible.

"Don't get your back up, Kate," Jason said with a smile. "I've already gotten an earful from Carolina when I phoned earlier today and asked to speak with David. Has it ever occurred to you Amazons that I just wanted to shoot the breeze with him?"

"You're always welcome at the ranch, Jason," Kate told him. "But you know Dad. If it were left up to him, he would be back in the lab right now doing exactly what his doctors advise him not to: continuing his research. Two more months, Jason. Then, you can have him. Until then, he's ours."

Jason held up both hands in a conciliatory gesture. "All right, Kate. Like I said, I only wanted to chat with David about personal things. Not work."

Jason regarded Rafe. "Nice meeting you."

"Likewise," Rafe replied with a sympathetic smile. He didn't understand why Kate had been so hard on the guy. But then he didn't know Jason Edmonton, while she did.

"Bye, Jason," Kate said. "Enjoy your evening."

"You, too," said Jason.

Kate and Rafe hurried to his car before they could be waylaid by anyone else. At the car, Kate leaned against the passenger-side door and crooked a finger at Rafe. "I've got something for you."

Rafe went to her, slipped his arms about her waist, and gently pulled her against him.

"I dreamed about holding you all night long."

"I dreamed about your kisses," Kate told him. "Refresh my memory."

Rafe lowered his head and claimed her mouth. They kissed softly, but intensely, as if they were lovers who had been denied each other's touch for months instead of less than a day. Rafe's mouth was a marvel as far as Kate was concerned. His tongue never invaded or plundered, but enticed and mesmerized.

He turned his head, thereby breaking off the kiss. "Was that familiar to you?"

Kate gazed up at him with a contented smile. "Vaguely."

Rafe redoubled his efforts. He gathered her in his arms and, bending her slightly backward, kissed her deeply, ending with the gentle suckling of her bottom lip. Kate gave a satisfied sigh when he let her go. She didn't know what he'd done but whatever spot he'd hit upon with his tongue had nearly made her have an orgasm.

Rafe had a self-satisfied smirk on his face. "I see you recognize me now."

"Oh, yeah," Kate breathed.

Rafe could see her pulse beating on the side of her neck. He leaned close and planted a kiss there. "You're too sexy for your own good. It's going to be hell resisting you."

They were alone in that section of the parking lot. The

sun was going down, and Arizona's famous orange-streaked sky was about to put in an appearance.

Kate looked him straight in the eyes. "Why would you want to resist me?"

Rafe smiled at her. "What are you saying, Kate?"

"I'm saying I've never felt this way before and, as a scientist, I feel duty-bound to conduct an experiment and record my findings for future generations."

Rafe laughed. "That's the most inventive invitation to a woman's bed I've ever had."

Rafe busied his hands by unlocking the passenger-side door and handing her in.

Before closing the door, he said, "But the answer's no, Kate. It's too soon to make love to you."

He firmly closed the door, and Kate immediately reached over and unlocked his door for him. As soon as he got inside, Kate said, "It's my family, isn't it?"

They buckled up.

Rafe put the key in the ignition, but didn't immediately start the car. He met her eyes. "Yes, and no. I like your family. Meeting them told me something about you, Kate. You love your family and you're passionate about protecting them. I can relate to that because I've always felt that way about my sister, Jenny, who is just about all the family I have left. But the main reason I won't take you to bed any time soon is that I know rushing into sex can ruin a relationship faster than anything else, and I want you in my life longer than a few weeks. So, to quote you, the only thing that separates us from the animals is our ability to control our impulses."

Kate had no reply to that. After all, the man made perfect sense, while she had obviously misplaced a few IQ points in the last few minutes.

"Do you feel me?" Rafe asked.

"Apparently I won't be doing that for a long, long time," Kate joked.

Rafe laughed and started the car. "How long has it been?"

"Since?" Kate asked, playing dumb.

"You know what I mean."

Rafe backed the car out of the parking spot and pointed it north.

"You have to be more specific," Kate said.

"Sex, Kate. How long has it been since you made love to a man? Is that specific enough for you?"

"How do you define 'make love'? Because, as you know, there are different degrees of making love. Kissing can be defined as making love because we exchange bodily fluids while engaging in it."

"In this day and age, if you're safe, there is no exchanging of bodily fluids during intercourse. That's what I'm referring to. Coitus, Kate. It's when a man and a woman interlock bodies, for however short a period of time." His tone was amused, not in the least bit irritated.

"Then, technically, I have never had sex with anybody."

Rafe felt that statement deserved his full attention, so he pulled the car over at the earliest opportunity, which turned out to be the parking lot of a McDonald's. He parked the car and simply sat there a couple of minutes looking at Kate.

Then, he broke the silence with "Never?"

"Well, you see, most of my blossoming years were spent with my nose in a book. And to be honest, I never missed sex. Riding horses has its advantages. Haven't you ever wondered why so many young girls love to ride so much? Let's just say my needs were being met, okay?"

"Then you have had an orgasm?"

"I'm not a *virgin*," Kate said, aghast. "I just haven't had sex."

Rafe mulled that over a bit. "Mmm, I see."

"I shouldn't have told you. Now you're going to think I'm some kind of a freak," Kate said, looking at him for some sign that he truly did think she was nuts.

Rafe had a slight scowl on his handsome face, and he was chewing on his bottom lip as he looked at her. "What about oral sex?"

"No. I've never given it or had it done to me."

"Masturbation?"

"Yes, of course. I experimented like any normal adolescent. I'm pretty good at it now. Don't you do it?"

"Yes, but I'm not a technical virgin. Has a man ever brought you to orgasm by touching you 'down there,' or anywhere else?"

Kate sighed. "If you count your tongue in my mouth just a few minutes ago, then almost. Otherwise, no."

Rafe smiled at her. "Kate, you are a challenge."

"You like challenges?"

"Love them."

"Good, then you can introduce me to all those little things I've been missing."

Rafe smiled even broader at the prospect as he turned the key in the ignition. "It would be my pleasure."

Kate put her hand high on his thigh. "Mine, too."

Five

The Puma was minding his own business, methodically chewing up one of Carolina's old sandals with his sharp teeth, when he was rudely interrupted. The noise came from downstairs. For a moment, The Puma entertained the thought of hiding under the bed until he had the chance to sneak outside again. He was not supposed to be in the house. When the humans were preparing to leave, one of them had left the front door open for a few minutes while she went back inside to get her coat and that's when he'd stealthily entered the house and hidden under the sofa.

Frankly, if the humans didn't want him in their precious house they shouldn't have built it on a spot he was fond of. He was a mountain lion. His mountains, the Catalinas, were only a day's run from here. That was where the human, Kate, had found him, half starved, three years ago. She referred to him as a tomcat, but he'd known what he truly was ever since that day the other humans, the ones who'd left him in the mountains, had driven off in their car. To survive, he'd had to become one with the mountain. Kate had seen it in him the moment she'd set eyes on him and dubbed him The Puma, which was Spanish for "mountain lion."

The Puma purred irritably as he languidly rose, abandoning the chewed-up sandal, and went to investigate the noise. He sniffed the air. That human aroma wasn't anything like his regular humans' smells. Leaving the bedroom, he paused when he reached the landing. He heard voices. Those definitely were not the voices of *his* humans.

He positioned himself between two slats in the railing on the landing and peered down onto two dark heads belonging to males of the human species, males he'd never sniffed or seen before.

This was where things got tricky. On the one hand he wasn't supposed to be there himself, so keeping his presence in the house a secret would be to his advantage. On the other hand he was a mountain lion and there was nothing mountain lions enjoyed more than leaping onto their prey from a superior height. Although the landing could not double for a mountain ledge, it would do. Poised on the precipice, The Puma waited.

Soon a head appeared just below him. Bombs away. . . . The Puma screeched a war whoop on the way down. The human whose head he'd targeted looked upward, and screamed loud and long, especially when The Puma's claws dug into his face.

"Argghhhhh. . . ." The man continued to scream in terror as he dropped everything he had in his arms and began pulling at the maniac cat on his head. "Get it off me, man. Get it off!"

The other man was so startled he'd tripped and fallen over a chair. Pushing himself up now, he looked at the scene unfolding in front of him. He looked around frantically for something he could use to dislodge the cat from his partner's head. He certainly wasn't going to touch the animal with his bare hands. It could be rabid!

But before he could find anything, The Puma grew bored with the game, leaped from his prey's head, and shot out the door, which the humans had left ajar.

Laughing, the guy who had escaped the wrath of The Puma said, "I had no idea they had an attack cat."

"Very funny," said the victim. He gingerly touched his face and examined his hand. He was bleeding. "Somebody ought to skin that cat."

"Stop whining and pick up the disks you dropped. I've got the hard drive."

"This is heaven," Kate said.

After a meal in a soul food restaurant in Tucson, Rafe had driven into the desert and now they were parked near a saguaro that measured nearly sixty feet tall, looking at the stars. Maxwell's latest CD was playing softly in the background and the two of them were cuddling on the front seat.

"Let me guess," Rafe said. "You've never steamed up the car windows with a horny teenaged boy before."

"No, that's not entirely true. On prom night, Tomas Valencia and I parked. But the boy couldn't kiss. He literally choked me with his tongue. Turned me off of kissing for five years."

"You were in college before you let another guy get close enough to kiss you?"

"Yeah. He was a running back on the football team. He gave me my first good French kiss, and he was also the first guy I was tempted to make love to."

"What stopped you?"

"He was very popular. I didn't want to be another notch on his bedpost, so I broke it off. It wasn't as if he'd promised to be faithful or anything. He told me from the start that college was just a stepping-off point for him, and he didn't plan to make any permanent attachments there."

"He went on to play pro ball then?"

"He's still playing: George Sanders of the Dallas Cowboys."

"You mean I have old George to thank for the way you kiss? I'm going to have to send him a thank-you card," Rafe joked, pulling her closer to nuzzle her neck.

Kate fairly purred when he began trailing kisses down the side of her neck. "And you? Who taught you to kiss like that?"

"I went through a lot of girls before I came to my present technique," Rafe murmured against her neck. "I was probably as bad as Tomas Valencia was when I kissed my first girl at thirteen."

Kate had removed her boots, and her legs were curled up on the seat. If Rafe kept kissing her neck like this she feared she'd be tempted to remove some other article of clothing, and toss it onto the backseat with her boots.

She sat up suddenly and said, "Tell me about your work. Why did you join the U.S. Marshals Service?"

Taking his cue from her, Rafe sat up straighter and removed his arm from about her shoulders. If the lady wanted to cool it for a while, it was fine with him. He was becoming too turned-on by her anyway. He could use the time to concentrate on reducing the amount of stretching the material in his crotch had undergone.

"I went into the navy at seventeen, right out of high school. Mom and Dad were gone and there was no money for college. Besides, I needed money to help support Jenny. We had few relatives who were willing to take in a nine-year-old. In fact, no one volunteered except an elderly great-aunt. She was eighty-three then and not in the best of health. But she was willing to look after Jenny. I arranged with the Navy to have part of my salary sent to Jenny. After I was discharged, I went to Temple University, and majored in criminal justice. I wasn't sure what I wanted to become, a cop, or maybe go to the FBI academy? It was by accident that I ran into a brother who was a deputy marshal. He introduced me to the program. It sparked my interest and after I graduated, I applied. I think it was the thought of actually enforcing the ruling of the courts that attracted me to the work. I like bringing the bad guys to justice. And I also like protecting the innocent."

Kate had thought listening to him talk about his job would be mundane, something to take the edge off her arousal, but the passion with which he spoke made her even more aroused. It was perhaps fifty degrees outside. Therefore the windows were up. Kate reached over and lowered her power window a bit. "It's getting hot in here."

Rafe couldn't agree more. It was indeed hot in there. The sexual tension was so thick that he felt the weight of it in every cell of his body. His *hard* body. He wanted her, and wished he hadn't been such a boy scout earlier. But that was lust talking. He would deny himself satisfaction, but maybe he could satisfy Kate.

"Do you trust me, Kate?"

"Absolutely," Kate told him, looking at him. He noticed she was breathing through her mouth, a sure sign of sexual meltdown.

"Then come here and kiss me."

Kate turned to him and went into his arms. Rafe pulled her onto his lap, his big hands handling her gently but firmly. Their mouths met in a slow, sensual dance of giving and taking. Kate's arms were around his neck. She could not get enough of his sweet mouth. Nor the feel of his powerful hands as they moved over her body. She felt his right hand on her left thigh as she sat on his lap. *What is he doing?* Ah, but what he was doing with his tongue was making her insides quiver, and she momentarily forgot where his hand was. But, then, even as he continued to bring her to near-orgasmic heights with his tongue, his hand moved sinuously between her legs. Kate sighed and wantonly opened them wider to give him easier access. She might feel guilty in the morning, but for now curiosity as to what would happen next had her in its grip.

Rafe gently pulled back from the kiss. "Don't be shy, Kate. I want you to move if the spirit hits you."

Then he was kissing her again. His hand traveled up her dress and settled on her bottom, where he busied himself with lowering her silken bikini panties. Skin touched skin. Kate moaned deep in her throat. Rafe's arousal was immediate. Kate's nipples hardened in response to the act of sitting on his erection; then his hand was inside her panties and his fingers were testing the warm, welcoming place between her thighs.

Kate was so wet Rafe had to close his eyes and concentrate on her pleasure instead of the images that were going through his mind. Thoughts of putting her on her back and making passionate love to her here and now. He managed to rein in those thoughts and returned his attention to giving Kate her first manual orgasm.

"Let me know if you want me to stop," he said between kisses.

Kate could do nothing but pant.

His tongue had found its spot again, the one that had almost driven her to distraction. And the pad of his thumb had found her clitoris. Using two fingers now, he gently massaged the sides of her clitoris until Kate was inspired to move her hips up and down, matching the rhythm of his movements.

"Oh, my God," Kate said loudly as she was rocked by an orgasm the likes of which she'd never experienced before.

Rafe's mouth didn't leave hers, nor did his hand leave

the spot until Kate had stopped moving with the spirit. With a contented sigh, Kate sat up and looked at him. "Now I know the meaning of the caveat 'You don't know where his hands have been!'"

Rafe just laughed.

Davida came dragging back to her grandma's booth at a quarter past nine. Josefina and the ladies were engaged in a lively game of bid whist when she showed up, but Josefina put her cards down and swatted Davida on the behind a couple of times just on general principle.

"Where have you been? And don't lie to me, or I'll put you over my knee right here and charge admission to the beating!"

Davida stuck out her lower lip and rubbed her bottom. "I didn't leave the grounds, Grandma. I just took in a few shows, went to get something to eat with Sherry and Kyle, and then I came back here."

"Nearly four hours later!" Josefina said, still steamed. "I have a good mind to tell your parents just how helpful you were to me tonight. You think just because I spoil you rotten and take your side in disputes with your parents you can get away with anything! But this takes the cake, young lady. No self-respecting fifteen-year-old, especially a girl, and especially in this day and age, should be floating around this place by herself, and you know it. That's why you took off the moment my back was turned!"

Davida stood with her eyes downcast, taking her medicine. "I deserve to be punished, Grandma. I didn't mean to stay away so long." She glanced at what was left of her grandmother's inventory. Apparently Josefina and the ladies had enjoyed brisk sales, because there weren't many flowers left, just some anemones and poppies. "I'm glad to see you've just about sold out."

"No thanks to you!" the ladies at the card table chimed in.

"I'm going to have to think of an appropriate punishment for you, Little David. Something you won't soon forget," Josefina said with a mischievous glint in her eyes.

Davida might not have been intimidated by her great grandmother's threat if not for the sudden appearance of her parents, back from a night of the cinema and a romantic dinner together.

David and Carolina were walking with their arms about each other's waists. They smiled at Josefina as they approached. "How did it go?" Carolina asked warmly.

Davida held her breath. If her grandmother informed on her, her parents would ground her indefinitely. She might be seventeen before she would be allowed to date if then.

"You can see for yourself," Josefina said, indicating the few flowers that were left. "We had a good night. Such a good night that Davida has been inspired to come to my house every Sunday from now on and learn the art of paper flower making."

Carolina hugged Davida to her breast and kissed her cheek. "I'm so pleased. Another family tradition handed down to the next generation."

While in her mother's embrace Davida grimaced at her grandma and mouthed the words "You're mean!"

Josefina and the ladies laughed, and Josefina went back and claimed her chair at the table. "Take the child home now," she told her granddaughter. "She needs to rest up for our first lesson tomorrow."

In the car on the way home, Carolina drove while David occupied the passenger seat. Compared to her normal behavior, Davida was glaringly quiet in the back. So much so that her behavior piqued her mother's cu riosity. "So, Little David, how did you like helping your grandma tonight?"

Somewhere between the festival and the outskirts of Tucson, Davida had decided that nothing her parents could do to her could compare to the fate of having to learn to make crepe paper flowers. That was an old woman's hobby. "I ran off as soon as you and Dad left," she confessed.

"I see," said Carolina, not in the least bit surprised. "Where did you go?"

"All around the festival with Sherry and Kyle," she said. She paused. "And Cory Jackson." She waited for her mother to explode with fury.

Her parents' laughter freaked her out more than their anger would have.

After a couple of minutes, she timidly asked, "What's so funny?"

"The thought of you learning to make paper flowers," her father replied. "I'll have to take pictures to commemorate your first lesson."

"Punish me!" Davida begged them. "Anything. Take away my computer privileges for a month. Don't let me go to the mall with friends for two months. Don't give me an allowance for six months. Anything except the paper flowers. Anything!"

"That clinches it," Carolina said with a chuckle. "The paper flowers it is."

"I don't see why you can't just punish me severely instead," Davida cried.

She pouted the rest of the way home.

David was always the one who unlocked the door whenever they returned home. He stood with the key poised in his hand at the front door, but he didn't put the key in the lock. His senses were tingling. David, though a man of science, was very attuned to his emotions. Something simply didn't *feel* right to him. He glanced down and when he did, he noticed a single drop of what appeared to be blood on the flagstone, right next to the woven welcome mat.

He tried the doorknob before attempting to unlock the door. It was locked. Carolina and Davida were coming up the walk. "What's wrong?" Carolina asked instinctively. She knew David's mannerisms well. When he was frowning he was thinking, trying to put two and two together.

David unlocked the door and stepped into the foyer. "I guess it's nothing. There's a spot down by the welcome mat that wasn't there when we left. Looks like blood."

Carolina went to take a look. "Could be The Puma's on the warpath again. He could've killed another mouse, brought it up here as an offering, then changed his mind and taken it back. You know he's done it before. That cat's neurotic."

"I don't think it was The Puma," David said. He was bending over, picking up something. As Carolina came farther into the house she saw he was holding a 3.5-inch disk, the old kind he still preferred using. David was pretty set in his ways.

A little concerned now, though not panicked, Carolina said, "He could have gotten into your office. If he somehow sneaked in before we left he could have been in here all this time getting into mischief." She turned and said to Davida, "Sweetie, call him. If he's still in here, he'll come to you."

The Puma doted on Davida. Hers were the only legs he would rub against, and even lie atop and fall asleep. Davida spoiled the fat cat.

"I'm going upstairs to check the bedrooms," Carolina said. "David, you should check your office. If he got into your disks there's no telling how much damage he's done in there."

"Okay," David said, sounding skeptical, as he turned to cross the living room and make his way to the back of the house where his office was located.

"Humor me," Carolina said.

The three of them walked off in different directions.

In the master bedroom, Carolina slowly opened the door and reached in and switched on the overhead light, which they rarely used, preferring individual lamps on their nightstands. Her fears were confirmed when she saw one of her favorite leather sandals lying in the middle of the room with telltale tooth marks imprinted on it. She bent and triumphantly picked it up. Something had to be done about that rogue cat!

She hurried downstairs to David's office.

"I told you it was The Puma. Take a look at my shoe," Carolina was saying as she walked through the door. She stopped in her tracks. David was sitting at his workstation, in front of the computer monitor with his head in his hands.

He looked up at her as she walked farther into the room. "They're gone, Caro. All of my notes. Years of research." His face fell. "They even took the hard drive."

Carolina went to him and pressed his face to her breasts, holding him tightly. "Damn them!" she cried fiercely. "They're not gonna get away with this." She bent to look into his dear face. "We'll get everything back, David."

She could hear Davida calling for The Puma. Her heart ached for her husband. She knew, better than anyone besides him, how much blood, sweat, and tears had gone into his work over the years. It would be impossible to start from scratch. And with his recent stroke, how much of that knowledge had been lost forever? No one knew. David had not told her, but she was aware of his fear of never being his old self again. Now, this!

"Little David!" she yelled when she heard Davida's voice getting closer to them.

Davida came running. She was through the door of the office in a matter of seconds. "Yes, Mama?"

"I want you to call Kate's cell phone number and tell her to come home. Your father's research has been stolen. I'll use my cell phone and call the police."

"Oh, no!" Davida said, looking pitifully at her father. Tears stood in her eyes. Fear had been a constant visitor to this family after his stroke and during his recovery. For this to happen on top of everything else seemed too much for him to take. Davida was reluctant to leave his side.

"Go, baby!" Carolina said urgently.

Davida turned and hurried down the hall to her bedroom where she would use the phone to do as her mother had instructed. She batted her eyelashes to clear away the tears before picking up the receiver and dialing.

Kate answered immediately. Being a worrier, she was not one to let her phone ring incessantly. Someone could need her.

"Yeah, Kate here."

"Kate, Mama says you should come home. Someone broke into the house and took Dad's research. I don't know everything, but I'm sure they must have taken his disks, because when we came in the house, Dad found one on the foyer floor."

"What?!" Kate said, astonished. "Okay, Little David. I'm on the way."

Flipping her cell phone closed, Kate, who was still parked in the desert with Rafe, said, "Somebody broke into the house tonight and took Dad's research."

Rafe immediately started the car while Kate straightened her clothes and went into her purse to get the packet of moist towelettes she always carried. Opening the packet, she got one and handed it to Rafe. He wiped his fingers and deposited it in the small trash bag he kept in the car.

"What does this mean?" he asked as he drove across the bumpy terrain toward Highway 10, which would take them to the ranch. "Didn't your dad have backup disks?"

"Sure, he has backup disks," Kate said. "But it doesn't matter. You see, whoever took the disks can now proceed with his experiments, and succeed before my dad can finish recovering from his stroke. Nobody cares about theories anymore, Rafe. All they care about are results. I'm gonna break it down for you. We're now in a race against time. Using my dad's research, the people who stole it can now build the matter-transference pods Dad has constructed only in his mind. They, depending on the amount of financial backing they have access to, can be the first to bring the theories my dad has about teleportation to life."

"Damn," said Rafe. "What about the fact that they stole the information from your dad? They can be brought to justice for doing that."

Kate laughed coldly. "You're a lawman, Rafe. You know how often the guilty go unpunished."

"Too often," Rafe said regretfully.

"The only way we're going to make certain Dad gets full credit for his work is to catch whoever stole his research red-handed or, barring that, go into the lab and finish Dad's research before they can do it. The last option may not be an option at all, because without Dad at full capacity he may not be up to the challenge."

Kate felt like pounding something, she was so mad. "This really stinks! Kicking him when he's down." She felt manic with the desire to hit back at those who had

attacked her father while he was in his most vulnerable
state. "You don't know what he's been through, Rafe. At
first they laughed at him when he proposed that quantum entanglement might be the key that would allow us
to transfer one physical object to another place in time.
Beam me up, Scotty! was the headline in a science maga-
zine when Dad first let his peers in on his theories. Then
a few years later, other teams eagerly jumped on the
bandwagon. Teams all over the world are now convinced
his theories can work, but no one was as far ahead of the
game as he was. Until now."

"I don't understand, Kate. If your dad's research was
that important, why didn't he keep it locked in a vault
somewhere? Why at home?"

"Because he's a throwback to another era, that's why,"
Kate said. "He lives in his own world. A world in which
you can trust your fellow man. I doubt if it ever occurred
to him that a colleague would steal from him. And that's
the truth."

"Then you think it's a colleague," Rafe said.

"It would have to be someone who knew he kept the
bulk of his research at home," Kate theorized. "Because,
like you said, wouldn't most scientists guard their research more carefully than that? Hey, I tried to talk Dad
into putting a security system in the house several years
ago, but he wouldn't hear of it. 'We live way out in the
middle of nowhere,' he said. 'Who's gonna bother rob-
bing us?' See what I mean about his being gullible? He's
the stereotypical absentminded professor. But I love him
to death! And right now, the way I feel, I could seriously
kick somebody's butt."

"I could seriously *help* you kick somebody's butt," Rafe
said as he finally reached Highway 10 and stomped on
the accelerator.

They rode in silence for a few minutes.

Then Kate exclaimed, "Oh, no!"

"What?" Rafe asked, concerned.

"Dr. William Allen," Kate said, remembering. "I'd forgotten all about him. He's the physicist who approached me at the conference. He told me to tell Dad that he ought to do the altruistic thing and turn over his research to a scientist who was capable of bringing his ideas to fruition."

"You think he was desperate enough to come all the way to Arizona and break into your family's home to get his hands on it?"

"Well," said Kate, "he wouldn't have to come very far. If memory serves, Dr. Allen is a member of the team at the Phoenix Institute of Technology."

"Mmm," Rafe said. "This gets more interesting by the minute."

It took Kate and Rafe nearly half an hour to reach the ranch. Two black-and-whites were parked on the circular drive when they pulled up. "Would you like me to come in?" Rafe asked. He didn't want to overstep his bounds, but he sincerely wanted to help catch the thieves if he could. There was always the possibility that he could see something in the physical evidence the thieves left behind that the local police might overlook.

Kate must have been thinking the same thing. "We could always use another pair of eyes, and another pair of brains."

"Pair of brains?"

"Humans are two-brained creatures. We have a right side, and a left side. Everyone calls it 'a' brain, but medically it's two brains. If you cut it in half, a person could still, conceivably, function."

"You're weird, Kate."

She smiled at him. "Thank you."

"So, the whole family was out for the evening," said Detective Soledad Montenegro. She was in her mid-thirties, dark-haired and dark-eyed, tall, trim, and all business. Her hair was in a smooth chignon at the back of her neck, and she was wearing a navy blue skirt suit in lieu of a uniform.

Carolina looked up when she heard Kate and Rafe entering the house. She, David, and Detective Montenegro were sitting in the living room, right off the foyer. "That's our daughter, Kate, now and her friend, Deputy Marshal Grant. Kate, Rafael, this is Detective Montenegro of the Tucson Police Department."

Detective Montenegro keenly regarded the newcomers. "U.S. Marshal?" she asked.

"Yeah, that's right," said Rafe.

He and Kate took seats on the sofa opposite David and Carolina. The room was large and airy, the furnishings were upholstered mostly in high-quality brown leather and had been in the family for years. Southwestern touches like multicolored handwoven Pascua Yaqui rugs, accent tables in blond wood, huge terra-cotta pots with small trees in them that Carolina had grown from seedlings made the home unique and comfortable.

"You have no jurisdiction here," Detective Montenegro blankly told Rafe.

"I'm aware of that. I'm here as a friend of the family."

"Just so you know," Detective Montenegro said, satisfied. She turned again to Carolina. "You say you think the cat might have scratched one or more of the perps. Why is that?"

"When my husband was coming into the house he noticed a drop of blood by the door. And when I went upstairs I found one of my sandals chewed up by our cat. The sandal wasn't there when we left. The blood wasn't either. Plus, there's the fact that our cat, The Puma, has a habit of leaping on people from high up on things like shelves, the refrigerator, or the stairs. He gets a real kick out of it."

"I thought you said he only jumped on you," Rafe said to Kate in a low voice.

"I said that to put you at ease," Kate told him.

Detective Montenegro shot them an impatient look as if she were a teacher silencing two talkative students in her class. "Okay, I'll take that into consideration. The perp might have scratches on or near his face. I take it the cat aims for the head?"

"That's right," said Kate

The detective made a notation to that effect.

She then looked at each of them in turn, her eyes settling on David. "Dr. Matthews, can you name anyone in particular who might want to steal your research?"

David slowly shook his head in the negative. "I don't have any enemies."

Detective Montenegro smiled. "Come now, Doctor. We all have enemies. A colleague who envies you, perhaps? Someone you might have inadvertently teed off?"

"I get along with all of my colleagues at the university," David stubbornly avowed.

Kate spoke up. "I have something to say on that subject."

Detective Montenegro acknowledged her with a nod. "Go ahead."

"I attended a conference in San Francisco a couple of days ago, and as I was leaving, Dr. William Allen pulled me aside. The man rudely suggested that my dad should turn over his research to him."

"Kate, why didn't you tell us about this before?" asked David, incredulous.

"I'm sorry, Dad. You have enough on your mind. I

didn't want to add to your worries by telling you what some blowhard had said."

"Stop protecting me, Kate," David said with barely contained anger. "You"—he looked at Carolina—"and your mother have both gone overboard with your protective attitudes. I'm nearly fully recovered from the stroke. I don't want to be kept in the dark about anything that concerns me."

In his frustration, David rose and began pacing. "Now tell me exactly what William Allen had to say. Word for word."

Kate calmly related her encounter with Dr. William Allen, after which everyone sat silently for a few minutes, thinking. David broke the silence with "Jason was there, too. Funny that he didn't mention seeing William Allen at the conference. They are not the best of friends."

"They seemed friendly enough to me," Kate said.

"No," David insisted. "Allen made a derogatory comment about Jason at a conference some years ago to the effect that Jason couldn't cut it as a scientist and had to become an administrator instead. Jason has never forgiven him for it."

"That seems kind of petty," Detective Montenegro said.

"Not really," David said. "What he was doing was saying that Jason knew his limitations as a scientist, and in order to achieve any kind of recognition in the field he would have to ride on the coattails of someone more brilliant than he."

"Meaning you," Kate said.

"He didn't mention me in his tirade, but yes, I believe he was referring to me," David admitted.

Detective Montenegro was scribbling furiously on her pad. "You scientists can get down and dirty when you want to, can't you?" she said with a smile. "Okay, let's see what I have: Dr. William Allen tells your daughter to encourage you to give him your notes. Dr. Jason Edmonton shows up just in time to break up what could have been a fight." She smiled at Kate. "I think you coulda taken him." Back to business, she added, "Kate leaves the two scientists standing in the lobby."

She wrinkled her nose. "Something doesn't smell right. It looks kinda like a setup to me, you know? Like Dr. Edmonton might have planned it so that Dr. Allen would take the fall. He doesn't like him. Dr. Allen was egotistical enough to go after Kate at the conference and give her enough of a reason to wonder about his motives following the robbery. But what if Dr. Edmonton planted the thought in Dr. Allen's frenzied brain, huh? I'm going to have to go to Phoenix tomorrow and have a nice chat with Dr. Allen."

"I found him!" Davida announced as she came into the room with The Puma clutched in her arms. "He was in the stables taunting the horses."

"Lord, does that cat ever stop?" Carolina said.

Detective Montenegro cautiously approached Davida, who had The Puma in her arms.

"Hello," she softly said to The Puma. "Aren't you a handsome puss?"

The Puma cocked one eye at her and purred at her as if she had his attention, but he needed more convincing before he would allow her near him.

"I've never seen such a handsome feline," Detective Montenegro said as she gently rubbed his head. She reached for him after The Puma failed to rip her hand off, and Davida placed the fat cat in the detective's outstretched arms.

"You're a big fellow," Detective Montenegro said as she continued to rub The Puma's head. She looked closely at his paws. There was dried blood on both forepaws.

"You've been a naughty kitty tonight, haven't you? Or were you a hero, protecting hearth and home?"

The Puma looked up at her with what could only be described as a self-satisfied smirk.

"A hero it is," said Detective Montenegro.

Six

"Excuse me, Detective Montenegro, but there's no way that Jason Edmonton had anything to do with this," David said, interrupting Detective Montenegro's rapport with The Puma. Cat and human looked perfectly content. However, she did have a case to solve, so Detective Montenegro reluctantly handed the now happy cat back to Davida, walked over to her abandoned chair, and sat down again. "Then why did you bring up the fact that he and Dr. Allen are not the best of chums?"

"Because it's the truth. However, Jason would never steal from me. We've been best friends for more than thirty years. We met when we were both earning our doctorates at MIT. He's Kate's godfather. I refuse to believe he'd stab me in the back."

Detective Montenegro had been looking David in the eyes the whole time. She made a habit of this because over the years she'd become very adept at reading peoples' emotions by the expression in their eyes. Dr. David Matthews sincerely believed his friend was incapable of betraying him.

"Tell me something, Doctor," Detective Montenegro began. "How rich would a discovery like the one you all have described to me tonight make someone who gets it into the marketplace first? I'm just curious."

David narrowed his eyes. He didn't like the direction

she was heading in. "I know you're thinking that anyone would turn against you if the money was good enough. But, I'm telling you, Jason Edmonton is not your man."

Detective Montenegro's expression was impassive. "For your sake, I hope you're right. However, he will definitely be investigated. I wouldn't be doing my job if I failed to check him out."

"Well, you can start doing that soon because I phoned him a few minutes before you arrived. He should be here shortly," Carolina put in.

"Excellent," Detective Montenegro said, rising. "I should go see what my colleagues have found in your office, Dr. Matthews. I have to say, the thieves were pretty sloppy to have left that one disk behind like they did." She left them.

Recalling that Davida had mentioned the disk earlier, Kate asked, "What was on it?"

"It's the last disk I was working on before the stroke," David told her. There was a hopeful light in his eyes that made Kate's heart leap with hope too.

The doorbell rang and Kate sprang up. "It's probably Jason."

She hurried to the front door and opened it. Jason looked as if he'd dressed in a rush. He had on a pair of well-worn jeans, a University of Arizona sweatshirt, and a pair of Nikes without socks. He scowled at her. "Is it true, Kate? Someone's stolen David's files?"

Kate felt guilty for doing it, but her eyes went to his face and neck to see if he had any recent scratches on him. He didn't. "Yes, it's true, Jason."

"Damn it to hell!" Jason said as he walked past her. "Where is everybody? How is David taking it?"

Kate closed the door and followed him. "Everybody's in the living room."

Jason, who was used to instantly assessing a situation

and immediately taking charge, strode into the living room, went straight to David, who stood when Jason entered the room, and firmly clasped his hand in the manner in which they usually did. They were men from the old school who did not embrace under any circumstances. Their emotions could be read from the firmness of their handshakes and the expressions on their faces.

"We'll catch the rotten bastards who did this, David," Jason said with force.

Kate observed her father and Jason, as she sat down next to Rafe. Her mind was taking her places she probably shouldn't be going, but Detective Montenegro's comments about Jason setting up William Allen to take the fall had her imagination going wild.

She'd never known a time when Jason Edmonton hadn't been a regular visitor in this house. His feet had been under their dinner table more times than she could count, and he'd been present at most of the milestones in her life beginning with her baptism when she was an infant.

"I'm glad you're here," Kate heard her father say. "Maybe you can help Detective Montenegro compile a list of suspects."

"David can't think of anybody who'd want to steal his ideas," Carolina put in.

The Puma yowled, and Carolina looked at Davida. "Little David, put the cat out and go get ready for bed."

"Aw, Ma, I want to hear what's going on, too," Davida protested.

"Do as I say." Carolina raised one eyebrow.

Knowing exactly what that meant, Davida hastily turned and left the room with The Puma held tightly in her arms.

"I can think of five or six right off the top of my head," Jason said. "David happens to be a firm believer in the inherent goodness of mankind." He was speaking for Rafe's benefit because David, Carolina, and Kate, as evidenced by the rolling of their eyes, had heard it all before. "I am more suspicious and cynical."

He cleared his throat and looked around them. "Where are the Keystone Cops, anyway?"

"Did I hear someone ask after me?" Detective Montenegro inquired as she reentered the room. She zeroed in on Jason. "Dr. Edmonton, I presume?"

Jason rose and shook the detective's hand. Soledad Montenegro got the impression that Jason Edmonton could charm the stars from the sky. For a second, when he glanced down at her hand, she thought he was going to kiss it. When he didn't, she figured he'd been checking to see if she was wearing a wedding band. She wasn't.

With eyes narrowed, Soledad reclaimed her hand and said, "Why don't we all get comfortable? I have a few questions for you, Dr. Edmonton."

"Certainly," said Jason with a smile. He looked directly into her eyes.

Soledad was momentarily speechless. She thought he could pass for a younger Billie Dee Williams. She snapped out of it. "What is your opinion of Dr. William Allen?"

"I think he's a competent physicist who missed his chance to be brilliant. And I pity him because of it. He isn't a very happy man."

"I see," said Soledad. "Did you have the opportunity to speak with him in private when you saw him at the physics conference a couple of days ago? And, if so, what did you talk about?" She knew he had been alone with Dr.Allen, because Kate had told her she'd left them standing in the lobby when she'd gone upstairs to get her luggage.

Jason nodded. "Yes, I did. I told him that if he ever put his hands on Kate again, I'd break him in half. He knew I meant it. I don't like the man for personal reasons."

Soledad was impressed. He might be a scientist, but he looked like he was in better shape than a lot of policemen she knew. She bet he could handle himself in a fight.

"Do you think he was serious when he suggested that Dr. Matthews should turn over his research to him?" Soledad asked next.

"I think he was deadly serious. But if you're asking if I think he has the guts to carry out a burglary or even hire someone to do it for him, my answer would have to be no. William Allen is all talk and no action."

Frowning slightly, Soledad considered his comments, then scribbled something on her pad before speaking again. She brightened. "That's all for now, folks." She rose. A gentleman through and through, Jason rose as well. "If I have any more questions, how can I reach you, Dr. Edmonton?"

Jason instinctively patted his left breast pocket where he usually kept his business cards. He was attired in a sweatshirt tonight, though. Therefore he gave her his home and office numbers and watched as she wrote them down.

This done, Soledad looked at David. "We lifted several prints from the surface of your computer. If you're right and only you and your wife ever used the room, we should be able to determine whether the perps left behind any prints sometime tomorrow. Thanks to both of you for allowing us to fingerprint you tonight. That'll save us a lot of time." She ended with a smile in Carolina's direction. "Good night, all."

Kate got to her feet. "I'll see you to the door."

Three other officers, all male, two of them carrying black bags with the tools of their trade in them, were waiting in the foyer. "Thanks for coming," Kate told them.

"You're welcome, ma'am," one of them murmured.

"We're here to serve," another said.

"We just hope we're able to catch whoever did this," Soledad said as she followed the men across the threshold.

"We have faith in you all, Detective," Kate told her. "And, please, no matter what time it is, call us if you think we can help with anything."

"I will," Soledad assured her.

She and her men left then, and Kate returned to the living room where David and Jason were having a lively conversation about security.

"I don't want to add to your stress levels," Jason was saying as she reentered the room. "But if you'd taken my advice and gotten a security system put in this place, we would probably not be having this conversation."

Kate went over to Rafe and touched his shoulder. "Come with me," she said.

Rafe rose and looked down at her. "Do they always argue like that?"

"Ever since I can remember," Kate told him, crooking her finger at him. "I thought you and I could take a look at the scene of the crime together."

Rafe followed Kate through the living room, down the hall, and to the back of the house. The office was large and had one huge window that looked out on the deep backyard. The blinds were open. Kate went to close them.

"Whoever did it didn't come in through this window. There isn't a scratch on it. This is all so surreal. This house has stood on these grounds for at least a hundred years, that I know of, and I don't think I've ever heard any of my relatives mention it being broken into before. I sure hope the police went away with evidence tonight."

"I really doubt they found any viable prints," Rafe told her regretfully, as he walked around the large room that looked like any other home office you might see anywhere, except there was an old-fashioned blackboard on wheels, for easy movement, standing in a corner of the room with calculations written all over it in white chalk.

Kate saw Rafe looking curiously at the blackboard.

"Dad likes to write problems down on the blackboard and let them sit there until he solves them. He calls it saturating the brain. The problem looks at him from the blackboard, he looks at it until one of them finally capitulates, usually the problem, and the solution comes to him."

"And you? How do you work?"

Kate smiled at him. "We're talking about my dad."

Rafe grinned, and Kate's heart did a crazy staccato beat in her chest. She peered at the floor in order to break eye contact. Given the nature of their budding relationship it was a little late for her to get shy in his presence. He had touched her intimately in a place only her gynecologist had gone before. Her cheeks grew hot at the thought of what they'd done in his car only a little while ago.

While she was looking down, she saw a bright blue something sticking out from under the edge of her father's desk. She bent and looked more closely. It appeared to be the cellophane wrapper from a package. She went to pick it up, but Rafe told her, "No, wait."

He went and got a sheet of typing paper from the printer next to the computer and a pencil with an eraser, then placed the sheet of paper beside the wrapper Kate had found, using the eraser end of the pencil to nudge the wrapper onto the sheet of paper. Rising, he handed the sheet of paper with the wrapper on it to Kate.

"Oh, my God," said Kate, smiling broadly.

"What is it?" Rafe asked. He was stumped. He had no idea what the Japanese symbol on the tiny wrapper was.

"It's a coupon from a digital game called Aminatu's Daughters. Players collect the wrappers and can redeem

them for new games. It's a game about a secret society of
black Amazons whose mission is to champion the rights
of women and children the world over."

"Sounds pretty noble," Rafe, who wasn't into digital
games, said.

"The women players in the game wear practically
nothing. It's very popular with adolescent boys, and men
who simply refuse to grow up," Kate said.

"You don't think the wrapper belongs to your dad,
do you?" Rafe joked.

"We can ask," Kate said as she walked over to the desk
and carefully folded the sheet of typing paper with the
wrapper inside. "But I don't think so. I think it belongs
to whoever dropped in for a visit tonight."

"Then we're looking for a man who is into digital
games," Rafe said, not sounding optimistic. "There must
be millions of those to pick from."

"Maybe," Kate said. "And maybe not. Let's go see what
Dad has to say about it being found in his office."

David, Carolina, and Jason had moved their conversation to the kitchen where they could have a cup of coffee
and some of Carolina's homemade cinnamon buns
while they argued.

Kate and Rafe found them there. She paused for a
moment at the entrance, looking at the smile on her father's face. Perhaps she and her mother had been wrong
to keep Jason at arm's length for so long during her father's recovery. Maybe that's what he'd needed,
someone to argue with.

"Would you two break it up long enough to take a look
at this and tell me what you know about it?" Kate asked as
she moved forward and placed the paper in the middle
of the kitchen table. Opening it, she added, "Rafe and I
found this under your desk, Dad. Do you have a secret
digital game habit?"

"It's not mine," said David.

"Could it belong to either Dave or Kent?" Kate asked. Her two brothers hadn't been home from college in months, but they might be into Aminatu's Daughters. They were appropriately immature in her opinion.

"I just cleaned in the office two days ago, Kate," Carolina said as she went to stand in front of Rafe with a steaming cup of coffee in one hand and a plate with one of her cinnamon rolls in the other. "Midnight snack, Rafael?"

"Thank you," Rafe said, accepting her offerings.

He joined the other men at the table.

Jason had been busy chewing part of his roll. He took a sip of coffee now, and looked up at Kate. "One of your father's research assistants is very fond of that game. I should know, the boy came to my office and played it the entire time we talked about the direction in which his academic career is headed: down the drain."

"Now we're getting somewhere," said Kate, feeling truly optimistic for the first time that evening. She went and poured herself a cup of coffee, got a cinnamon roll, and joined the men at the table. "Jason, you should call the detective and tell her about it first thing in the morning."

"Oh, no," said Jason. "I know that look in your eyes, Kate. And I know the Huerta women's penchant for matchmaking. *You* call the detective tomorrow and tell her about it."

"Chicken," said Kate.

The next morning, right after a nice chat with Soledad Montenegro, Kate decided to work off some steam by putting in a day's work on the ranch. Because the Circle M was a working ranch, the horses had to be exercised, trained, fed, and groomed on a regular basis.

Kate had gotten back into the routine when she'd returned home four months ago. She'd been living on the northern coast of California, in Sonoma, where she still owned a small house in the charming community that was set smack-dab in the middle of wine country.

As she put Stony, a two-year-old palomino, through his paces in the corral she thought back to how she'd ended up in Sonoma. After earning her doctorate in quantum physics she'd come home for a while. But she was restless. For some time she'd been entertaining the notion that she really didn't want to work in the field of physics. She didn't want to disappoint her father, whose fondest wish was for her to follow in his footsteps. However, after several obsessive-compulsive episodes during which she'd lost herself in the pursuit of a solution to a physics problem, she'd come to the difficult conclusion that, though she loved physics, it would be her downfall in the end. That is, unless she learned to curtail her tendency toward total absorption in it. She talked to her father about it. He told her that if she was like him, she might never stop being compulsive about her work. The only thing that kept him grounded was his love for his wife and children. He encouraged her to find something to balance her life. If it meant she had to postpone beginning work in the field of physics, then so be it. Kate latched on to the only other thing she was good at, writing. Of course the subject she knew best was science. A new career was born.

She was a success right out of the gate, selling articles to science magazines across the nation. One of her editors, Sean Young, who was senior editor at *Everyday Science* out of San Francisco, convinced her that she should put her talent and expertise to work writing a college textbook introducing students to physics in a hip, modern manner that would pull them into, instead of chase them away from, the subject. Kate wrote the book and was shocked when a publisher actually wanted to print it. College textbooks might seem boring, but when several hundred colleges and universities in the U.S. decided to use the book in their Physics 101 courses, that particular textbook proved to be very lucrative for Kate. Commercial publishers were eager to publish her second book, which explained quantum physics for everyday people who dared to dream about another reality that was not ruled by normal time constraints. It had debuted as number ten on the *New York Times* Best Sellers list, and rapidly climbed to number two, where it had topped off. Kate was working on a third book about inventions that exist today that were first introduced in works of science fiction. Like the rocket ship that H.G. Wells wrote about in his 1933 novel, *The Shape of Things to Come.*

Due to those two books, Kate was a moderately wealthy twenty-eight-year-old. Her sudden windfall gave her the one thing she hadn't formerly had—time. She would no longer feel compelled to take a job as a physicist somewhere simply to make ends meet. Now, she would only return to the discipline for one reason alone: for the love of it.

She'd purchased the house in Sonoma because in many ways the small town had reminded her of home. The weather was temperate most of the year, with plenty of sunshine. It had historic adobe buildings. The people were warm and friendly, and it was quiet. She could really write there.

But, deep down, she knew she was running away from her dilemma. When her mother had phoned and told her her father had suffered a stroke, it took Kate less than a minute to decide she was going home to stay until her father was well again.

Now, as she felt the sun on her face, and the powerful palomino beneath her, she knew she'd made the right decision. She looked toward the horizon. This land had been settled for over twelve thousand years. Her mother's people had been here for hundreds of years. She felt she was a part of the land. It was in her blood.

And now there was the matter of her father's missing research. What if the culprits were never caught? What if her father's only hope was to build the matter-transference pods before the thieves could best him? Could he do it alone? She doubted it. He would need help. If he asked for her help would she be up to the task?

Only time would tell. All she knew now was, she would be there for him.

Kate let up on the reins a bit. After twenty minutes of taking Stony through his paces it was time for his daily run. The powerful animal was almost dancing in place as Kate coaxed him close to the gate of the corral. She bent and unlatched it, and the palomino pushed it open with his nose. He knew the drill, and was raring to go.

Kate made certain her headgear was on securely, and let him take the lead. She could use the exercise herself. It was a surefire stress reliever.

The day was one of those glorious autumn days in the Southwest, a clear blue sky, cool, crisp weather, and a panoramic view of the Catalinas to the east. Stony followed the white fence that surrounded the ranch all the way to the end of the road, a good mile. Kate's hair was flying out behind her, and with every passing minute she felt more alive. Besides her family, she'd missed riding more than anything else while she was living in Sonoma. Sitting high up on a horse, with the wind in your hair and the sun kissing your face, was the closest you could get to flying without actually being in the air.

Stony kept going once he reached the end of the fence,

and Kate gently pulled back on the reins and pulled right to turn him around. "I'm sorry, boy, but I have things to do today. I can't go for a long ride in the desert."

On the way back, Kate heard the sound of a car's motor, and peered over her shoulder to see who was visiting at—she glanced down at her watch—eleven-ten in the morning.

It was a FedEx truck.

Kate slapped Stony's rump with her hand and he picked up speed. He didn't even slow down as he suddenly turned and went straight for a portion of the fence. Knowing what he was preparing to do, Kate leaned into the jump. She and Stony soared across the four-foot fence and landed on the other side without mishap. "No more funny stuff," she cautioned the palomino. "You're not supposed to be jumping fences. Mama will have your hide *and* mine. What if you injured yourself?"

That was the thing about horses, you simply never knew what they would do. They could be cooperative one minute, and take you on the ride of your life the next.

Kate patted his muscular neck as they cantered toward the house. She pulled back on the reins, stopping Stony near the corral. After dismounting, she led him into the corral by the reins and quickly removed the saddle and the bit with the reins attached.

This done, she patted his flank. "Thanks for the workout. Go play with your friends."

There were four other young horses in the corral.

Curious about what the FedEx guy could be delivering, Kate went to the house.

She saw her mother at the front door signing for the package. The FedEx guy smiled at her and said hello as she passed him on the walk.

"Good morning," Kate said with a smile.

Carolina was standing in the doorway reading the

label on the package. She looked up at Kate. "It's addressed to you," she said, handing the package to Kate.

"I can't imagine what it could be. I haven't ordered anything," Kate said.

"Oh, open it already," said Carolina. "Must you have a logical explanation for everything that happens in your life?"

"Yes," Kate said seriously.

Carolina laughed and went back inside, leaving Kate standing in the doorway.

Kate went inside and closed the door to read the label. The *from* section was not filled out, so she couldn't tell whom it was from or even where it had been sent from by reading the label. She pulled the tab and opened the package.

Inside was a short stack of paper. It felt to Kate as if there were around twenty sheets of paper altogether. She pulled it out and read the top sheet. It was a copy of her father's notes from the first disk he'd started in 1995, when he'd begun the project.

She riffled through the rest of the pages. They were numbered 1–22.

Strange, thought Kate, no note? Just the pages?

She ballooned the envelope and peered inside. Yes, there was another piece of paper inside. It looked as if it had been ripped from a yellow legal pad.

If you want your father's disks back, come alone to the Frog and Firkin Friday night at seven. Sit at a booth in the back and order the vegetarian appetizer, the lionheart lovash. I might be late. If you tell the police about this, your father will never get his disks back.

The Frog and Firkin was a college bar and grill near the campus of the University of Arizona. Kate had been there a number of times. It was a popular hangout for students who could be seen finishing homework assignments while chowing down. Whoever had sent the package must have known Kate was familiar with the place. He hadn't bothered to give her the address.

Kate shoved the papers back into the envelope and went in search of her father.

"There is no way you're going there alone," David told her a few minutes later.

They were in his office. Paranoid after yesterday's goings-on, he was testing all of his backup disks to make sure the information he'd put on them was still there. Kate thought he looked as if he hadn't slept very well last night. His medium brown skin had acquired a healthy glow during his recuperation. Today, however, it appeared ashen and there was the beginnings of dark circles under his dark brown eyes.

He'd risen and was pacing in front of the blackboard, which, Kate noticed, had new calculations on it. "It must be someone from the university," David said, guessing at the identity of the person who'd sent the note. "I hate to think it's Paul Knowles. He may be having some academic problems at the present, but I think he has the makings of a fine physicist if he can pull himself together."

Over the years David had mentored several students who'd gone on to earn their doctorate degrees in physics. He was generous and patient with them. He couldn't fathom one of them turning on him, stealing his research, and holding it for ransom, as the person who'd sent the package this morning seemed to be doing.

"I'll ask Rafe to go with me," Kate suggested. Nine times out of ten, she was thinking, unless the culprits had been keeping her under surveillance for some time they would not know that Rafe was connected to her. "We can go into the Frog and Firkin separately. He can observe everything that goes on. Then, if I get into trouble he'll be there to help me out of it."

"I still don't like it," David said. "But if Rafe woul[d]
agree to do it, I'd at least feel better about your safety."

"How would you like some company?"

Rafe was standing in his bedroom still slightly damp
from a shower. He'd cycled for ten miles that morning
and he felt good. The towel wrapped loosely around his
waist hung low, gravity threatening to pull it to the floor.
He held it up with one hand while he held the receiver
to his ear with the other.

"I'd love it," he told Kate. "I just got out of the shower
after a workout. Give me a few minutes to change."

"How many minutes?"

"Where are you, exactly?" Rafe asked, suspicious. With
Kate, you never could tell.

"In your driveway," Kate said. "I'll drive around the
block a couple of times to give you time to change."

"No, you don't have to do that," Rafe said with a short
laugh. "Come on in. I'll meet you at the door."

Rafe's house was in an older Tucson neighborhood
where the houses and the lawns were well kept and
much loved by its residents. Rafe's house had hardwood
floors throughout, high ceilings, and the original wood
moldings. He'd furnished it sparingly, preferring a lot of
space instead of material possessions.

Kate's boot-clad feet made clicking noises on the floor
as she strode into the foyer. Rafe had slipped on a
bathrobe but was barefoot. He didn't think she'd mind,
she'd seen him in pajamas, after all. Kate went right into
his arms. He wound up kicking the door closed.

She smelled heavenly, a mixture of exotic flowers and
spice. Her hair was loose and fell in waves about her
lovely face. His hands were in it, the strands between

his fingers. It was incredibly soft and silky. He had the instant desire to feel it all over his body.

Kate pulled away and looked up at him. "You smell divine."

"Funny, that's what I was just thinking about you," he said, taking her by the hand and leading her into the living room. Monochromatic colors in brown and beige made the room appear even larger than it was. Masculine, but not overpoweringly so.

They sat on the dark chocolate couch where Rafe bent forward and kissed her hello. Kate returned the greeting with enthusiasm. Coming up for air, Rafe said, "I hope you're here for your second lesson in manual orgasms." His hand was on the top button of her jeans. She placed her hand atop his to prevent his going too far, too soon.

"Oh, my," Kate breathed. "I can hardly wait. But first, while I'm still clear-headed, I need your opinion on something connected to the theft."

Already in the throes of passion, Rafe had to take a couple of deep breaths in order to compose himself before asking, "Have there been further developments?"

Kate nodded. "Yes. I received a note this morning telling me to meet him at a local bar and grill Friday night if my dad ever wants to see his research again."

"You can't do it, Kate," Rafe said without hesitation. His brandy-colored eyes met hers. "I mean it. It's too dangerous."

"It'll be in a public place."

"I don't care, Kate. It's still too dangerous. Have you told Detective Montenegro about this?"

"No, the note said not to involve the police."

"A ransom note always warns you not to involve the police. But the only way this guy is going to get caught is if you involve the police, Kate. Do the right thing, ca[l] Detective Montenegro and let her do her job."

"Hear me out before you condemn my plans," Kat[e] said, pleading with him with her eyes. "Dad and I wer[e] thinking the thief is probably one of his students. Now the reason behind his behavior is a mystery to us but w[e] figure that, at the very least, we may be able to get mor[e] information by meeting with him and listening to hi[s] terms."

"I disagree," Rafe told her. "By agreeing to meet hin[m] you're putting the ball in his court. How do you know h[e] isn't some deranged lunatic who isn't in it for the mone[y] but has a grudge against your father and wants to ge[t] back at him by harming someone close to him? You[,] Kate! No, this is a bad idea all around."

"No, Rafe," Kate insisted. "It could work. If you coul[d] be there in the restaurant the whole time, watching us, [I] think I would be perfectly safe. He doesn't know you[.] You could sit at the next table. That would be clos[e] enough for you to stop him if he tried anything. But, re[al]ly, the Frog and Firkin is extra busy Friday nights[.] There's a live band, and it's usually packed. He isn'[t] going to try anything in there."

"I won't do it, Kate," Rafe said, firm in his stance. "I'v[e] seen too many scenarios like this shot to hell in an in[s]tant. The authorities have used innocents as bait before[.] In some cases the innocents got killed during the exe[]cution of the operation. Kate, I would never forgiv[e] myself if something happened to you."

Kate realized, now, that she hadn't fully considere[d] the consequences of her actions. For example, wha[t] would happen to Rafe's career if he was caught helping her negotiate with the thief without the knowledge o[f] the police? She couldn't put his career in jeopardy.

"You're right," she said softly as she leaned in to kiss hi[m] cheek. She tilted his chin up with a finger as she kissed his other cheek, the tip of his nose, which was healing nicely, and the corners of his generous mouth. "I really need to give it more thought."

"I don't like the sound of that, Kate," Rafe said against her mouth. "I want to hear you say you're not going through with it. Otherwise, I'm going to phone Detective Montenegro and tell her what's going on myself."

Kate couldn't have that. "I'm not going through with it," Kate said, kissing him full on the mouth.

Rafe reluctantly pulled away to say, "You'd better not be lying to me, Kate." Then he gave all of his attention to her delicious mouth, and the feel of her body pressed against his, because by that time Kate was straddling him on the couch.

"Kate," Rafe cautioned, "I'm not wearing anything under this robe. Be careful, or we'll end up doing something we don't want to."

Kate held up her hands. "What if I promise not to touch you with my hands?"

"That would be good, because I'm the one who will be doing the touching. This is not about me, darlin', it's about slowly changing you from a technical virgin into a woman who's in touch with her sensuality. That is, if that's what you want."

"I'm your willing pupil," Kate said, looking at his mouth. She licked her lips. "Now, teach me." She closed her eyes and thrust her breasts forward.

Rafe could not help noticing how firmly her nipples were pressing against the material of her bra. She was exceptionally responsive to sexual stimuli. He remembered how wet she'd been the last time, and he immediately hardened. This teacher was definitely going to suffer greatly during the course of giving his lessons.

But, martyr that he was, he willingly made the sacrifice.

He slowly unbuttoned her emerald silk blouse. Under it was an emerald lace bra. Fortunately it clasped in the front. It took a mere five seconds to undo. Her full breasts spilled into his eager hands. He couldn't wait to taste her. Taking one breast between both hands he suckled, his tongue firm and oh, so warm and stimulating. Kate writhed in his lap, which made his erection that much more difficult to keep under control.

Holding her breast to his mouth with one hand, he grasped the top button of her jeans with the other. He licked her dark bud with the full length of his tongue, then said, "Kate, do you know where your G-spot is?"

"No," said Kate. "But, gee, this feels good!"

Seven

Rafe was antsy. For one thing, Kate hadn't told him what time she was expected to show up at the Frog and Firkin. Just the night, Friday. For another, he hated checking up on her, even if it was for her own good.

Perhaps he should simply have trusted her to keep her word. She'd phoned him the day after she'd shown up on his doorstep to reassure him that she had, indeed, told Detective Montenegro about the note, and would let the police handle it.

However, when he'd asked her out to dinner for Friday night she'd said she was sorry, but she had a previous engagement. How about Saturday? That's when he'd become suspicious and *this* plan had been hatched.

"The plan" had him sitting in the Expedition across the street from the Frog and Firkin by six P.M., waiting for Kate to put in an appearance. Used to surveillance, he had his trusty binoculars and a thermos of black coffee with him. He was prepared for a long night. He was also prepared to look foolish. In fact, he was *hoping* to look foolish. He desperately wanted Kate to be elsewhere tonight. Anywhere, but here.

Kate had been right about the popularity of the Frog and Firkin, on East University Avenue and extremely close to the university. The door of the place got quite a work-out, couples, arm-in-arm, groups of students out to toss back a few brews. When he'd looked up the place in the yellow pages the ad had read that the bar and grill boasted thirty different draught beers and another fifty kinds in bottles. A firkin, the ad had explained, was an English term for a three-quarter-keg of beer. Hence the name, the Frog and Firkin. Where the Frog came in, Rafe had no earthly idea.

At ten till seven he spotted Kate walking across the street headed toward the bar and grill. "Damn it to hell," Rafe muttered as he got out of the car, locked it, and waited until he saw her go inside.

Inside the Frog and Firkin, Kate was looking around for an empty booth in the back.

She'd worn all black tonight. A black turtleneck sweater, black jeans and boots, and her black leather bomber jacket. Her hair was in a ponytail. The place was packed, as she'd expected it to be. Patrons occupied the bar stools, all of the booths (she'd have to wait until she saw one open up), and most of the tables. She sat down at a table near the kitchen. Whenever a waiter or waitress came through the kitchen door, she felt the breeze from the door opening. She wasn't overly concerned that the writer of the note would have trouble finding her. She was one of the few black people present, the other two being college men, one of whom was giving her the once-over. He smiled from across the room. She smiled back. He took that as an invitation to join her, and he started walking across the room.

He was built like a jock, tall, muscular, broad-shouldered, and slim-hipped. A jawline that appeared sharp enough to cut diamonds. His gait was influenced, Kate imagined, by years of never being turned down by a woman he showed an interest in. The brother was confident.

"Hello, pretty lady," he said, flashing straight white teeth and a killer pair of dimples.

"Hello yourself," Kate said.

"Want some company?" He sat down without being invited, his smile never wavering.

Kate smiled at him. Even if she weren't seeing Rafe, this guy wouldn't be her type. He was too young, too cocky, and too presumptuous.

"I'm waiting for someone," she said sweetly.

"I'm here," he said. Those dimples were doing overtime.

"Yes, you are. But I advise you to make yourself scarce, because the person I'm waiting for is big, short-tempered, and"—she glanced at her watch—"since he's never stood me up, going to be here in about two minutes."

The guy immediately got up from the table. "Okay, pretty lady. Maybe another time. Enjoy your evening."

"Yeah, you too," said Kate.

Nice, she thought as she watched him leave. *He takes rejection like a real man.* Some guys would have insulted her in parting in an attempt to soothe their wounded egos.

On the opposite side of the room, Rafe watched as some big dude with a player complex walked away from Kate's table. Apparently that wasn't whom she was supposed to meet tonight. One of the waitresses, a petite blonde, approached his table.

"Good evening, sir. Welcome to the Frog and Firkin. What can I bring you?"

Rafe had quickly perused the menu. They served mostly Mexican and Italian cuisine. He settled on the tortellini toss that was made with spinach, tomato, and cheese tortellini with artichoke hearts, mushrooms, tomato, red onion, and basil pesto mixed in. He didn't have to starve while watching Kate.

On Kate's side of the room, the waiter had just left her

table with her order. She'd followed the writer of the note's instructions and ordered the vegetarian appetizer, the lionheart lovash. She thought she should play it safe. Maybe he had a connection in the kitchen who would tip him off that she'd arrived after the order got back to the kitchen. Or, he could be a vegan himself and wanted her to order it for him.

At any rate, she ordered it and waited not only for it to arrive, but for him to show up as well. The order arrived before he did. Kate sat at the table, stirring the ice in her Diet Coke with a straw. She was too nervous to eat.

She was looking down at her Coke when someone loudly cleared his throat next to her table and gave a huge sigh. "Boy, this place is hopping tonight. I would have been here sooner, but I couldn't find a parking space."

Kate raised her eyes. He was short, white, and average-looking in every conceivable way. He was of average height and weight. His hair was dark brown and a little on the shaggy side. He wore glasses that were too big for his face, which was narrow. His light brown eyes were watery and red-rimmed as if he had an allergy. Trim to the point of gauntness, he wore a white long-sleeve shirt, black trousers that looked like they were made of polyester to Kate, and black shoes that needed shining.

He plopped down on the chair across from her and extended his hand in a friendly gesture. "Kate, isn't it?"

Kate reached across the table and shook his hand. It was cool and dry. "That's right. And you are?"

He wagged his finger at her. "None of that, *Dr.* Matthews. You do have your doctorate in physics, don't you? But you're not using it. Smart girl. We have too many scientists as it is."

"Are you some kind of radical?"

He smiled sheepishly. "You think I took your father's notes to make a political statement? The answer is no,

Kate. I took his notes in order to sell them to the highest bidder. I'm here because I'd like to give you and your father the opportunity of making the opening bid."

"You expect us to *pay* you?" Kate asked, angry.

"Isn't that what you expected when you got my ransom note?"

"You didn't mention anything about money in the note."

"I prefer to talk about money face-to-face so there will be no misinterpretations of my terms," he said. "I want one hundred thousand dollars. Now, that's not asking too much, is it? You see, I'm not greedy. All I want is to be treated fairly."

There was something in his tone, and in his choice of words, that made Kate think he wasn't the brain behind the operation. He wasn't greedy, he'd said. All he wanted was to be treated fairly.

"No," Kate said emphatically.

"No?" he cried. "No to what? No, you won't pay me one hundred thousand dollars, or no, you won't pay anything to get the files back?"

"No, I won't give *you* one hundred thousand dollars. What kind of assurances do I get that you are going to turn over the research to me after I hand over the money? I want to talk to your partner, too. You might be trying to go behind his back and make a deal with us when you're not even in possession of the files and the hard drive. We know that there was more than one of you, because our cat scratched *somebody* that night, and you, Mr. high-water pants, don't happen to have any scratches on your face or neck that I can see."

Kate saw by the startled expression in his eyes that she had him.

"I'm speaking on behalf of my partner and myself," he said, not trying to deny he had a partner.

"Well, I still want to meet your partner. Otherwise, no money," Kate firmly told him.

"Don't make me angry, Kate," he warned, his eyes growing steely. "You don't want to see me angry. I came here on good faith tonight to give you and your father first crack at his files, but now I think I'll go back and tell my partner the deal's off and we should sell them to the highest bidder."

Kate felt like snatching him bald, she was so mad. "You are here because whoever hired you to steal the files was offering you and your partner less money than what you could get if you sold them back to my father," she guessed. "And the person who hired you offered you less money because he was powerful enough to offer whatever he wished, and you'd *better* be satisfied with it. But you decided to double-cross him, get a little extra money, and head for the border. Am I right? So, you need the money, and you need it fast, or else your boss will settle with you in a manner not suited to lying on a beach in Acapulco. Ah, no, you'd probably end up at the bottom of a lake somewhere."

"Shut up!" he hissed. "Just shut your trap." He trembled with rage. Meeting her eyes, he said, "You're grasping at straws, Kate. I knew where to find your father's files because more than six months ago, I overheard Dr. Edmonton and your father on the phone discussing putting a security system in the house. Your father should have listened to him. I saw my chance and took it."

"Then you *are* one of my dad's students."

"No, dear Kate, I was a janitor. I quit a few months ago."

"You're not a janitor. You're a computer geek," Kate confidently said. "If I'm not mistaken, that scar on your right wrist is due to having surgery for carpal tunnel syndrome. Plus, there's the wrapper for the Aminatu's

Daughters game we found underneath my dad's desk in his office. Are you the one hooked on that game, or is it your partner?"

He laughed shortly. "It's me. What can I say, I have a thing for black chicks in skimpy outfits. I bet you'd look good in one, Kate."

Kate ignored his comment. "Okay, now we're getting somewhere. There is no big boss breathing down your neck. This is a scheme you cooked up for some easy money. Fabulous!"

He looked smug. "You don't have to be a physicist to be smart, Kate."

"No," Kate said, smug too. "But it helps."

She rose and said into her cleavage, "Would someone please come get this guy?"

Across the room, Rafe watched as four police officers in plainclothes descended on Kate's table and took the little guy into custody. One of the officers was Detective Montenegro, dressed in a rather tight pair of jeans and a midriff blouse.

Soledad gave Kate a high five. "You did great, Kate. I heard everything you two said." She held up a microphone receiver in her hand. Earlier, Kate had been thrilled to have been fitted with a wire. She didn't feel so alone in there since she knew Soledad was listening to everything that was going on. "When I saw your friend, Rafe, come in I thought, for sure, he was going to come over and call you on your deception, but he was cool."

She had lost Kate when she'd mentioned Rafe's name. Kate was busy looking around the room for him. Diners were applauding the police officers, and craning their necks trying to catch them in action as they practically lifted the perp and carried him out of the Frog and Firkin.

Noticing Kate's preoccupation, Soledad laughed and said, "Behind you."

Kate spun on her heels. Rafe stood a few feet behind her smiling and shaking his head in mock consternation.

Kate ran and launched herself into his open arms.

Still laughing, Soledad went outside to join her fellow officers for the ride downtown where they would book and question the perp. Things had gone quite well tonight.

"I could strangle you," Rafe said in Kate's ear.

"I didn't lie to you," Kate said. "I did tell the police about the note. But when I did, Detective Montenegro suggested we do it this way."

Rafe squeezed her tightly in his arms, and set her down. "Let's get out of here, okay?"

Kate was perfectly cool with that. They hastily paid their checks and left the bar and grill. Rafe held her close to his side all the way to her car, where he took her keys, unlocked her door, and handed her in. "Follow me to my place," he said.

He jogged across the street to his car, and soon Kate saw the Expedition pulling out of a parking space. She followed in her Toyota Camry.

"I'm in for it now," she said aloud. Meaning he was undoubtedly angry with her for not telling him what she was up to. It was his opinion that she'd behaved recklessly tonight. She'd seen it in his eyes. She, however, was glad she'd done it, because now they knew the thieves were small-time. She and her family had gotten a good scare, but all was not lost. Her father could rest easy now. For that, Kate would do it all over again. Plus, she was extremely relieved to know Jason had nothing to do with the caper.

Soon, she was pulling the Camry behind the Expedition in Rafe's driveway. He got out and walked back to open her door and hand her out. Kate's body reacted in its usual manner whenever he got within ten feet of her, she got tense with excitement.

"Um, before you start in on me, I should phone my folks and tell them it's over," Kate said. "They'll be worried about me."

Rafe didn't offer comment as she reached in her shoulder bag, retrieved her cell phone, and flipped it open. "Matthews residence," she said, giving it a spoken command.

The phone automatically dialed her parents' house.

Her father picked up. "Kate, are you all right?"

She didn't wonder why he knew to whom he was speaking. They had caller ID.

"Yes, the guy's in custody. And, Daddy, it wasn't Paul Knowles. We don't know who he is yet, but they should have him spilling his guts in no time."

"Just so you're all right, Kate," her father said.

"I'm fine," she assured him. "I'm with Rafe. He showed up at the Frog and Firkin."

"He's a good man," was her father's opinion.

Kate smiled up at Rafe. "Yes, he is, Daddy. I'm going to say good night now. I think he's getting ready to bless me out for not filling him in on what we were planning to do tonight."

Her father laughed shortly. "Can't say you don't deserve it."

"Oh, so now you're on his side," Kate joked. "Men! Night, Daddy."

"Good night," said David, a note of laughter still evident in his voice.

They rang off, and Kate slipped the phone back into her shoulder bag. She looked at Rafe. "I'm ready to take my punishment now."

"And I'm ready to punish you until you plead for mercy," Rafe told her just before he threw her over his shoulder fireman style and carried her onto his front porch. "Stop wiggling," he said as he put the key in the lock and pushed the door open.

"Your hand is on a sensitive part of my anatomy. It tickles," Kate said.

Rafe set her down in the foyer. He switched on the light before closing and locking the door behind them. Turning to look her in the eyes, he sighed. "Caring for a woman like you could drive a man to drink."

"I wasn't in any real danger. There were four cops there, *and* you!" Kate said, going to hang her shoulder bag and her jacket on the hall tree. "It was worth the risk, because now we know there wasn't a scientist or an institute behind the theft."

Rafe took off his jacket and hung it up, too.

Facing him again, Kate earnestly said, "Don't be angry with me. I was the only one who could draw him out. He asked for me in the note. I had no other option but to do it." She smiled slowly. "To tell you the truth, it was damned exciting. The adrenaline rush was incredible when I realized that he was not working for someone else, and that there was a good chance my dad would get his research back."

"I know all about adrenaline rushes, Kate. You can get addicted to the high that goes along with risking your life."

"Are you?" Kate asked, walking over to him, reaching up, and gently caressing his cheek with the back of her hand.

Rafe pulled her fully into his arms. "No, I'm not. The only thing I'm swiftly becoming addicted to is you, Kate."

Kate tilted her head up, admiring the curve of his lips, enjoying the feel of his hard body against hers. "I literally ache for your touch all day long. Sometimes I can be doing something as routine as running the vacuum and I'll think of you and start tingling all over. Then, I'll dream about you at night and awaken with my entire body tense with desire."

Rafe bent his head and kissed her lightly on the mouth. "I want to make love to you, Kate—"

"Good, because I want you now."

"But I'm going away for a while in the morning. I have to go to Baltimore to pick up a prisoner who's going to stand trial here in Tucson. And I don't want to make love to you until I can take the time to wake up the next morning with you in my arms."

"Do you know how long you'll be?"

"Three days, four at the most. Then I'll be assigned to the courthouse where I'll be in charge of getting him into the courtroom each day. I asked for the assignment. I just didn't know it'd be coming up this soon. I wanted to spend the weekend with you."

"Why did you want this particular assignment?"

"Because I was among the deputies who captured him in Philly nine months ago, and before we could get the drop on him, he shot and critically wounded my partner, Craig Jackson. Craig's in a wheelchair now. I want to see this one to the bitter end."

"I'm so sorry about your partner," Kate said sympathetically. She laid her head on his shoulder, and sighed. "Yes, I can see why you'd want to be a part of this." She raised her gaze to his. "But, please, be careful."

"I always am, darlin'," Rafe said before leading her over to the sofa and pulling her down on top of him for a long, slow, wet, deep kiss. Kate felt intoxicated and light-headed when they parted. "You must think I have the willpower of a nun on Valium," she said, her voice husky. "What are you going to do, whip me into a frenzy of passion, and then send me home?"

"No way, my eager little student," Rafe said with a lascivious gleam in his golden brown eyes. "Lesson number three, coming up. And you can use your hands tonight. In fact, I heartily encourage you to use them."

The entire length of Kate's body was on top of his. His big hands were grasping her buns, and she could feel his erection on her stomach. "You mean I get to touch you?"

"Wherever you wish, whenever you wish, as often as you wish."

"Okay," Kate said, very pleased with his invitation, "I want to start here." She sat up and unbuttoned his pale blue denim shirt. This done, she spread it open and ran her hands over his hairy chest, being certain to tease his nipples with the palms of her hands. They hardened nearly instantaneously. She smiled, her full lips drawing back to reveal white teeth and pink gums. Licking her lips, she bent her head and tongued his right nipple. She felt him tremble. She slowly ran her tongue around the nipple, held it between her lips, and then captured it between her teeth without biting down.

She felt his penis grow even harder beneath her, and heard his breathing quicken. She smiled and treated his other nipple to the same treatment. She'd always been curious about a man's reaction to nipple stimulation. She knew she loved it. Now she knew he did, too.

"Ah, Kate," Rafe breathed. "You're learning so fast."

Kate didn't have time to chat. She was too busy working on the top button of his jeans. She was going to slip her hand down the front of his pants and feel the length of him. She was going to . . .

"You don't want to unleash anything you can't control right now, Kate," Rafe interrupted, his hand on her wrist. "I applaud your willingness, but I'm only a man and if you unzip me, fondle me, and spread your legs, I'm going to make love to you whether we're ready for that step or not. And I really don't believe we are."

Kate closed her eyes and breathed deeply. Opening her eyes, she withdrew her hands and sat up. "I should go, because I'm in deep trouble here, Rafe. We can talk about holding off until we're blue in the face, but the fact is I'm beyond the age of consent, and so are you. Whatever happens here tonight is between us, and us alone."

She got up off of him, and stood a few feet away from him. Rafe got to his feet as well and took a couple steps backward. "I'm trying to be a gentleman. That's what's happening."

"I don't want a gentleman tonight, Rafe. I'm a twenty-eight-year-old virgin and I'm ready to hand off my flowery crown to the next gal. I've chosen you for that honor. Deflower me, or send me home. Your choice."

"Girl, *please*, get your fine behind over here," Rafe said, his voice rife with passion.

He didn't wait for her to come to him. He went and picked her up in his arms.

"I think a shower together is the place to start. The sooner I see you naked, the better. Plus, there's something wildly erotic about soaping each other's bodies. I think you're gonna enjoy this."

Kate was laughing as he carried her down the hall. "I thought you were going to send me home."

"I'm many things, Katharine Matthews. A fool isn't one of them. I'm going to make love to you until we're both faint with exhaustion."

"We're young," Kate said. "That won't be happening any time soon."

In the bathroom they raced each other getting out of their clothes. Finally they stood in their underwear, their eyes drinking each other in. Kate's skin was a deep coppery brown. Wanting to see if she was that shade all over, Rafe went and pulled down her bra straps. Her skin was lighter beneath them, as he'd expected it would be. She obviously enjoyed being in the sun. Kate turned her back to him so he could unhook her bra. This done, she turned back around and helped him off with his sleeveless T-shirt. Now they stood solely in their panties and briefs. Kate felt her first twinge of nervousness. She put it aside, though, and pulled off her panties. Rafe removed his briefs. They both glanced down at the same time, and smiled, pleased by what they saw. Kate's belly was flat, but not rippled with muscles. She'd never done a stomach crunch in her life. Rafe's belly, however, was flat *and* rippled. His six-pack was fully loaded, as was the heavy equipment below. He was very well endowed.

Rafe watched her as she wound her hair on top of her head in preparation for the shower they would soon be taking together. "You should always be naked, Kate. You're unbelievably gorgeous."

"Ditto," Kate said, meeting his eyes. She didn't trust herself to say more at this point. She was more nervous than she'd ever been in her life. Her insides felt jittery with nervousness. She hoped she was managing to appear calm on the outside.

She went into Rafe's arms and they held each other. His embrace was warm and solid. "Kate, you're trembling. Is it too cold in here? I can turn the heat up."

"No, no," Kate said. "It isn't the temperature. I'm not as brave as the bravado I was displaying a few minutes ago might have led you to believe, that's all."

"There's nothing to be afraid of," Rafe said with a smile. He kissed her forehead. "Don't think I'm not a little nervous, too, because I am. I want your first time to be memorable, Kate. I want it to be something you will look back on and smile about, not laugh about. We men have our vulnerable spots too."

Kate felt a little better knowing she wasn't the only one with a case of the nerves.

The bathroom was large and had a walk-in shower, plus a bathtub. Decorated in shades of blue, the room had a calming effect on Kate. Rafe went and got two fluffy washclothes and a new bar of Zest soap. "I hope this is okay with you, it's all I use," he told her, handing her the bar of soap.

"It's one of my favorites," Kate said. Yikes! They really were nervous, discussing the type of soap he used as if it were important at this juncture. She would have used lye soap if that's all he had on hand.

"All right," Rafe said, stepping around her and switching on the shower's spray. A shower massage unit was attached to the showerhead. He pulled it up and out of its holder and adjusted the spray to "vigorous" remembering that's how Kate liked it.

"Come on in, the water's nice and warm," he said. Kate stepped in and took the shower massage from him and wet her body and the washcloth. Rafe did the same, then turned off the water and soaped his washcloth.

Kate began by gently rubbing the washcloth all over his upper body. Neither of them needed a shower for hygienic purposes; they'd showered earlier in the evening before going to the Frog and Firkin. Like Rafe had said, this was an exercise in erotic stimulation. Therefore Kate abandoned the washcloth in favor of her hands.

His body proved to be an erotic exercise unto itself. She moved her hands all over him, while she grew tenser with anticipation and Rafe sighed with satisfaction. Her golden brown skin color nicely complemented his darker chocolate-brown skin. And their heights proved advantageous too, as Rafe pressed her against the shower wall and kissed her. He only had to bend a little, and she didn't have to get up on her toes, which might have been unadvised in the shower.

"Kate, Kate, you taste so good to me. I want to taste you all over."

Kate wanted that, too. She wanted to feel his mouth all over her body, kissing her, licking her, bringing her to the peak, and stopping just before she reached it in order to deliciously torment her, make her wait until the moment she could no longer hold on, and then they'd experience bliss together.

They got out of the shower and dried off without saying a word, but their eyes were on each other's every movement. Kate could feel the tension in the air. Her nipples were hard and she felt an urgent throbbing between her legs. And all she'd done was kiss him and look at him unclothed.

Rafe went and got another dry towel to place about Kate's neck. In spite of their efforts not to get her hair wet, it had gotten damp. He dabbed the towel behind her neck where most of the dampness was. "Take it down, Kate."

Kate reached up and unwound her hair, removing the ponytail holder. It fell in waves about her shoulders.

Rafe imagined that the first woman, Eve, in all her beauty, had nothing on Kate at this moment. He was looking at her with such love that Kate felt naked, exposed, raw, and extremely blessed, all at once, to have someone who looked at her that way.

When he reached for her, she placed her hand in his and they walked into the outer room. The hardwood floor was covered with Berber carpeting in a wheat-colored shade. It felt soft beneath Kate's feet. However, her feet were on the carpet one instant and up in the air the next. Rafe had swept her into his arms with the intention of carrying her to his bed.

Somewhere in another part of the house, a phone rang.

Rafe lowered Kate to the bed. She looked up at him. "That's my phone." She knew the distinctive ring. Insistent two-note rings that irritated the listener into wanting to hurry up and answer it, or smash the darn thing to smithereens.

She looked in the direction of the sound, then back at Rafe, who was smiling at her.

He reached for her hand and pulled her to her feet. "You'd better get that. It could be something important."

Kate blew air between her kiss-swollen lips, frustrated. "I won't be long. Promise."

She hurried from the room, and Rafe threw himself onto the bed in a fit of disappointed angst to await her return. "Lord, don't let it be an emergency," he said under his breath.

In the living room, Kate got the cell phone that was in a pocket of her shoulder bag, flipped it open, and brought it to her ear and mouth. "Hi, it's Kate."

"Kate, Estrella just phoned and said your grandma collapsed a few minutes ago. She was taken to Northwest," her mother's anguished voice said. "Your father and I are on the way into Tucson, but I thought since you're already there you could get to the hospital faster."

"Oh, my God," said Kate. "Of course, Mama. I'll leave now."

"Okay. We'll meet you there," Carolina said, and hung up.

Kate replaced the phone in its pocket and hurried back to Rafe, who was reclining on the bed, his hands behind his head, without a stitch on. He sat up when Kate started gathering her clothes, which were flung all over the room, in her arms.

"It's Grandma," Kate said as she turned and left the bedroom, going into the bathroom to get her bra and panties. "She collapsed a few minutes ago. Mama said they took her to Northwest Medical Center, it's on La Cholla Boulevard."

"Yeah, I know where it is," Rafe said, right behind her.

They pulled on their underwear while standing in the bathroom; then they returned to the bedroom to finish dressing.

"I'll drive you," said Rafe as he pulled on his jeans.

"No, I have my car."

"Then I'll follow you."

Kate was buttoning her blouse. She locked eyes with him from across the room. Hers were filled with regret. "I'm sorry about tonight, Rafe."

Rafe smiled at her silliness. "Baby, don't be. Family comes before pleasure."

Kate went and kissed his chin. "You really are a good man."

For a moment, they gazed tenderly into each other's eyes; then they were back to business. "God, I hope she's gonna be okay," Kate said, worried as she pulled on her jeans. "We conveniently forget she's eighty-eight years old. She's so active, full of life. She never complains about aches and pains."

"Some seniors are like that," Rafe said. "They don't want you to worry about them."

By now they were fully dressed, shoes and all, and moving down the hallway. Kate collected her shoulder bag and coat from the hall tree. Rafe helped her on with her coat, she helped him on with his, and Rafe went to hold the front door open for her.

"Don't speed," he told her. "La Cholla's only ten minutes away. We'll get there in plenty of time."

"Seven if you take the shortcut I know," Kate said, and bounded down the front steps. The night air was bracing, and the black sky was covered with stars that glittered like diamonds. Kate gratefully breathed in the fresh air while she silently prayed that when they reached Northwest Medical Center, Josefina would be her old lovable, feisty self. Kate felt her world would never be the same again if she wasn't.

In spite of Rafe's admonition not to speed, she burned rubber after she'd backed out of the driveway and put the car in drive. In his car, Rafe smiled. He'd known all along that she was going to speed.

Eight

"Pneumonia!" Kate said, staring into the tired face of the emergency room doctor.

"It sounds bad, but she's lucky, really. We caught it in the early stages," the doctor, a young Chinese woman, said. "Advanced age usually works against patients with it, but she seems unusually strong for one so . . ."

"Decrepit?" Josefina suggested, pushing up on her elbows, and smiling weakly.

Kate was standing next to her bed in the examination room, holding one of her hands.

"Will you just lie back and rest?"

"I fainted, I didn't have a heart attack," Josefina said. She looked up at Kate. "Tell her to give me a prescription for an antibiotic, and send me home."

The doctor—Kate could see the name stitched onto the pocket of her white coat now, Lim Took Chuen—wagged her finger at Josefina. "There will be no going home tonight, Miss Thang. You will be spending the next few days in an oxygen tent, with copious amounts of antibiotics being pumped into your system."

"You really have a way with words," Josefina said. "Tell her she has a way with words, Kate."

"You just did," Kate said, laughing softly. She let go of her hand to gently take her by the shoulders and force her back onto the bed. "Now, lie down like a good girl, or I'll sic Mama on you when she gets here."

"Why'd you leave Rafe in the waiting room? One look at him and I'd feel young again," Josefina joked. She obeyed Kate, though. She didn't want Carolina in behind her. She yawned. "What time is it?"

Kate consulted her watch. "It's nine forty-five. Why?"

"Friday night," Josefina said. "I missed *Providence*."

Kate laughed. "I'm sure Sidney and the rest can get along without you for one night."

Dr. Chuen had been off to the side writing in Josefina's chart. She looked at Josefina. "If you're very good, you may be able to go home in a couple of days after we determine that the type of antibiotic we give you is working. Don't want to send you home if we're not certain the treatment is appropriate for you. I'll go set things in motion now. Following admission, we can poke and probe you at our leisure."

"Sounds like fun," Josefina said.

"Oh, it will be," replied Dr. Chuen with a grin.

In her absence, Josefina said, "I think she likes her job."

"It would appear so," Kate agreed. Getting serious, she sternly looked at her great-grandmother. "Why didn't you tell anyone you were feeling bad, Gram?"

"To be perfectly honest, Kate, I didn't know myself. I've been feeling less than energetic lately, but I thought that came with, as the doc put it, advanced age. I figured it was my time to start feeling puny. I've enjoyed robust health all my life."

"Of course you aren't going to be able to leap tall buildings in a single bound like you did in your youth, Gram, but you should enjoy good health as long as you don't have a chronic disease, which you didn't until now. You've got to pay closer attention to changes in your body. You know you're going to have to come stay at the ranch until you're fully recovered, right? Mom is going to insist on it, and I'll be backing her up."

Josefina, who had been asked to come live with Carolina and David many times over the years, preferred living in her small house on the Pascua Yaqui reservation there in Tucson. She had all of her old friends and neighbors around her. It was the last home she'd shared with her beloved husband, whom she still had conversations with every day thanks to a vivid imagination. And it was where she expected to die.

"I guess a short visit won't kill me," she said now. "Especially if I get to have The Puma for company. He and I both like to raise hell."

"I think that can be arranged," Kate said.

A nurse came into the examination room with a clipboard and pen in her hands. "It's time to sign the admission forms," she announced with a pleasant smile. "Then we will be taking you upstairs to your room. You can have one overnight visitor. The rest will be asked to leave at eleven." She'd ended with a glance in Kate's direction.

Josefina scribbled her name on the two pages where the signature lines were marked with a red X, and handed them back to the nurse. "Thank you, dear."

"You're welcome," said the nurse. "I'm going to get a wheelchair now. I'll be back in a few minutes."

Kate said, "Wait. Do you know what room she'll be going to? She has friends and relatives waiting to hear something."

"Room 406," said the nurse.

By the time Kate got back out to the emergency room's waiting area, her parents, Davida, the three "aunts," Estrella, Vera, and Gloria, plus several of her great-uncles, aunts, and various cousins, had joined Rafe in the crowded room and were fervently hoping for good news about the matriarch of the family, Josefina. Kate was delighted to be able to give it to them.

"It's pneumonia," she told them. "But her doctor is optimistic that they caught it before too much damage could be done. She estimates that Gram'll be here for about three days at the most."

"Can we see her?" asked her great-uncle Sebastian. He was Josefina's eldest son at seventy.

"Sure," said Kate. "They're taking her up to room 406 now. Give them a few minutes and go on up. The nurse says visiting hours end at eleven, so there's a good hour left."

The consensus in the room was that the gathering would reconvene in room 406. After they started moving toward the bank of elevators, Kate took the opportunity to pull Rafe aside.

"You should have heard her. 'Why did you leave Rafe in the waiting room?' she asked. You're a hit."

Rafe smiled slowly. "That's good to know. I think she's something else. Makes me miss my grandmothers. Unfortunately, they've both passed away."

He looked into her tired face. "Look, sweetheart, I'm going to go home. This is a time for family. Give Miss Josefina my best, and tell her I'll come to see her when I get back in town in a few days."

"All right," Kate said, trying to conceal her disappointment. She understood perfectly: They'd met only a week ago and he'd already been introduced to several members of her family. Now, ten more of them were gathered in her gram's hospital room. Any guy would feel uncomfortable and out of place. However, she was selfish enough to want him to stick around. The night was still young, and she wanted to eventually get back to what they'd been doing before the phone rang earlier in the evening.

She wondered if he'd changed his mind about making love to her tonight. He *had* suggested that they wait until after he returned from Baltimore. She was the one to give him an ultimatum, make love to her or send her home. Had she been mistaken?

Standing there, she recalled everything they'd done together in the past seven days. She'd let down her guard with Rafe almost immediately, committing intimate acts with him that she'd never done with another man. And tonight, she'd nearly jumped his bones. No wonder the guy was backing off. She was behaving like a desperate, love-starved female.

"I'll walk you to your car," she offered.

"Okay," said Rafe.

Kate was convinced he was distancing himself from her. What had happened when she was in the examination room with Josefina? Had a cousin ribbed him about being Kate's boyfriend? Boyfriend? It was much too soon to put that label on him. But that's how it had felt to Kate almost immediately with Rafe. She'd been drawn to the kindness in him. What other sort of man would have put up with what she'd put him through the night they'd met?

"I take it Mom introduced you to everybody in my absence," Kate said, seemingly making small talk, but really fishing for clues.

"Yeah, she did," Rafe said. "Everybody was very nice. You have a great family, Kate."

They were walking through the double electric doors of the emergency room. Once outside, Kate took his hand in hers. The night was quiet. Traffic on the street adjacent to the hospital was light, and all that could be heard was their footfalls on the sidewalk.

Rafe's car was only a few feet from the entrance, parked next to Kate's. At his car, he stood with his back to the driver's-side door and pulled her into his arms. "I'm gonna miss you, Kate. You have no idea what you've given me these past few days."

"I nearly gave you a broken nose," Kate said, her full lips curving in a sensuous smile.

"Well, that too," Rafe said. "But what I'm referring to is, you've given me a glimpse at what a real family is. I haven't had that in a very long time. A family is something that's lasting. Something you can count on. I love my sister, but since I went into the navy at seventeen, Jenny and I didn't get the chance to spend much time together. I didn't get to see her when she was growing up. I wasn't there for her first date, or her prom, that sort of thing. Seeing you with your family makes me realize what I've been missing. And it makes me realize what I want in the future."

Kate's head was on his shoulder as she listened to him. So, that's what was on his mind. She was very relieved he wasn't about to dump her because she'd scared him off with her enthusiasm. Her zest for living, as her mother called it. "Kate," she'd say, "slow down. You're bouncing off the walls. Life isn't a race. It's a journey. Take your time getting to your destination."

She peered into Rafe's eyes. *Slow down and savor this man,* she thought. "I'm glad. You've given me a lot these past seven days, too."

"Really?" Rafe said as he bent his head and kissed her high on the cheek. "What?"

"For one, I now know where my G-spot is," Kate joked. "That info will come in handy in the future."

"Yeah," Rafe agreed. "I'll show you just how handy in a few days. Don't start without me."

Then, they kissed good-bye.

* * *

The next couple of days found Kate dividing her time between going to visit Josefina at the hospital and pestering Soledad Montenegro about her father's case. To the Matthewses utter disappointment, the police had not been able to glean much more information from the man besides his name, Stephen Erwin.

Kate was sitting across from Soledad now, voicing her displeasure at the outcome of the investigation so far. "I can't believe this. He struck me as a rank amateur. He is an amateur, isn't he?"

Detective Montenegro squinted, struggling with what to say next. "It would appear so. But appearances can be deceiving. No amount of deal offering made him give up his partner. Up until now, Erwin's managed to maintain a low profile. He has no priors. Not even a traffic violation. But it's true what he told you about being a janitor at the school. He quit about the time your father had the stroke. We know everything we need to know, and more, about his life outside of a life of crime. He is originally from Santa Monica, California. He has a bachelor's degree in English, and a master's degree in education."

"Then he used to be a teacher," Kate ventured.

"No, he's never worked in the field," Soledad said.

Kate sighed and leaned forward. "But he *is* working alone, isn't he? He's not working for someone else?"

"That's not what he's saying now," Soledad said regretfully. "He insists that the reason he isn't talking is that the man he's working for would have him killed if he implicated him in any way."

"So, what are you charging him with?"

"Burglary," Soledad told her.

"What would he get? Five years, tops?"

"That's about it," Soledad said.

"And my dad's research, in the meantime, is floating around out there somewhere."

"Possibly already in the hands of his boss, or maybe still with his partner," Soledad said, giving her the options.

Kate thought of something. "What I don't understand is why he asked me to meet him at the Frog and Firkin. Why me? And why did he get so familiar with me, calling me 'dear Kate' in such an insolent way, as if he were taunting me?"

"Kate, you're probably imagining that," Soledad suggested. "It's true, the guy was cocky at the beginning of your conversation, but that could be because he thought he had you where he wanted you."

"It was also the way he looked at me," Kate insisted. "It was as if he knew things about me. Personal things."

"Okay," Soledad said. "Now you're getting paranoid."

Kate didn't think so. And she would rack her brains until she came up with a plausible reason why the little twerp had made her feel that way.

"I want to talk to him again," she told Soledad.

Soledad sat twirling her pen between her thumb and forefinger for several long seconds before she said, "I don't think so, Kate. I don't see any good coming from it."

But Kate's mind was already clicking. She knew she would get nowhere if she antagonized Soledad, so she tried another tack. "Okay, if you don't think it's advisable I'll forget about it. But up until nearly five months ago, I lived in California. In Sonoma. How long did he work at the university as a janitor?"

"Maybe two months," Soledad replied, wondering where Kate was going with this line of questioning. "It looks as if he stayed there long enough only to get the information he needed in order to break into your family's house."

"I don't understand it," Kate said. "Why did he wait

An Important Message From The ARABESQUE Publisher

Dear Arabesque Reader,

I have some exciting news to share....

Available now is a four-part special series **AT YOUR SERVICE** written by bestselling Arabesque Authors.

Bold, sweeping and passionate as America itself—these superb romances feature military heroes you are destined to love.

They confront their unpredictable futures along-side women of equal courage, who will inspire you!

The **AT YOUR SERVICE** series* can be specially ordered by calling 1-888-345-BOOK, or purchased wherever books are sold.

Enjoy them and let us know your feedback by commenting on our website.

Linda Gill, Publisher
Arabesque Romance Novels

**Check out our website at
www.BET.com**

* The AT YOUR SERVICE novels are a special series that are not included in your regular book club subscription.

THE "THANK YOU" GIFT INCLUDES:

- 4 books absolutely FREE (plus $1.99 for shipping and handling).
- A FREE newsletter, *Arabesque Romance News*, filled with author interviews, book previews, special offers, and more!
- No risks or obligations.

INTRODUCTORY OFFER CERTIFICATE

Yes! Please send me 4 FREE Arabesque novels (plus $1.99 for shipping & handling). I understand I am under no obligation to purchase any books, as explained on the back of this card. Send my **FREE Tote Bag** after my first regular paid shipment.

NAME _____

ADDRESS _____ APT. _____

CITY _____ STATE _____ ZIP _____

TELEPHONE ( ) _____

E-MAIL _____

SIGNATURE _____

Offer limited to one per household and not valid to current subscribers. All orders subject to approval. Terms, offer, & price subject to change. Tote bags available while supplies last.

Thank You!

Accepting the four introductory books for FREE (plus $1.99 to offset the cost of shipping & handling) places you under no obligation to buy anything. You may keep the books and return the shipping statement marked "cancelled". If you do not cancel, about a month later we will send 4 additional Arabesque novels, and you will be billed the preferred subscriber's price of just $4.00 per title. That's $16.00* for all 4 books for a savings of almost 40% off the cover price (Plus $1.99 for shipping and handling). You may cancel at any time, but if you choose to continue, every month we'll send you 4 more books, which you may either purchase at the preferred discount price. . . or return to us and cancel your subscription.

THE ARABESQUE ROMANCE BOOK CLUB
P.O. BOX 5214
CLIFTON NJ 07015-5214

PLACE
STAMP
HERE

four months before attempting to steal the notes? And how did he know we were all going to be away from the ranch that night?"

"That's easy enough to do, Kate," Soledad told her. "All he had to do was watch the ranch for a few days. In the course of a few days he would learn how many people lived on the ranch. All he had to do was wait for an occasion when all of you vacated the premises. His patience paid off."

Going back to how long Stephen Erwin had been in Arizona, Kate asked, "Do you have solid proof he was in California up until he moved here six months ago?"

"Yes, we have records showing he'd rented an apartment in Santa Monica. We also have copies of pay stubs from his former workplace, Thrill Seekers, Incorporated. It's a sporting goods chain specializing in—"

"Equipment designed for risk takers like sky divers, scuba divers, boogie boarders, snowboarders, and any other kind of sport where the risk of breaking your neck while doing it is high. I know the place. And I know the owner," Kate finished for her.

Soledad's eyebrows went up in amazement. "You mean there *could* be a connection between you and that little weasel?"

"Scientists don't believe in coincidence," Kate told her. She explained, "Have you ever truly regretted meeting someone? I mean totally wished you'd never set eyes on them before?"

"My ex-husband," Soledad said without hesitation.

"Well, that's how I feel about Rick Solano. I was in my favorite market one Saturday afternoon doing a little shopping and he comes up to me and introduces himself. He has a place in Sonoma. The place turns out to be a winery that has been in his family for generations. He asks me out. I turn him down because he isn't my type. The way he looks at me makes my skin crawl. You've probably met the type: he's a white guy with plenty of money and he thinks a brown chick can be bought for his amusement. And that's the truth of the matter. Don't misunderstand me, I'm the product of a mixed marriage. But there are those men who can respect and cherish your differences, and then there is the type who simply wants to make you his toy until he tires of you. Rick Solano was from the last group."

"Been there," Soledad agreed. "That attitude made me swear off dating white men for years. So, you told him to get lost."

"Not that nicely, I'm afraid," Kate told her. "At any rate, when I told him I wouldn't touch him even if I were dying of some horrible flesh-eating disease and he were my only hope, he told me I'd be sorry. Those were his exact words, 'You'll be sorry.' I didn't think anything of it. I was just happy to be rid of him. And get this, when I told my elderly neighbor, Mary Chase, about what had happened she told me I was lucky that I hadn't gotten involved with him, because it had been rumored for years that he was connected with organized crime."

"Mmm," said Soledad, sounding as if she'd just bitten into something delicious. "Then Erwin could very well be telling the truth about being afraid he'll be killed if he informs on his employer." She picked up the phone. "I'm on it, Kate. Now, you'd better split so I can get to work."

Rising, Kate smiled down at the formidable detective. "Can't I just have five minutes with Erwin? I know I can make him talk."

"If you don't get out of here . . ." Soledad said menacingly.

Kate laughed shortly. "I'm going, I'm going."

"And don't say anything about this to anyone until I get back to you. Not anyone!"

When Kate got back home, she stopped at the big house to check on everyone. It was nearly noon on a Tuesday so Davida was in school.

Kate spied her mother in the kitchen, through the window, preparing lunch.

She rapped on the window.

"Hey, have you spoken with Gram today?"

"Yeah, she's feeling better and she's complaining about the bland food. Her doctor says she can have spicier fare now so I'm going to take her something for dinner."

"Good," Kate said. "See you later."

"No news about the investigation?" Carolina asked hopefully.

"Not yet. Detective Montenegro's optimistic though."

"Your dad was up half the night scribbling on his blackboard. I'm worried about him. You ought to come over and see what he's up to."

"I will," Kate promised. "I need to try to get some writing done this afternoon. I'll come by in the morning."

"'Kay. Bye, sweetie."

Kate jogged to the Camry, got in, and drove around back to the guest house. When she walked into the house through the kitchen a couple of minutes later, her eyes had to adjust to the darkness. She'd neglected to open the curtains at the windows in the room before she'd left that morning. She went and opened them now. Light spilled into the room. She went to the refrigerator and got a small bottle of cranberry-grape juice and drank half of it standing in front of the fridge. Out of habit she then glanced in the direction of the answering machine sitting on the counter next to the phone. The red light was blinking.

Hoping the message was from Rafe, but wondering why he hadn't used her cell phone number if it was, she walked over and pressed the button.

"Hello, Kate, you'll never guess who called me." It was Sophie.

Kate immediately felt guilty for not phoning before now to see how she and Renata were doing. She hadn't spoken with Sophie since she'd done her hair for her first date with Rafe.

"Vance!" Sophie said with a guffaw. "Vance. Can you believe it?"

"Frankly, no, I can't," Kate said, talking back to the machine.

"He phoned to ask me out," Sophie's voice continued. "And my Jessie . . . dead only nine months! I almost cussed him out! I *should* have cussed him out. But he was so nervous he wouldn't let me get a word in edgewise. He went on and on about how he'd always been in love with me. And he never would have said anything if Jessie had lived. He sounded like a teenaged boy trying to ask a girl out who he thinks would *never* go out with him. He sounded so pitiful, I couldn't cuss him out."

There was a pause and Sophie added, sounding angry, "You'd better set that crazy cousin of yours straight, Kate. Or I will. He has some nerve asking me out after what I've been through the last nine months." She sounded tearful now. "What the hell was he thinking, huh? I don't think I'll ever be ready to date anybody. Nobody can replace Jessie. Nobody!"

Kate heard Sophie's doorbell ringing in the background.

There was a quiet period during which Kate imagined Sophie was walking to her door with the cordless phone in her hand. "Kate, it's that fool cousin of yours with a big bouquet of flowers in his arms and a stupid grin on his face. I'm going to get my shotgun and blow him off my porch."

She hung up then.

Kate ran to check her caller ID to see what time Sophie had phoned her. She'd called only thirty-four minutes ago. Kate dialed Sophie's number.

"Hello," said Sophie.

"You didn't shoot him, did you?"

"No, but I would have if Renata hadn't come into the room and was instantly taken with the idiot. She loves him. They're playing on the living room floor right now. I'm in the kitchen. He impressed her when he knew every character on *Sesame Street*. He would, he's nothing but a kid himself."

"You're remembering the Vance you knew in school, Sophie. I think he's grown up since then," Kate told her. She was worried about Vance's relationship with Trudy Rodriguez, though. She'd just seen them together less than a week ago. How could she recommend Vance to her best friend when she wasn't sure of his intentions herself?

Sophie had been through enough.

"You hope so!" said Sophie skeptically.

"You're right," Kate agreed. "I hope so. You don't have to go out with him, Sophie. Tell him how you feel, you're just not ready to date yet. Tell him, and see what he says."

"He'd better say he understands if he knows what's good for him," Sophie said.

"Good luck," said Kate. "Call me back later?"

"You know it," said Sophie. "Thanks for listening."

"Thanks for talking," Kate said. "Kiss Renata for me."

Kate hung up the phone and walked over to get her shoulder bag off the kitchen chair she'd thrown it on when she'd come through the door a few minutes ago. Glancing down in it, she noticed the red light on her cell phone was blinking. Someone had left her a message. She checked the ringer on the cell phone. She usually had it set on "loud ring"; however, she must have inadvertently bumped against it. It was now on "vibrate." No wonder she hadn't heard the phone ring.

Quickly pressing a button that would allow her to hear her message, she placed the phone to her ear and waited. "Lawyers," said Rafe's deep voice. "They'll be the death of us all. Bainbridge's lawyer managed to postpone his change of venue. He's claiming that Bainbridge can't get a fair trial in Tucson. However, the prosecutor in Tucson is saying that because the murder was committed there, the trial should rightfully be set there. The result is, I'm going to be here a few more days until the judge rules on whether Bainbridge leaves or stays. I'm sorry, Kate. Call me when you get in. I want to hear your voice."

Kate checked the time of his message: eleven forty-seven A.M.

He'd phoned her while she'd been talking to Sophie.

Kate quickly dialed his number from memory.

Three rings later, Rafe picked up. "Deputy Marshal Grant."

Kate's toes curled at the sound of his live voice.

"It's Kate."

"Of course it is," Rafe said. "How are you, sweetheart?"

In Baltimore, he was descending the steps of City Hall at 100 North Holliday Street, on the way to lunch. It was cold, and he'd worn an overcoat over his gray business suit. Two other deputies were waiting for him in a dark sedan at the curb.

"I'm upset because you won't be coming home sooner," Kate said.

"Don't pout, it ruins the picture of you I have in my imagination. Believe me, I'll be out of here like a shot as soon as they say he goes or he stays. Either way I'll be coming home to you. And that'll make me a very happy boy."

"And when you're happy, I'm happy."

"See? I knew you were feeling me. I've got to go now. I'll phone you tonight. Stay out of trouble."

"As if!" Kate said. "All right, good-bye."

Rafe put away his cell phone and climbed into the passenger seat of the sedan.

"That must have been a woman," Deputy Marshal Robinson, a brawny African-American in his late twenties, said as he put the car in drive and pulled away from the curb. "Ain't no way a man could make you smile like that."

"It was," Rafe confirmed, still smiling.

"And she's hot, isn't she?" Deputy Marshal O'Malley, of Irish-American descent, said from the backseat.

"She is," Rafe said.

"She must be," Robinson joked. "Just the sound of her voice has reduced you to using two-word sentences."

All three of them laughed.

"She does have the ability to turn my brain to mush," Rafe admitted.

In Tucson, Kate put the cell phone on its charger atop the kitchen counter and went into the second bedroom, which she'd converted into an office, to begin work. As she sat in the swivel chair and switched on the computer, she wondered what her father was working on in his office that had her mother's curiosity up.

She supposed her mother was worried that her father was going back to work too soon after the stroke. Her mother had to realize that all her father needed was a good excuse to go back to work. The theft of his notes had been the catalyst.

Opening the new book's file, she made a mental note to go over to the big house tonight and talk to her father about what he was working on so furiously.

* * *

Kate felt as if she'd been in a time warp. When she glanced down at her watch she saw that she'd been at the computer more than five hours. It was the way Einstein had jokingly defined relativity: When you're doing something you love, time flies. When you're engaged in a less riveting activity, time seems to stand still.

She shut down the computer, rose on stiff legs, and yawned with feeling.

Her stomach growled. She'd missed lunch.

After a stop by the bathroom to relieve a full bladder, she washed up and headed out the door, thinking she could probably raid her mother's pots. Undoubtedly her mom would have something delicious simmering on her stove. She'd mentioned taking Gram something spicy for her dinner. Kate hoped it was chili rellenos. She had a taste for the stuffed chilis. By the same token, she wouldn't wish that much work on her mother. The recipe was intricate, and ate up a good chunk of your time.

Kate inhaled the wonderful smells as she came through the big house's back door.

Her mother was sitting at the kitchen nook enjoying a cup of coffee and watching the local five o'clock news on the nine-inch color TV installed in the cabinet above the nook. Carolina glanced up. She was attired in jeans and a long-sleeve white blouse over which she'd tied a multicolored apron. She wore tan loafers.

"Thought you would be showing up pretty soon," she said to Kate.

Kate walked over to the stove and began lifting lids on the pots. The aromas were enough to clear her sinuses if they needed clearing. Everyone in the Matthews family loved their food hot, and Carolina knew just how to spice it so that it was so scrumptious going down, you didn't think twice about your burning tongue.

"Chili con carne," Carolina said, "corn bread, and steaks on the grill."

Kate's hopes had lifted at the word "chili," and then her mother had tacked on "con carne" and they had fallen. *Still*, she thought, as she gazed down at the chili simmering in the Dutch oven, *that chili con carne smells divine.*

"Taste test?" she said, asking for permission to partake.

"Help yourself," Carolina said with a smile.

"Where's Dad and Davida?" Kate asked as she spooned some of the chili into a small bowl. Come to think of it, she hadn't seen Davida all day. She hadn't joined them for breakfast, and Kate had been working when she had gotten home from school.

"David's in his office. He didn't even stop for lunch. I took him a tray, and went back to get it two hours later. He hadn't touched it. At that point I blew up at him, and he sat down and ate his lunch. I tell you, Kate, he's behaving like he used to before you and the other kids came along. He was a driven man back then. You kids helped mellow him out a lot. He says I am the reason he was able to stop being obsessed with his work, but I was there. I know it was having children that did it. He finally came to understand that there were things more important than his work. That not only did I need him, but his children needed him even more."

"He's been a good dad," Kate said.

Carolina nodded. "Yes, he has been. And I should stop worrying about his becoming obsessed with work. I wouldn't be if he were not recovering from a stroke. After all, this is his time. You kids are grown, except for Little David, and he has every right to go after his dreams. I want him to. Honestly."

"I understand, Mom," Kate assured her. "You want Dad

to be happy in his work. More than that, though, you want him to be around for a long, long time."

"That's it, exactly." Carolina reached over and switched off the TV. "Nothing's positive on the news anymore. I'm a nervous wreck after watching it. Why can't they have a segment called Good News where all they report are the positive things that are going on in the world? Feel-good news, if you will. It would be a pleasant antidote to all the poisonous negative news we're fed on a daily basis."

Kate was busy shoving a piece of chili-dipped corn bread into her mouth.

"I see you can't talk now," Carolina said. "How is the chili?"

"Mmm," said Kate, relishing the juxtaposition of spices with the hearty flavor of the corn bread. Since she couldn't speak, she gave her mom a thumbs-up sign.

"Have you heard from Rafael?" Carolina asked with a mischievous glint in her dark eyes. "I'd love for him to show up at one of my ladies' auxiliary meetings. Danita Flores is always bragging about her daughter, Alexis. I'd like to see old Danita's jaw drop when you walk in on Rafael's arm. Invite him to the Red and White Ball in December. I would pay good money to see that."

Kate swallowed. "Mom, we've just met. I don't even know if Rafe goes in for affairs like the Red and White Ball."

"It's a charity event. Of course he'd go," was Carolina's opinion. She looked Kate in the eyes. "What? Are you having doubts this soon? What happened?"

Kate laughed. "Chill, Mom. I think you're more worried about my relationship working with Rafe than I am." She sat down across from her mother.

Carolina laughed too. "It's not as if I've had a lot of chances to interfere in your past relationships, Kate. You were in college before you ever had a steady boyfriend, and you broke up with him before you could bring him home for Christmas vacation. That was my first missed opportunity to give you motherly advice on men. What was his name?"

"James, James McBride," Kate said with a contemplative smile. "I wonder whatever happened to him. The last I heard, he was engaged to Monica Harmon. Sweet girl. I hope they're happy together."

"Better her than you, huh?" Carolina said cynically.

"For your information, I was happy with James. He had a problem with *me*. He told me he couldn't be content with a woman who, at some point in the relationship, had the potential to outearn him. It was a matter of pride."

"Or insecurity," Carolina said. "If you want to know the truth, every woman on the face of the planet has the potential of earning more money than the man she's with. What most women value is the love and support her man gives her."

"To be fair," Kate said, "there *are* women who won't date anyone who earns less than they do. So, men are in a weird position. On one hand, they would probably love to be accepted for who they are and not for what's in their portfolios. On the other, they realize that a lot of women want financial security, and will not waste their time on what they call 'trifling brothers.'"

Carolina sighed. "I'm glad I'm an old married woman. I don't envy you singles. Things used to be so much simpler."

"What things?" David asked, coming in on the tail end of their conversation. "That chili drew me. I'm ravenous." He went and got a bowl from the cabinet. "Don't let me interrupt. Sounds like you were having an interesting conversation. What is it that men and women want nowadays?"

"If I knew that," Kate cracked, "I wouldn't be still looking."

"Are you still looking?" her father asked as he filled his bowl at the chili pot.

"That's a loaded question," Kate said. "You're wondering how I feel about Rafe."

"Yes, I am," David admitted. He went and claimed a stool beside Kate at the nook. He looked at her, waiting for her reply.

Kate squirmed a little on her stool, thinking. "All I know is, I'm very happy to be in his presence, and I miss him when I'm not."

David smiled. "I was hoping for something a little juicier. I've been going over calculations in my head all day. A bit of mushy love talk would've hit the spot."

Kate laughed. "Okay, you asked for it. He makes my ears tingle, and my toes curl. I've never felt this way about anyone in my entire life, and I think that if he asked me, I'd marry him tomorrow."

"Whoa!" said David. "You wanna give me another stroke?"

He would often make his condition the subject of a joke, thereby taking some of the sting out of it. It worked for him. However, Carolina didn't think there was anything amusing about it.

"Don't say that!" she cried.

"I was just kidding, baby," David said, trying to console her.

"I don't care," Carolina said. "Don't put it out there!"

"There is no empirical evidence that talking about something makes it happen," David said. "If that were possible there would be a hell of a lot more rich people in the world."

"I don't care," Carolina reiterated. "Call me superstitious all you want. I believe negative thoughts can be bad for your physical health. They've done studies on prayer, for example. It has been proven that patients who were prayed for recovered at faster rates than those who weren't. Prayer uses the power of positive thinking."

"That's ridiculous, Carolina. If that were true, then it proves that God only cares about those people whom others pray for. What kind of God is that?"

"A busy God," Carolina said, "who listens to prayers."

"Oh, you make me crazy!" David said with a grin.

"And you make me insane!" Carolina said with an equally broad smile.

David leaned in. Carolina leaned in. They kissed.

"You both make me think there must be something in this chili," Kate said, rising. "I'm gonna get another bowl, to go."

She did just that, and left the lovebirds alone to smooch in private.

Nine

It had happened so fast.

Friday morning, the morning after the judge's verdict, Rafe and fellow deputies Robinson and O'Malley were taking the prisoner, Thomas Bainbridge, out the back door of the county jail to a waiting department-issued van.

It must have been about forty degrees. Their breath could be seen in the moist morning air. Rafe was the point man. In front of Bainbridge, he led the way to the van. Robinson and O'Malley were on either side of Bainbridge. Each had hold of him on either side. Bainbridge's arms were cuffed in front of him. His ankles were also cuffed, with a short chain between them, preventing any quick movements on his part.

Another deputy marshal waited next to the van. He stood beside the driver's-side door. All of the deputy marshals were dressed in work gear, dress slacks, heavy-duty black shoes, short-sleeve polo shirts in light blue, and dark blue jackets with the U.S. Marshal insignia in large white letters on the back.

They were only about eight feet from the van when a woman dressed gangster-style, designer denims two sizes too big, a Tommy Hilfiger jacket, also too big for her, and an expensive pair of pristine white athletic shoes, emerged from the alley with a Smith and Wesson .357 magnum drawn.

Rafe didn't have to think about it. He'd instantly drawn his weapon, a standard-issue .38 Special.

For one split second Rafe had the illogical thought that the gun in her hand looked bigger than *she* did. She couldn't have been more than five feet two inches tall and a hundred and ten pounds.

"Easy now," Rafe said. "You don't want to do this."

Behind him, both Robinson and O'Malley still held on to Bainbridge. They would take their cues from Rafe.

The girl was shaking. Her eyes were wild. Rafe was afraid she could be on something. Liquid courage, or courage in the form of a more potent drug. He saw that the deputy marshal who had been waiting by the van had pulled the driver's side door open and was using it as a shield. His gun was trained on the girl.

"Oh, I do want to do this," said the girl. She drew her jacket flap aside to reveal a distended belly. "That there is the father of my baby, and I'm leaving here with him today, or we all die."

"Think about this," Rafe said calmly, even though he didn't feel very calm. "There are four lawmen here with weapons. Men trained to use them. How far do you think you'll get even if we do let Bainbridge go?"

Rafe's line of sight was on her trigger finger. Some said you could tell when a shooter decides to shoot by looking into his eyes. But in Rafe's opinion, while you're looking in the eyes, you could miss the minuscule amount of pressure being put on the trigger.

"There's a man behind you with his gun pointed at your back. If you shoot me, he's going to shoot you, and thereby hurt your baby. You don't want that. Put the gun down, *please.*"

The girl was crying now. "I can't. I've gotta do it, or

he'll have me killed." She held the gun firmer, steadier. "He can do it, too. It doesn't matter if he's in prison. One of his boys on the outside would do it for him. I've seen it done before. So, I'm sorry."

Her finger began moving on the trigger. Rafe shot her. She weighed so little, the impact knocked her off her feet and her body slammed into the concrete. The .357 magnum flew out of her hand, and at that moment Thomas Bainbridge violently wrenched himself out of the deputies' hold and dove for it.

Rafe had been in a crouch when he'd shot the girl. He now threw himself on the concrete, rolled, and trained his gun on Bainbridge, who was lying on his side with the .357 magnum in his cuffed hands and his finger on the trigger. He had the gun trained on Rafe. "Stinking cop. You've had it in for me ever since I shot your partner. Well, this one's for—"

Before he'd completed his last sentence, Rafe shot him in the chest. His electrical system shut down immediately and his hand no longer had the strength to hold the gun. He lay on his side, his head twitching. The rest of his body seemed to be paralyzed.

Deputy Marshal Robinson rushed forward and kicked the gun out of Bainbridge's reach, then knelt to look at him. He shook his head. He didn't think anyone would be transporting Bainbridge to a prison facility any time soon. More likely to the morgue.

Rafe got to his feet and went to check on the girl. She was lying still with her right hand pressed to her left shoulder. He was more than a little relieved to see he'd gotten her in the shoulder.

Behind him the deputy marshal at the van was already phoning for an ambulance.

Deputy Marshal O'Malley knelt beside Rafe and the girl. "She must have been terrified of him."

"My question," Rafe said, "is how did she know we'd be taking him out this way? We change our routine on a regular basis to prevent things like this from happening."

"Search me," said O'Malley. "But I imagine it's not hard to grease the palm of a public servant for information. Bainbridge was wanted for drug dealing and murder in three states. He probably had money stashed all over. Being his lady, she probably had access to it. You heard her, she knew how he operated."

Rafe frowned. He hated to be thinking what he was thinking: there was a leak in the department.

In Tucson, Soledad Montenegro was having a rather strange phone conversation with Rick Solano. She'd phoned him supposedly looking for information about an ex- employee of his, Stephen Erwin.

"Detective Montenegro," Solano said smoothly, "I have more than twenty-five stores. I don't know all of my employees by name. You would have to phone the store where he worked last and ask to speak with the manager. The manager could then pull the ex-employee's file. I'm sorry, but that's my suggestion to you."

"I've already done that, Mr. Solano," Soledad surprised him by saying. "Your manager was very forthcoming. She said not only did you know Stephen Erwin but that you and Mr. Erwin seemed to be personal friends. The present manager was the assistant manager when Mr. Erwin, who was the manager, worked there. I was told that you and Mr. Erwin often went to lunch together among other things."

"I take my employees to lunch when I want to speak with them in private. That's not an unusual occurrence, Detective Montenegro."

"No, it isn't. But when the lunch lasts three hours, that's a tad unusual, Mr. Solano. Also, when an employee routinely comes in late, insults paying customers, and boldly takes money from the cash register in plain sight, all without impunity, I would also label 'not usual' behavior. Do you want to tell me why he wasn't fired for that kind of behavior, Mr. Solano, or do I have to ask your local police to pay you a visit?"

"All right," said Solano with a bitter edge to his voice. "The little pain in the butt is my cousin. I was looking out for him, okay? His mother is my favorite aunt, and she has had nothing but trouble out of him all his miserable life."

Soledad sat perfectly still at her desk. She hadn't expected this. Solano's tone had the ring of truth to it. Could it be true that it was a coincidence that Stephen Erwin was connected to Rick Solano?

"He's in a lot of trouble here in Tucson," Soledad said.

"What has he done now?" Solano asked. To Soledad he didn't sound as though he really wanted to know, but felt duty-bound by family to inquire.

"He broke into a local scientist's home and stole his research, his disks and hard drive. The home belongs to Katharine Matthews's family. Do you know Ms. Matthews?"

"Yes, of course, I know Katharine Matthews. She's my neighbor in Sonoma. But I haven't seen her in months. You could say we had a falling-out."

"You asked her out and she turned you down flat. After which you threatened her."

"Now, hold on!" Solano cried. "I don't know what she told you but, yeah, it's true I was angry she'd turned me down. She's a beautiful woman, and my ego was shattered. I might have said some harsh things to her, but they were just words. I would never hurt anybody. Did he hurt her? Is that it?" He sounded genuinely concerned.

"No, nobody was harmed during the burglary," Soledad answered.

"Well, I don't know how I can help you, Detective. I

97979797

have no idea what Steve's been up to since he left here months ago. To tell the truth, I was relieved he was gone and hoped never to hear from him again. I know his mother isn't going to like hearing he's in jail in Tucson."

When he mentioned Tucson, Soledad thought of something else she wanted to ask him. "So, you haven't heard from him since he's been here in Tucson?"

"Yes, he would call whenever he needed to borrow money. Money he never paid back."

"When was the last time he phoned to borrow money?"

"It must have been four months ago, or around then," Solano said. "I think it was in May or June. He said the heat there was a killer. He was sweltering in that apartment of his and he needed money to buy a window air-conditioning unit. He was talking crazy, I figured the heat had gotten to his brain or something. Anyway, he said he would pay me back this time because his ship was getting ready to come in."

"Nothing specific? Just his ship was coming in?"

"That's all, Detective."

"Okay, Mr. Solano," Soledad said. "Thank you for your time."

"You're welcome. Oh, Detective?"

"Yeah?"

"Tell Kate I still think of her, and she has my number if she changes her mind about going out with me." He possessed a smarmy confidence that Soledad found loathsome. But, unfortunately, you couldn't arrest a man for that.

"Don't hold your breath," she said, and hung up.

A few minutes later she was sitting across from Stephen Erwin in the visiting area of the city jail. Seven days after his arrest he looked even more nondescript than he had when they'd brought him in. His skin appeared paler. His eyes were sunk in their sockets. His greasy hair lay limp on his head.

He looked at her. "Detective Montenegro. It's a pleasure to see you."

"I don't see why," Soledad said. "I only show up when I want to put you through the wringer. You should hate to see me coming."

He smiled. "On the contrary, seeing you is like looking at the Mona Lisa. You are lovely to look at, and you have an air of mystery about you. I love a good mystery."

"So do I," said Soledad. She even smiled back at him. "It's a mystery to me, for example, as to why you even came to Tucson when you were living so well off of your cousin Rick Solano in Santa Monica. He told me how he carried you for years."

Erwin sat quietly, but his breathing had become slightly more labored. Soledad noticed little things like that.

"I got a job offer," he said, his voice tight.

"Splendid," Soledad said. She licked her lips.

She noticed Erwin's cold eyes had followed the movement of her tongue across her lips. "A man with your qualifications must really be in demand. I mean, you have two college degrees but you have never used either of them in a legitimate job. You let your cousin take care of you. I'm wondering, Mr. Erwin, what goes on in a mind like yours? Are you too busy dreaming up 'the great scheme'? 'the big score'? to seriously apply yourself to an honest job? Is that it? The world of people who spend their lives going to a daily job bores you to death?"

"I could never get bored with you, Detective Montenegro." He said her name with the correct Spanish pronunciation, but he still made it sound vulgar to Soledad's ears. "I've been wondering about your investigation. If you never find evidence that I was in the Matthews house, will you have to let me go?" He smiled at her. "I mean, that little stunt at the Frog and Firkin could have been a hoax. I could have heard about the burglary, and what was taken. I still have friends at the university who work in Dr. Matthews's department, you know. One of them could have overheard Dr. Edmonton talking about it, and told me about it. Come to think of it, that's what happened. I saw the chance to make a little money on the side by holding the research hostage. Research that I never had in my possession. It was a stupid move on my part but, as you know, losers like me don't think straight anyway. I live off others. It would be just like me to dream up a get-rich-quick scheme like this."

"Oh, I'm not worried about that," said Soledad, her poker face intact. "Because we've found your partner, Mr. Erwin, and he's spilling his guts to my colleagues as we speak."

Soledad took great pleasure from the surprised expression on Stephen Erwin's face.

She rose. "Have a good day!"

Kate was ready to let loose and have some fun. Her gram's condition had improved and she was enjoying being pampered by all of them during her extended stay at the ranch. Kate's book was on schedule, and she believed she'd make the December 15 deadline.

So, when Rafe phoned her Tuesday night, the first time he'd called in days, her initial thought had been geared toward having a little harmless fun with him. That thought completely vanished and she swallowed the humorous remark she had on the tip of her tongue when she heard his tone of voice. She knew at once that something was wrong.

"Hello, Kate," he said with forced lightness.

Kate was standing in her bedroom attired in a voluminous pair of men's pajamas. In fact they were the very pair Rafe had worn the first night they'd met. She felt strangely comforted by the feel of them on her bare skin.

"You sound funny," she said, hoping she was mistaken.

"Funny, ha, ha, or funny, peculiar?"

"Funny, peculiar."

"Kate, don't take this the wrong way, but will you stop being so damned intuitive?"

"I can't help it," Kate said, her voice husky. "It's late, and I miss you, and I'm wondering why you sound as if you're getting ready to give me bad news."

Rafe laughed shortly. "Stop being dramatic. How is Miss Josefina?"

"She's lording it over all of us around here. She's doing so much better, I suspect she'll live to be a hundred and eight, at least!"

"Good, I'm glad to hear it," Rafe said. Kate was cheered to hear a note of laughter in his formerly somber voice.

Rafe was quiet for several long seconds; then he said, "I'm back in Tucson."

Kate breathed a sigh of relief. "That's great. You can come right over, it's not *that* late!"

"Kate, listen. Some things are going on. When we were transporting Bainbridge, there was a shoot-out. I shot two people. One of them was Bainbridge. He's dead. Now, there's an ongoing interdepartmental investigation. I don't know what the outcome is going to be. I'm at loose ends right now. I'm not much fun to be around. I'm having to see a psychiatrist because I killed someone. That's routine. What I'm trying to say is, I can't see you right now. I need time to figure some things out first. I can't put this burden on you."

"What if I say I still want to see you, Rafe? How do you know I can't help you get through this? At least let me try."

"I've got to do it alone, Kate. That's just the way I am. Try to understand."

"I do understand," Kate said quietly. She hadn't seen him in nearly two weeks. She had no photo as a memento of their time together. She had nothing except her memories of the week they'd shared. They felt suddenly bittersweet. "All right, Rafe, if that's how you feel about it, I won't bother you. I'll wait for you to call me."

She thought his sigh sounded rather sad and resigned. "Thanks for understanding, Kate. I'm really sorry, but my head's pretty messed up right now."

"Is that why you phoned instead of coming over?" Kate couldn't help asking. "Because you didn't want me to see you in your present state?"

She heard his sharp intake of breath. He hadn't expected her to ask that.

"That and the fact that if I saw you in the flesh, I knew I'd never be able to keep from touching you. I have been consumed by thoughts of your sweetness and of tasting you again, Kate. But the way I feel now, I would be taking advantage of your offer of comfort because I'm so damned needy right now I could burst!"

"I'd rather have you take advantage of me than have to face the prospect of not seeing you," Kate told him. "That's how I honestly feel, Rafe. I'm a big girl. I need you. And I think you need me right now. I just wanted to get that out in the open. If you change your mind about going through this alone, I'm here for you. But if you decide you can't see me then, okay. I don't agree with you, but I understand your point of view."

"This is so hard for me to do, Kate. But I believe it would be for the best."

"All right then," Kate said, her voice breaking. "You take care of yourself."

"You, too, Kate." He paused. "Good-bye."

"Bye," said Kate, and immediately pressed her thumb to the off button on the cell phone. "Damn," she muttered. "Damn, damn, damn!"

She sat on the bed in the dark. For some reason she thought of that old Etta James song, "The Soul of a Man." As elated as she'd felt upon hearing Rafe's voice again, she felt equally as bereft by the news he'd called to deliver. Why couldn't he let her comfort him? Wasn't that what a woman was for? Wasn't that what falling in love was all about? She was hurt to her heart that he'd chosen to ride it out with his personal demons on his own.

To her way of thinking this didn't bode well for them.

If he couldn't let her share in his sorrows, did that mean he was the type of man who liked protecting women from the harshness of life? That was no way to be, and it wasn't what Kate had come to expect from a relationship. You took the bitter with the sweet. You needed to see your man at his worst to appreciate him at his best.

She sat there and cried for what had died between them tonight.

Soledad had been pulling Stephen Erwin's chain when she'd told him they had his partner in custody. Two weeks later, though, they had found him. She was at the city jail now, preparing to question him. His name was Martin Penichiero. He, indeed, had The Puma's scratches on his face and neck. Unlike Erwin, he had a long list of priors. All for misdemeanors except for grand theft auto, which had landed him in Arizona State Prison for five years. He'd been released less than a month before he'd hooked up with Stephen Erwin. He claimed to have met Erwin in a bar where they'd started talking, and the next thing he knew he was agreeing to accompany Erwin in burglarizing the Matthews home.

"You had nothing better to do, huh?" Soledad asked when he said he'd agreed to break into the Matthews home upon meeting Erwin for the first time.

"I'd been out of prison for weeks. No one would hire me. My own mother had told me I couldn't come back to her house to live. When a guy offers you ten thousand dollars to break into a house just to steal some computer disks, you jump at the offer."

"Even if you could land back in prison?"

"He said there was little chance of getting caught. He had the house plans; plus it would be guaranteed that the house would be totally empty that night."

Over the years Soledad had heard so many sob stories from criminals that she'd learned to turn a deaf ear to everything they said except for the pertinent details. She met his bloodshot brown eyes. He sniffed, as if he was coming down with a cold. He lowered his eyes. Good liars didn't care if you looked them straight in the eyes. They knew they were well schooled in the art of deception. Maybe Martin Penichiero had never learned to lie convincingly.

"This guarantee that the house would be empty," Soledad said. "Where did it come from?"

"He said the guy who'd hired him to break into the house had told him specifically where to find everything. And Erwin only got the word an hour or less before we had to be out there at the house. He complained about the short notice the entire time we were in the house. As a matter of fact, I might have seen that stupid cat if I hadn't been distracted by his griping about every little thing. That guy ain't wrapped too tight, if you know what I mean." He paused, and raised his gaze to hers. "You think I could get a donut and some coffee? I haven't had anything to eat all day."

Soledad went and got the donut and coffee herself.

When she returned to the interrogation room, Penichiero had laid his head on the table and was sound asleep. Soledad loudly cleared her throat.

Penichiero jerked awake and smiled weakly. "I haven't been sleeping well since that night." He gingerly touched the scratches on his face. "And I think these scratches are infected."

"Well," Soledad said, "where you're going you'll get plenty of rest and access to the infirmary."

She'd meant her comment to be sarcastic, but Penichiero sighed with relief. "Thank God," he said. "At least I got three squares in prison."

"Back to the subject of where Erwin got his information," Soledad said. "Did Erwin ever tell you who had hired him?"

"No, he didn't," Penichiero told her. "I asked him, but he said it would be better if I didn't know. I don't think he trusted me much."

Soledad got to her feet. "Okay, Mr. Penichiero. If you continue to cooperate with us, I will see to it that the judge knows you were a help in the investigation of this case."

"Oh, Detective?" Penichiero called to her just before she summoned the guard outside the door to come and let her out. "I do remember something: he called the guy Billie Dee. I think because the guy reminded him of Billie Dee Williams."

Gotcha! Soledad thought triumphantly.

She walked back over to Martin Penichiero and enthusiastically shook his hand.

When she released his hand, Penichiero complained,

"Man, you've got some grip for a tiny lady. I bet my hand's gonna be sore tomorrow."

"They'll take a look at that in the infirmary, too," Soledad assured him on her way out. She had a certain department head at the University of Arizona to question, and the sooner she got to it, the better. But first, she needed to get some backup. Never underestimate a man when he's cornered. Then, too, she had to see a judge about a search warrant.

"Good Lord," Soledad said under her breath. "If I didn't know better I'd think I'd gone back in time to the sixties." Indeed, college students were as unkempt as the hippies she'd seen on campus throughout the sixties when her own dad had been a janitor here. Back then that was the only kind of job an uneducated Mexican could get. Her father, however, had given the job some dignity. It rankled that Stephen Erwin had also worked here as a janitor. He'd probably been a bad worker with his sorry attitude. Her father had always said that it didn't matter what sort of job you had. Always do it to the best of your abilities. Soledad tried to do that every day of her life.

Soledad had instructed her partner, Jim Bent, and Officer Duncan Oldham to follow her into the building but to maintain their distance. She wanted it to appear that she'd come alone. She wanted to put Jason Edmonton at ease when she began questioning him.

As she turned the corner leading into the final leg of the walk to his office she was surprised to see Kate coming out of an office down the hall. She had what looked like a printer in her arms.

"Hey, Kate, what are you doing here?" Soledad asked, keeping her tone even.

Kate grinned at her as she balanced the printer in her

arms. "Stealing equipment, as you can see. My dad's printer went kaput on him this morning, and I took it to the shop. We're borrowing this one until his comes out of the shop."

"I see," said Soledad, trying not to appear too eager for Kate to be gone.

"How is the investigation coming along?"

Soledad knew those were going to be the next words out of Kate's mouth. She smiled. "Looks like we might have a lead. I needed to ask Dr. Edmonton a few more questions. Have you seen him?"

Kate nodded her head to the left. "He's in his office. His secretary's at her desk, so you'll have to get by her. Watch out, she's tough as nails."

With that she smiled at Soledad again and said, "I'll get out of your hair."

"Okay," Soledad said pleasantly. "Take care."

"You, too," said Kate and took her leave.

Suddenly, Jason Edmonton came barreling through his door at that moment, and jokingly said to Kate, "Halt in your tracks, young lady. What are you doing making off with University of Arizona property?"

Soledad saw the delight on Kate's face when she heard her godfather's voice.

She felt a slightly regretful twinge at having to arrest him. Very slight.

Kate turned and walked back to chat with Jason. Soledad's fears were realized when her partner, Bent, and Officer Oldham came strolling down the corridor.

She didn't have to guess what was going through Jason Edmonton's mind when he spotted them, because he ran to Kate and grabbed her by the wrist, thereby leaving her trying to hold the printer up with a little hip action and one hand. "Jason, what's gotten into you?" Kate cried, confused.

Frustrated, Jason gave the printer a shove and it crashed to the floor. He then yanked Kate after him as he sprinted back into his office and shut the door. In the outer office where Mrs. Neal, his secretary, worked he shoved Kate toward the inner office and ordered Mrs. Neal, "Get out!"

The startled middle-aged woman was frozen in her chair.

"You heard me, get out!" Jason said with such viciousness that Mrs. Neal nearly fell off her chair. Hesitating no longer, she ran from the office, almost colliding with Soledad as she came into the outer office.

Jason dragged Kate into his office and locked the door. Kate lost her balance and was now looking up at him from the floor. "Oh, my *God,*" she said, disgusted. "*You* did it."

Soledad stood outside the door and calmly spoke to Jason. "Don't make this harder than it has to be, Dr. Edmonton. As it is, you'd get five years. Seven at the most. But if you persist in your present behavior, holding Kate in there against her will, the charge goes up to kidnapping and, well, you don't want to do *that* time. Twenty years. Think about it."

Kate got to her feet, but she didn't move from the spot.

Jason had gone to his desk and removed a handgun from the top drawer. He was holding it in his right hand as though the weight of it somehow surprised him. As if he didn't really know how it had gotten into his hand.

Kate knew he was in the grip of panic. She thought it best not to make any sudden movements, or to say anything that would upset him.

"Come on out, Dr. Edmonton," Soledad continued from her side of the door. "Consider this: if you give the disks and the hard drive back to Dr. Matthews it would work to your advantage during the trial."

"It's too late for that," Jason said as he raised the gun to his head. "I've already sold David's research. All I needed was the time to get out of town."

If he wanted to talk, Soledad would accommodate him. "And leave the men you hired to rot in prison, huh?"

"They're lowlifes," Jason said with a derisive laugh. "They deserve everything they get."

"What exactly did you promise Stephen Erwin for his silence? He hasn't said a word to us the entire four weeks he's been behind bars," Soledad said.

"I promised him a hundred thousand dollars," Jason said. "That's more money than he's seen in his entire miserable life."

Kate was watching him through slits, she was so angry with him.

"I'm more interested in what you got for stabbing your best friend in the back."

"David is too gullible, and way too innocent for the cutthroat scientific world. We're not living in a vacuum, we're living in an ever-changing environment. No one can afford to wait on him to fully recover from the stroke. By that time, someone could have had a breakthrough. Teams all over the world are working on going beyond transporting quantum states of photons. David's research showed the possibility of transporting massive particles. Imagine the military applications of such a device. Governments all over the world would pay through the nose for that type of technology."

"That's what you did?" Kate asked, feeling sick to her stomach. "You sold Dad's research to a foreign government?"

"No, I sold it to a company that will in turn develop the technology and, one day soon, sell the teleporters to foreign countries."

"You never did tell me how much money you got," Kate reminded him.

Jason smiled slowly as he lowered the weapon. He'd thought of another use for it. Why kill himself when he had a truckload of money waiting for him in a country where there was no extradition? All he had to do was get to the airport and onto a plane.

He went to Kate and grabbed her, pulling her fast against him. He held her there with his arm across her throat. Kate chuffed. "The answer to your question, Kate, is two million dollars. I can live like a king on that for the rest of my life," he said in her ear.

In the outer office, Soledad, Bent, and Oldham all had their weapons drawn and pointed at the door of Jason Edmonton's office. "Enough talking," Soledad yelled. "Come out now, or we're coming in!"

Looking at Oldham, a huge six-footer with shoulders like a linebacker's, Soledad nodded at the door. Duncan shouldered his way through while Soledad and Bent covered him.

When they got inside, Jason Edmonton and Kate were gone. They looked at the raised window only a split second before running to it and peering down. The window opened onto a fire escape. They had neglected to figure out if Jason Edmonton's office had an alternative exit. Jason and Kate were long gone.

After escaping, Jason shoved Kate behind the wheel of his Mercedes and ordered her to drive him to the airport. Kate insulted him all the way.

"Two million dollars? You sold my Dad out for a measly two-mil? William Allen was right about you. You *have* ridden Daddy's coattails all these years."

"Shut up, Kate!" Jason yelled. "Do you know how you

sound? Like the spoiled little girl you are. All of you Matthewses live in a dreamworld in which you actively try to make the world a better place. Carolina with her activism. You with your high ideals about not adding to a world of scientists who haven't managed to save the world yet. As if that could ever be achieved! So, you don't even use your degree. You write books instead. And, finally, David, who eschews everything military. He would rather cut off his arms than develop a weapon to defend his country with. He needs to take his head out of the sand. We're living in a world in which the country with the biggest guns rules. Why shouldn't I benefit from that? I've spent more than half my life trying to keep a bunch of losers going fiscally. Scientists. I hate the whole lot of them. Especially do-gooders like your father."

"Oh, you're ranting now," Kate taunted him.

"Just drive the damn car," Jason said through clenched teeth.

Kate glared at him. "You can go straight to hell, Jason."

"What a mouth you have on you," he said, seemingly pleased he'd caused the outburst. "But you were always just on the brink of wildness, Kate." His wistful tone only irritated Kate more. She was unaware of it, but the angrier she got the heavier her foot got on the accelerator.

"Don't talk about us as if you cared for us," she ground out.

"Oh, Kate, I don't want you to think I didn't genuinely care for all of you. You were my family. My haven, really. I would come to your house whenever I felt in need of some human kindness. You were all *full* of it. Do you remember when you were a little girl? You'd give me the best hugs and kisses. You doted on me, Kate. I think your father was a bit jealous of the attention you gave me. Then when you got in your teens you stopped hugging me." He paused. "It wasn't because you'd developed a crush on me, was it, Kate?"

"Of course I had a crush on you, Jason. But now I just want to smash your face."

"There's a thin line between love and hate," Jason said regretfully.

He happened to glance down at the speedometer. Kate had the car up to eighty-nine in a fifty-five-mile-per-hour zone. "Slow down," he ordered. "The last thing we need is to attract the attention of a cop."

"That might be the last thing *you* need," Kate said. "But a cop sounds pretty good to me right now."

Jason pressed the gun to her side. "I sure wouldn't want to shoot you, Kate."

Kate eased up on the accelerator.

Ten

"It pains me, bruh, that you're thirty-four years old and still doing stupid things like that." Jenny's words reverberated through Rafe's brain as he paced the floor at the airport. He was in the waiting area of the carrier Jenny had chosen.

She'd promised to be there this time. "I'm coming," she'd told him over the phone last night. "You can come pick me up, or you can *not* come pick me up. I don't care. You're not going through this alone. Why didn't you call me sooner?" She'd sighed heavily then, as if he were seriously the greatest burden in her life, or that's how he had interpreted it. Then, he realized what she was trying to do was mask the sound of her crying.

"Can't you see that when you denied Kate the chance to comfort you, you put a wedge between you two?" she'd said. "And now you haven't seen her in *two weeks?* If my guess is right, she's in nearly as much pain as you are right now. She's probably confused as to why you wouldn't come to her, or let her come to you. And, I'm gonna tell you, Rafe, the longer you wait to go to her, the harder it's going to be to do it. You're giving yourself a chance to talk yourself out of needing her altogether. I know you. You'll rationalize this thing to death. You've killed someone. A man who, in my opinion, gave you no alternative but to kill him! Still, it's eating away at you. You didn't get into this job to take anyone's life, but to preserve life. Now, you may be thinking that Kate deserves someone better than you. You're wrong if you're thinking that way. She deserves *you!"*

Rafe had felt like a big boob on the other end, listening to his sister sob her heart out over him. He was supposed to be the strong one. He was supposed to be the one to give her advice, not the other way around. Now, he had to be man enough to listen to his little sister.

Jenny had been right about one thing: he had been slowly talking himself out of ever calling Kate again. He'd come to realize the great chasm that separated the two of them. She was much better educated. Wouldn't he eventually bore her? She came from a big, loving family. He'd not been blessed like that. All he had was Jenny, and he'd failed her emotionally in many ways. After talking to Jenny he had to admit the biggest thing that separated him and Kate was not their intellects. It was her capacity to care for someone unconditionally. Look at how she'd welcomed him, a perfect stranger, into her home, her life, her family, in the blink of an eye. He was simply not that emotionally sound. But maybe there was hope.

"Rafe!"

The sound of his sister's voice interrupted Rafe's reverie. He braced himself. Jenny had dropped her bags and was running toward him just like she used to do when she was a little girl. Although, now, she weighed a lot more.

Whomp! He picked her up, no mean feat, and spun her around.

Setting her back down, he realized that Jenny had, indeed, put on more weight. Her normally trim figure was fleshed out and she had a potbelly.

"I'm pregnant!" Jenny said happily, her pretty brown face crinkled in a grin.

Rafe looked at his sister, mouth agape. "What?"

"Preggers, expecting, a bun in the oven, in the family way," Jenny said, her smile never leaving her face. "That's the main reason I didn't show up last time. I didn't know how to tell you. Especially when I have no intentions of marrying Zeke."

"Zeke!" Rafe hated that posturing baboon. He'd been in and out, mostly out, of Jenny's life these past two years. Living off her when he was with her. For the life of him, Rafe didn't know what Jenny saw in him.

Looking into Jenny's radiant face, Rafe didn't have the heart to rant and rave about Zeke. He simply hugged her again.

"Baby sister, if you're happy, I'm happy for you."

Tears sat in Jenny's large brown eyes that were the same color as her brother's. It was the one feature they shared. Where Rafe was tall and broad-shouldered, Jenny was petite and kind of a waif. Until now.

Rafe gently placed his hand on her round belly. A niece, or a nephew. Either way, he was going to be an uncle. He liked the sound of that.

He released her. "Come on, let's get your bags and go get you something to eat. You're probably starving. You always are after a flight, no matter how short."

Jenny watched him as he strode over and picked up her bags. She was so proud of her brother. His reaction to her news made her even prouder. Rafe was becoming mellower. She was glad she'd waited to tell him her news face-to-face.

They began walking toward the exit.

"So," Rafe said, "where exactly is Zeke living nowadays?"

"Oh, he's back in Los Angeles now. Hard at work in the studio. Why?"

"I'm gonna kick his butt, that's why."

Maybe he hadn't mellowed *that* much, Jenny thought

with a short laugh. "You're not gonna do any such thing. He isn't running from his responsibility. He's agreed to help me financially, and he even wants to be in the delivery room."

"Support you and the baby financially?" Rafe said. "You must have selective memory. Or have you forgotten you were the one supporting him when you were together?"

"That's all changed now," Jenny said. "Zeke's band finally signed a record contract. He's on his way."

"Oh, Lord," Rafe said. "Not only do I worry about your being an actor, I now have to worry about your child's father being in a rock band."

Rafe held the door open for Jenny to precede him. They were now on the walk in front of the terminal where taxis lined up hoping to attract fares. "Sometimes I think you're not happy unless you're worrying about me," Jenny was saying.

However, Rafe's attention was elsewhere. He was watching as Kate's godfather, Dr. Jason Edmonton, opened the door of a late-model Mercedes and began pulling someone from the driver's seat. He considered it pulling because whomever Jason was tugging on wasn't cooperating.

Then he watched as Jason yanked the person out of the car, and that was when his heart started thudding with apprehension, because he saw that it was Kate. Mind racing, he said to Jenny as he handed her his car keys. "You know my car." He pointed in the direction of short-term parking. "It's two rows over. Go get in it and wait for me. Something weird is going on that I need to check out."

Jenny did as she was told. She knew her brother's instincts about his job were usually on the money. "'Kay. You be careful." And she was gone.

Rafe saw Jason, with Kate directly in front of him, walking toward him on the sidewalk. Rafe kept his head down, hoping not to be recognized until he was right on him.

He was in luck because Jason's attention was diverted by the sound of sirens. While Jason was looking nervously back at what turned out to be an ambulance, Rafe walked past him and Kate, then turned around and followed them.

Kate, for her part, noticed Rafe right away. Her legs had gone slightly weak at the sight of him. She wondered what he was doing there. And if he knew Jason had a gun. Panic seized her. She couldn't bear it if Jason shot him. She began praying that he wouldn't be the hero that she knew in her heart he was, and not do something risky like try to rescue her. Jason was holding the gun inside his coat with it pointed at her rib cage. She had no doubt he'd shoot her. This wasn't her Jason anymore. This was a man who'd taken a flying leap off the deep end and would now do anything to salvage what was left of his life.

Jason poked her in the side with the gun now. "Walk faster, Kate. You'd better not try anything foolish like try to delay me until the police get here."

"Why would I do that?" said Kate. "No one wants you gone more than I do."

"Good. Let's go directly to American Airlines, shall we? They usually have flights out of here on the hour. If you're good, I'll let you go as soon as my flight is called. I can't get through security with a gun, after all. I'll have to ditch it somewhere. Then you're free as a bird."

"Sounds like a plan," Kate said, playing along with him.

Feeling more relaxed now that the sirens he'd heard hadn't been Detective Soledad Montenegro and her colleagues, Jason loosened up a bit and lowered the gun at her side. "I'm sorry you had to find out about this, Kate. I never meant for your family to ever know what I'd done. I was simply going to disappear. There would've been talk about my sudden disappearance, but soon things would have gotten back to normal and you would have gone on with your lives. David will be fine. Look at him. Yesterday he phoned me and told me he'd never felt better about his work. This episode has inspired him. It's challenged him. It's put the spark back into him. We didn't get the last disk he was working on, you know. Who is to say that David won't come through before the company I sold his notes to can decipher them? I'm rooting for David."

"Yeah," Kate said. "Because of your thievery, Dad is back at the blackboard dreaming up theories and tossing them out. Furiously coming up with miraculous calculations that seemingly explain his theories, then erasing them when they prove inadequate. Yes, Jason, your actions definitely got results. It made him terrified that thirty years of work is down the drain. He's had to reevaluate his life's work, figure out if it all meant anything, after all. Because in spite of your optimism, he may never find the strength to go that last mile of the way and emerge triumphant. That's what you've given him, Jason, more self-doubt."

"If you believe that, Kate, then you don't know your father very well."

"Admit it, Jason. You're saying all this to try to ease your conscience. It makes you feel better to believe your actions won't have lasting negative effects on Dad."

They were inside the terminal now. Kate had a bit more freedom of movement and when she turned to her right, she saw Rafe coming through the door behind them, keeping his distance. She turned her gaze on Jason again.

"So, where are you going?"

Jason laughed shortly. "This isn't some romantic suspense novel where the villain tells all just before he gets caught, Kate. I'm not telling."

"Let me guess. Not Mexico, because they tend to cooperate when it comes to extraditing prisoners."

Jason grabbed her by the hand and pulled her along. "Have you forgotten I'm in a hurry? This way, Kate."

They arrived at the American Airlines desk and got in line behind three other people.

Kate wondered where Rafe had gotten to. He'd disappeared after Jason had taken her hand and led her here. She glanced down at her hands. Her left one was abraded. Probably from when she'd been pushed to the floor of Jason's office. There was light bleeding where the skin had broken.

She looked up again, and there was Rafe, walking toward them with a big smile on his face. *Oh, Lord, he's just gonna walk up and pretend nothing's going on and then try to disarm him,* she thought nervously.

It was Jason's turn, and while he was speaking with the woman behind the desk, with Kate's hand still held firmly in his, Kate mouthed to Rafe, "Go away!"

Rafe simply smiled at her.

Quite desperate now, Kate mouthed, "Are you crazy?"

Rafe mouthed, "Yes, about you."

Then he was upon them. "Kate!" he said angrily. "How dare you leave me for this dinosaur? He's old enough to be your father." He jerked her toward him, thereby breaking her connection with Jason, and then he rapidly walked away with her in tow.

To her utter surprise, Jason did nothing but try to rush the woman behind the desk through the tedious process of finding him a seat on the next plane.

Though relieved to be safe again, Kate stared up at Rafe bug-eyed. "How did you know that would work?"

"The last thing he wants is to draw attention to himself," Rafe said. "But, wait, you'll see what happens."

Kate and Rafe stood several feet away and watched as Jason was surrounded by airport security led by her cousin Vance. Bringing up the rear were Soledad and two male police officers. Jason didn't even put up a struggle. He handed over his gun and allowed himself to be handcuffed and led away.

Kate's mind seemed to come back to the present from a distance. She had been more panicked than she'd realized. Especially when she'd looked up and spotted Rafe. Now she inhaled the male scent of him, felt the warmth emanating from him. The very aliveness of this beautiful man. Her head was tilted up, her eyes taking all of him in, that square chin, those wide-spaced brandy-colored eyes with those killer lashes. That mouth that she'd been longing to kiss for a month now. No, a month and two days!

Foolish woman that she was, she threw her arms around his neck and started sobbing simultaneously. "God, I've missed you so much!"

And there in the middle of the terminal, Rafe kissed her, tasting her tears, hardly able to contain his emotions he was so relieved to have her in his arms again.

Someone loudly cleared her throat behind them. Rafe and Kate parted.

"So, this is Kate."

"What are you doing here? Didn't I tell you to wait for me in the car?" Rafe asked.

Jenny swung her heavy shoulder bag back and forth. "I thought you might need reinforcements. This has gotten me out of some tight spots."

Rafe motioned her over and then he hugged the two most important women in his life. "Kate, meet Jenny. Jenny, meet Kate."

Kate looked into Jenny's eyes and saw Rafe. She instantly liked her.

Jenny looked into Kate's eyes and saw how much she loved her brother. She considered her a sister from that moment on.

* * *

Kate went with Rafe to his house so that he could get Jenny settled in. From there, he drove her back to the university, where she went to the science building and upstairs to Jason's office. She found that Mrs. Neal had picked up her shoulder bag from the floor and put it safely away in a drawer. She thanked the still-shaky secretary and told her how sorry she was about what had happened that afternoon, not giving her too many details. News of Jason's arrest would be circulating around the campus soon enough.

She allowed Rafe to lead her out of the building, and away from unpleasant reminders of the past hour and a half.

Rafe walked her to her car, handed her in, and closed the door. "I'll follow you." He bent, leaned in, and briefly kissed her lips. "Drive slowly so I can keep up with you," he joked.

Kate smiled at him, grateful. "Whatever you say."

Rafe placed the back of his hand on her forehead. "That doesn't sound like you, Kate. Let's get you home and into bed."

Kate turned the key in the ignition. "Now you're talking."

A few minutes later, they were met at the door of the big house by a relieved David. He pulled Kate into his arms and hugged her tightly. "If he had hurt you . . ." he began, so full of emotion that he had to take a long pause. "I don't know what I would've done."

Carolina, Josefina, and Davida all took turns hugging her.

"When Detective Montenegro phoned and told us what

Jason had done, I was so shocked," Carolina said. "I, like your father, would never have suspected he could be so greedy." She peered into Kate's beloved face. "You look worn out. Stay here tonight so I can watch over you."

Kate smiled tiredly. "I'm okay. I just want to go to sleep in my own bed tonight."

Carolina turned to Rafe. "You will stay with her until she falls asleep?"

"I don't mean to leave until she's sound asleep," Rafe promised.

When Kate and Rafe had gone to the guest house, David told Carolina, "That boy's in love with our daughter."

"Good," Carolina said. "Because I don't think there's gonna be that much sleeping over there tonight."

David laughed. "Is that all you Huerta women think about, sex?"

"That and paper flowers," Carolina joked. Josefina and Davida were out of earshot at the kitchen table cutting out shapes in crepe paper. "How is she doing, Gram?"

"She has potential," Josefina said, holding up a misshapen red paper rose. "My roses didn't look half this good when I first started."

"What's happening with the internal investigation?" Kate said as she and Rafe came through the kitchen door of the guest house. She wanted to get all business talk out of the way, because she had some seriously unprofessional things to say to him tonight.

"They found the leak, and plugged it," Rafe told her. "I was cleared in the shooting. No matter how by the book a lawman is, he is always investigated after something like that happens." He still hated to say the words. He'd killed someone. That would never sit right with him. Some part of him would always regret the way things had turned out that morning.

Kate hung her shoulder bag and coat on the hall tree. Rafe did the same. They turned and regarded each other with serious expressions on their faces. "How're you doing?" Kate asked. She observed his every nuance as he formed the words in his mind. He was at war with his emotions. When he said, "I still feel like crap sometimes," she knew he'd won. She went to him, put her arms around his waist, and laid her head on his broad chest. "Let me make it better."

"I'm all yours, Kate," Rafe told her, cupping her face between his big hands. How he'd missed her sweet face. Their eyes met and held. "Forgive me for not coming to you the night I phoned. I thought I was sparing you my ugly side."

"I tried to understand, Rafe, but it still hurt. And when days turned into two weeks, I began to really worry that I'd never see you again. Each night I'd sit looking at the phone willing myself to call you, but I remembered I'd promised you I wouldn't. Then I started willing *you* to call."

Rafe bent and kissed her cheek. "I wanted to phone you so many times. But, I thought, what would you think of me? We'd only known one another a week before I had to go to Baltimore. Maybe you didn't want to be involved with someone with baggage. Maybe you'd be better off with someone you have more in common with."

Kate put her arms about his neck and smiled up at him. "You were right, I didn't know you well. I didn't know you with my head, I knew you by heart, Rafe. It felt so good being with you. I'd never been happier with anyone else. When you decided you wanted to be left alone, I wondered what I'd done that made you think I wasn't strong enough to support you in your time of need. But that's not what you were thinking, was it?"

"No," Rafe said. "I was thinking you'd be better off without me. That you should go find some physics type and make little physics type babies and live happily ever after."

"Now, Rafe," Kate said with a sexy smile, "if I limited myself to dating physics types, I'd never date. I prefer men who can bring to the table adventures that I'm not familiar with. Men who can teach me something about the world that I don't already know. In other words, a man like you."

"Then quit talking, and kiss me, Kate," Rafe said with a wicked grin.

"It's really gonna happen this time?" Kate whispered against his lips. Then his mouth came down on hers and all she could think about was tasting him. She sighed deep in her throat and opened her mouth to allow him entrance and there it was, that spark of electricity that began at the base of her spine and spread to every pleasure point in her body until her head felt light and she became intoxicated with him. He was like a potent drug designed to induce sensual pleasure.

Raising his head, Rafe said, "I must have been nuts not to come to you that night."

"No, baby, you were just hurting," Kate said, and pulled him down for another kiss.

Rafe molded her lush body to his hard form. Kate was wearing an orange long-sleeve pullover body shirt with a pair of button-fly jeans. The shirt clung to her, and her nipples were clearly visible beneath it. Rafe wore a short-sleeve polo shirt in ice-blue and a pair of well-worn Levis Kate had pulled the hem of the shirt up and out of the waistband of his jeans and was running her hand over his six-pack. "You would think," she said, "that after all this time they would have invented clothes that tear away easily in instances like this."

"Oh, no, sweetie," Rafe said. "Anticipation is a good thing."

He pulled her shirt over her head. "What do you say we start with a shower? Think that angry shower massage of yours will leave me unscathed this time?"

"You go on," Kate said. "I want to put on some CDs." She kissed him again before going into the living room and selecting CDs by Eva Cassidy, Sarah Vaughan, and Dinah Washington. She loved the romantic classics those ladies sang in their heyday. There was something poignant about their voices and they always made her feel good.

Clutching the orange pullover in her hand she went to join Rafe in the shower.

Strains of Eva Cassidy singing Sting's "Fields of Gold" filled the house.

Rafe was already in the shower when she walked into the bathroom. "Hey, I'm getting lonely in here," he called to her when he heard her enter the room.

Kate made short work of removing her clothes. "Everything's just like you left it," she joked. "Be patient."

"I'm not feeling very virtuous tonight, Katharine Josefina. So, get your butt in here."

"How'd you know my middle name?" Kate asked with a laugh.

"I saw your driver's license the first night we met, remember?"

In fact, she hadn't remembered. For some reason she was glad he had. Maybe he was one of those rare men who didn't forget birthdays or anniversaries.

"Okay," she said, removing her panties. "When's my birthday?"

"January thirty-first," Rafe answered confidently.

Kate grabbed her shower cap hanging on the hook

behind the door and put it on before sliding the shower stall door back and stepping inside. "You have a great memory."

Rafe looked her over. "Funny, I don't remember your being quite this beautiful." For a moment such a serious expression sat in his golden brown eyes that Kate felt herself holding her breath. Rafe bent his head and began nibbling on her lips, first the top, then the bottom. He liked everything about her sensuous mouth, how sweet she tasted, how soft her lips were. And that little sound she made when she was in the throes of passion. It came from down deep, and it never failed to arouse him even more than he already was. He pulled back, deciding that Kate in large doses would not be good for a starving man. He didn't want the curse of the overeager male visited upon him tonight: premature ejaculation. No way. He planned to make love to Kate until she fell into a sound sleep.

Just like he'd promised her mother. Well, not *exactly* like he'd promised her mother.

Kate looked dreamy-eyed when they parted. "If you keep kissing me like that, I may still be a virgin for my next orgasm."

"Can't have that," Rafe said. He soaped both hands and began rubbing them all over her torso. Her nipples were so hard now they were slightly painful to the touch. Rafe did not pause to manipulate them further, though. He moved his hands along both sides of her hourglass figure. Enjoying the tone and texture of her buttocks. Then soaped his hands some more and gently turned her back to him. He came up close behind her. Kate sucked in air when she felt his engorged penis low on her buttocks where her thighs came together. Rafe grasped her breasts from behind, and bent his head to rain kisses on the side of her neck. "I love touching you.

Your skin is so silky I can hardly wait to get you in bed so that I can feel the full length of your body against mine."

Kate relaxed against him. Her eyes were closed. His touch, his voice, and the feel of his body on hers were hypnotic. Then his hands moved to her inner thighs. Her eyes sprang open. Rafe's warm breath was on her neck. But his hands, his hands were delving into that soft, feminine throbbing place and it felt so good she wanted to shout. But she muffled any noises in favor of a silent orgasm.

Rafe felt her body quiver, in spite of her attempts to keep the orgasm under wraps.

"Number one," he said in her ear.

Then while she was coming down, he finished bathing her, bathed himself, and rinsed both of them. He stepped out of the shower stall onto the bath rug and gave Kate a hand out. "Kate?"

"Mmm?" she asked with a satisfied sigh.

He toweled her dry while he talked. "Do you have any condoms in the house?"

"Top drawer of the bureau. Left corner. I bought them the second day after meeting you." Her eyes looked starry even as she removed the shower cap, freeing her wavy hair.

"Wanted to be prepared?" Rafe asked about the purchase of the condoms.

"Wishful thinking."

He laughed as he bent and worked the towel between her legs, drying her with a gentle hand. "You're good for a man's ego," he told her.

"I just know what I like, and I liked you from the beginning."

"You'd chosen me to deflower you, as you put it."

"Yes, and I think I chose well."

"I do, too. It's just that your methods are a bit unorthodox, Kate. I certainly hope you're going to teach our daughters not to bring strange men home with them."

Seemingly not paying close enough attention to what he was saying, Kate replied, "My parents taught me, and look what it got them? I still brought you home with me."

Rafe rose and looked into her eyes. He smiled at her, but let slide the fact that she hadn't paid any attention to his subtle marriage proposal. He handed her a fresh towel.

"Would you?"

"Gladly," Kate said, taking the towel and patting him dry with it. While he stood there, she slowly moved around his tall, muscular form, dallying here, placing a stray kiss there. After a while, she dropped the towel to the floor and walked around to stand in front of him. She boldly grasped his penis in her right hand and gently squeezed. She felt him move in her hand almost immediately. "The answer is yes, Rafe, I'll marry you. But not before you make me a woman. You don't want an inexperienced bride on your wedding night, now, do you?"

Rafe shook his head in the negative. "No, ma'am."

Kate let go of him, and Rafe took her hand. "I've been meaning to have a little talk with you about how to handle a man's, uh, privates. Especially when a man is as ready to make love to you as I am right now. The way you were holding me just now was a bit too much. I almost came in your hand. We don't want that because whereas a woman can come sometimes three times in succession, a man has to take several more minutes to recover before he's good to go, if you know what I mean."

"Absolutely," Kate said. "But, I like touching you." She actually pouted, which was extremely funny to him.

"Top drawer, left side?" he said, laughing, pulling her after him.

In the bedroom, Kate went over and turned down the bed. Her bed was queen-size with an extra-firm mattress on it. After doing that she hopped onto it and drew her legs up, watching Rafe as he walked across the room toward her. His thigh and leg muscles flexed powerfully when he walked. His buttocks were so fine, they had that indentation on the sides that you saw in well-conditioned athletes. She could watch him all night.

Eva Cassidy was singing "I Know You by Heart" in the background. Kate rose.

"I love that song. Would you dance with me?"

Rafe tossed the foil-wrapped condom onto the bed and pulled her into his arms. Kate laid her head on his shoulder as they slow-danced.

"That's a sad song," Rafe said.

"Yes, it's about loss." Kate looked into his eyes. "My mother once told me that love between a man and a woman is a fire that burns hot enough to melt steel at first and then gradually adjusts to a lower heat. It can be turned up or turned down at will, depending on how you tend its embers. I love you, Rafe. Right now I'm burning up, and I want to know if you're the man who can fan my embers for a lifetime."

"I'm your man," Rafe said, whereupon he bent and kissed her. Kate's arms went around his neck, drawing him ever closer. Love began to heal the self-doubt that had kept them apart.

Rafe lifted her straight up from the floor, and Kate wrapped her legs around his waist. He walked with her to the bed, and knelt on the edge of the bed. Kate let go and fell backward onto the bed, spreading her legs. The vision before him made him grateful to have been in the airport the night they'd met. Her deep coppery skin glowed, and the dark hair between her legs glistened. She was wet with anticipation.

Rafe felt on the bed next to his knees for the damned condom. He knew he'd tossed it onto the bed. Where the hell was it? Ah, there it was. He tore it open, and his hands shook a bit as he found the right side before placing it at the tip and rolling it onto his now throbbing penis.

He leaned over and kissed her mouth once more before placing his penis at the entrance of her vagina. Kate's breathing was labored. He thought she might be bracing herself, expecting penetration to be painful.

On his knees between her legs, he grasped both her legs. "Kate, try to remember the pleasure I gave you with my fingers." He demonstrated by gently massaging her clitoris with the pad of his thumb. He felt her inner muscles begin to relax. He felt her becoming more lubricated. While his member grew ever harder.

Withdrawing his thumb, he replaced it with his penis and pushed. Kate let out a breath and with her exhalation, her muscles relaxed and he was farther inside her. Kate's muscles contracted around him, accepting him. Rafe pushed a bit more. She felt so tight, so warm, so good to him that he had to concentrate in order to control the amount of pushing, when what he wanted was to completely fill her up.

Kate felt a bit of friction at first, but soon that sensation passed and all she felt was the urge to push. She imagined her vaginal lips were pulling Rafe toward her, eagerly drawing him inside.

Rafe felt the change in her and pushed harder. He groaned because she felt so good to him. "Kate, don't let me hurt you."

"It doesn't hurt," Kate assured him. "You feel good to me. I want to push back."

"Not yet."

Now he was fully inside her, and gently pumping her. In and out. Kate's vaginal muscles quivered each time he pulled out. She felt the need to increase the momentum.

But Rafe said, "Slow is good, baby. Feel the intense

pleasure deep inside. Roll with it. Let it sneak up on you." He felt her letting go. "That's good."

Kate moaned. Rafe pulled his shaft out of her and placed the tip on her clitoris, rubbing it. He whipped them both into a passionate frenzy with that little game, and then he went back inside her warmth, his penis feeling cooler to Kate now, which also heightened her arousal. Sweet, was all she could think. So sweet.

It was just as he'd said, it gripped her suddenly, and she could no more keep it at bay than hold back the night. She screamed. It was out of her before she knew it and then her body was drenched in pleasure. She imagined it as a nuclear explosion. The warmth spread from her center to the rest of her body. She felt Rafe rocking with her, and she knew he was coming too. He howled. Yes, the man howled. She wasn't mistaken. He sounded like a wolf up in her bedroom!

Kate's kiss-swollen mouth curved in a self-satisfied smile. She was relieved he had enjoyed himself as much as she had. She could admit to herself now that she was afraid she might not be that good in bed. She was, after all, a bit inexperienced.

Rafe lay spent between her thighs.

She kind of liked him in that position.

"I'm glad I waited for you," she said after a long pause.

"Me, too," Rafe said. "You would have killed a lesser man."

Kate laughed. "You're joking. You were so gentle with me, we barely broke a sweat."

"That's not what I'm talking about," Rafe explained. "What I meant was what you have between your legs is so damned pretty, a lesser man would have expired when you first spread your legs."

Kate laughed louder. "You're incorrigible, Rafael Grant."

Rafe got up and disappeared into the bathroom. When he returned, he got back into bed with her and drew her into his arms. "I ain't pulling your leg, sweetheart. You have some powerful stuff."

Kate turned in the crook of his arms to look him in the eyes. "You like my stuff, huh?"

"It's some mighty sweet stuff," he said, his smile boyish and charming.

Kate returned his smile. "So is yours."

Rafe briefly kissed her. "Close your eyes now, Kate."

"You'll be here when I open them again?"

"I'll be here."

Kate awoke to the smell of something delicious cooking. She rolled over to check the readout on the digital alarm clock on the nightstand: ten thirty-one P.M. She had slept over three hours. She must have been more tired than she'd thought. But, having a gun pointed at you definitely took something out of you. She thought her untroubled dreams could be attributed to Rafe's closeness. All of her dreams had been wonderfully positive. She'd awakened with a warm feeling inside.

Getting up, she rose, slipped into her bathrobe, and went in search of Rafe.

She found him in the kitchen busy stirring what looked like scrambled eggs with chopped onions, peppers, and cheese in the mixture. She came up behind him and put her arms around his waist. He was attired in the pajamas he'd worn the night they met.

"You cook, too?" Kate asked, pressing her face to his broad back.

"Sorry, but no. Scrambled eggs and toast are my complete repertoire, I'm afraid. But, I do them very well." He reached over, turned off the fire beneath the skillet, and lifted it from the stove. Kate's arms were still around his waist. He simply walked about the kitchen with her attached to him, not seeming to mind at all. He dished the scrambled eggs onto two plates, Kate clung. He went to place them on the table, Kate clung. When he went to the cabinet above the sink looking for glasses, he asked, "I noticed you have orange juice and grapefruit juice. Which do you prefer?"

"Orange," said Kate, and sighed contentedly.

He collected the glasses, went to the fridge, withdrew the carton of orange juice, and took it and the glasses back to the table. "Kate, I would rather you sat on my lap, than vice versa."

Kate happily obliged, letting go of him and coming around to sit on his lap. Rafe smiled up at her. She looked so young with her hair mussed up, sleep barely gone from her eyes, and those dimples winking at him. He could see their children in her eyes. Funny, the prospect of having children with any of the other women he'd been in relationships with had never crossed his mind. But twice tonight he'd had those thoughts about Kate. With her he felt at home, finally. As if this was where he belonged.

"I love you, Kate."

She smiled at him. "I know you do."

"Just wanted to make sure you knew. When you told me you loved me earlier tonight, I was so stunned, I neglected to tell you I loved you, too. I do, Kate. I adore you."

"I knew you loved me this afternoon when you mouthed the words 'Yes, about you' after I'd asked you if you were crazy," Kate told him. She went on to explain, "When I saw you at the airport, I assumed that Soledad had somehow gotten a message to you and you'd gotten to the airport before she could get there. I had no idea you were there picking up Jenny. But then I got a sick feeling in the pit of my stomach: what if Jason shot you? That's when I started praying that you wouldn't try to do anything. That you'd just wait until Soledad and the other policemen got there. Jason had told me he would let me go as soon as his flight was called. But you went ahead and acted anyway."

Rafe held her a little tighter. "I told you, all Jason wanted to do was get away. He couldn't very well keep holding you against your will. He would have to get rid of the gun at some point before preparing to get on the plane. Everyone's obliged to walk through the metal detectors these days. And I couldn't wait until Soledad got there, because he could have changed his mind about letting you go and forced you to get on the plane with him, even without a gun. I couldn't have that."

"There's no way I would've gotten on that plane," Kate said.

"Oh, you're tough," Rafe said, tickling her below the rib cage.

Giggling, Kate got off his lap. "Eat your food before it gets cold. You need your strength." She went around to the other side of the table, sat down in front of the second plate of scrambled eggs, and began to eat. "This is good!"

Kate and Rafe did not tell anyone about their engagement, deciding to wait until Christmas because Kate's brothers would be home, and Jenny had promised to return then, too. They spent the last two weeks of November so wrapped up in each other that Kate nearly missed her deadline. She did mail her manuscript on December 14, though, and after that she was free as a bird. Rafe, however, wasn't. He went back to work full-time after being given some time off following the shooting. Therefore, Kate had time to fill. She spent most days debating with her father in his office.

She was glad to see him in fighting form again. His speech had returned to normal, and his thought processes were also gaining acuity. Soon his rapier-sharp intellect would be back, and she would no longer be able to beat him at chess or any other game of skill he enjoyed playing between the times he was scribbling formulas on his blackboard.

All of this made Kate hopeful that he would be able to finish his work. Some scientists speculated that teleporting single atoms and molecules could be perfected within ten years. Her father believed he was closer than that. If he could just pin down the formula that would explain his theories mathematically, then he would be making real progress. Unless he could prove his theories mathematically, there was no way mechanical engineers would be able to build the teleportation pods he imagined. Visualizing and drawing up the plans the mechanical engineers would use to build the pods was Kate's area of expertise. She thought in terms of mechanics.

If her father could devise the right formula, she could take it from there and build the pods in her mind. From her mind, she could put the plans on paper. From her blueprints, mechanical engineers would construct the physical pods.

It was a long, drawn-out process. Thrilling only to scientists who could foresee the practical applications of such a device: medicine could be instantly teleported anywhere in the world where sick people were in need of it. Only small items could be teleported at first. But, eventually, larger items like imaging equipment could be teleported to medical facilities anywhere on the planet. Perhaps even humans could be teleported from one place to another in an instant, à la *Star Trek*. Imagine the implications on the travel industry and transportation systems. The possibilities were endless. That's what Kate loved so much about physics. It was almost like magic. But magic you could break down in scientific and mathematical terms.

One day in mid-December, she and her father were in his office going over some of his notes from the final disk, the one the thieves had not gotten their hands on. David was at the blackboard, his eyebrows furrowed in concentration, talking to himself, while Kate sat at the computer going through the file page by page. The file was over three hundred pages long. She'd been studying it for more than two weeks, trying to figure out what the satori moment had been that her father said he'd gotten toward the end, but didn't write down before his brain had misfired and the stroke had him in its grip.

Throughout history sudden discoveries in science had oftentimes come to scientists during sudden enlightenment, or satori moments. Years of research, years of study prepared their minds for the instant when all of a sudden everything fell into place. Everything made sense. Kate understood perfectly her father's obsession with recovering that moment in time.

"Kate," her father said, still standing in front of the blackboard with a worn-down piece of chalk in his hand, "look at this."

Kate's eyes had grown grainy sitting there in front of the computer screen. She was glad for the respite. "Coming."

David, attired in his favorite pair of brown corduroys, white long-sleeve cotton shirt with a button-down collar, and a multicolored knit vest with a harlequin design, had chalk in his hair, on his face, and on his fingers. Kate smiled at the image he made. Then she perused the calculations he'd asked her to come check out.

David watched her facial expressions closely because he wanted to know if she would see what he'd seen. His own eyes held an amused glint in them. His daughter's smile slowly faded. Then she cupped her chin in thumb and forefinger, really concentrating. Finally, she grinned and looked up at him. David was grinning like an idiot, too, while he nodded excitedly. He recognized that she'd gotten it.

"They're digging in the wrong place!" they cried in unison in a crazy tribute to their favorite movie, *Raiders of the Lost Ark.*

What they meant was their competitors, which is how they considered the company that had bought David's notes from Jason, did not have the final disk. And because they didn't have it, their conclusions as to the interpretation of David's notes would lead them in the wrong direction. In other words, David's carefully documented research would be absolutely worthless to them.

David and Kate did a high-energy do-si-do around the office, whooping at the top of their voices. David stopped abruptly and held Kate by her arms, peering into her face.

"Kate, do you know what this means? I can still do it. With your help, I know I can come up with the correct calculations. You and I think alike. Look at how you saw, right away, what I was trying to get across to you. As for your ability to draw up plans for the pods, once I have the mathematics down pat, I have no doubt you can do it. What do you say, will you help your old man out?"

"Do you really think I can do it, Dad? I'm a little rusty."

David laughed. "You're young and you're strong. You think outside of the box, which is why I know you will be good for me. I tend to be too traditional in my thinking."

"I'll try," Kate said, doubting herself.

"That's all I ask," David said, and hugged her tightly.

Carolina appeared in the doorway. "What was all that racket?"

Kate kissed her dad's cheek, and did the same to her

mom on the way out of the room. "Dad'll fill you in. I've got to go throw up."

Carolina moved out of her way.

"What's got *her* all nervous?"

"I just asked her to work with me," David told his concerned wife. He went to her and drew her into his arms. "Carolina, I know where I went wrong now. Kate and I are going to finish the project together."

Carolina hugged her husband back. Hearing David was going back to the work that had stressed him out to the point of a stroke did nothing to quell her fears. But, at least, he was going to be working with Kate. Kate wouldn't let him work too hard.

"Wonderful," Carolina said enthusiastically. "This means you'll be going into the lab at the university every day from now on, right?"

"I'm afraid so, sweetheart," David confirmed.

Carolina pulled back and looked him straight in the eyes. "But you won't miss Christmas? Even mad scientists get Christmas off."

David smiled at her. "I promise, my darling wife, I will take the whole day off."

"And no late, late nights," Carolina bargained.

"Nothing after ten P.M.," David said.

"Nine P.M.," Carolina haggled.

"Nine-thirty," David said. "And that's my final offer."

Carolina tiptoed and kissed his cheek. "Deal."

Eleven

The new head of the physics department was more than happy to cooperate with David when he requested the use of a lab on campus. She assured David that not only would it be a pleasure to have him back, but she wanted to do anything she could to lessen the blow of being betrayed by a colleague.

The physics department as a whole had responded with shock and disbelief when rumors of Jason's duplicity had spread, and then the local paper began running a series of articles about it. The case was a source of avid speculation.

For Jason's part, he was not forthcoming about the identity of the company to which he'd sold his pilfered information. However, Stephen Erwin was eagerly informing on Jason. His willingness to talk now did little toward persuading the prosecution to let up on him. Soledad Montenegro saw to that. She reminded the prosecutor that she'd had to work her tail off to bring those two in, and if he let them get off he would have to answer to her.

He didn't want to have to do that, so he sought to build a rock-solid case against the two defendants. Martin Penichiero, however, was being considered for a lesser charge. In the meantime, he was enjoying a safe, dry place to live and three meals a day. Soledad even took him some paperback novels to help occupy his time. He thanked her for her kindness with, "Much obliged, Detective. Do you think you could get me some of Melanie Schuster's novels? She knows how to tell a good story."

"Nobody borrows my Melanie Schuster novels," Soledad said. "I'd never get them back." She punctuated her comment with a stern expression directed his way.

Martin looked bereft at her pronouncement.

Taking pity on him, Soledad said. "I'll drop by the book-store on the way home and buy you a couple, all right?"

Martin perked right up. "Thanks, Detective. Did I ever tell you you remind me of Cagney of *Cagney and Lacey*?"

"Keep your flattery," Soledad said with a short laugh. "I'm gonna bring the books."

Graduate students were coming out of the woodwork offering to serve as lab assistants. David chose four able-bodied specimens, two males and two females, and worked them to the point of exhaustion, which was how hard he worked himself and Kate.

Kate dragged herself to her car each night, thankful to be out of the lab and on the way home to a hot bath. Oftentimes she would phone Rafe en route to see if he was up to a late dinner or something more. He usually was, but occasionally he'd have to go out of town early the next morning to pick up a prisoner, and those times he'd beg off.

Two days before Christmas, Kate was leaving the lab with her coat held closely around her, the sudden chill air making her long for the warmth of her bed, when she looked up and saw Rafe leaning against his Expedi-tion, waiting for her.

"Hello, Doc, are you always the last to leave?" he asked.

Kate didn't say a word, she simply walked into the circle of his arms and kissed him soundly. "Just follow me home, please."

Home meant either his place or hers. It didn't matter.

"My place," Rafe said. "I want you all to myself tonight. I plan to pamper you and then put you to bed right."

Kate kissed his mouth again. "Sounds good to me." She walked over to her car, got in, and shut the door. A few seconds later she was pulling out of the parking lot with Rafe's headlights reflected in her rearview mirror.

At his house, Rafe unlocked the front door and let her precede him inside.

Kate was coming out of her coat the moment she stepped into the foyer. Underneath she wore a pair of black slacks and a camel sweater. On her feet were a pair of black athletic shoes. She was on her feet a lot at the lab, and these shoes were comfortable.

Her hair was pulled back in a ponytail.

Rafe's boots made crisp sounds on the hardwood floor as he crossed the room and took her coat from her. He hung it in the foyer closet and removed his own brown leather jacket, hanging it beside Kate's lined coat. He wore a pair of khakis and a long-sleeve shirt in off-white denim.

They stood looking at each other for several seconds.

"I haven't seen you in four days, Kate. My trip to Houston was uneventful, thank God, and then when I got back two days ago you were too busy to see me. What's going on in that lab?"

"The closer we get, the harder Dad wants to work. I have to force him to take breaks. I have to remind him he's already had one stroke and is courting another before he'll slow down. I'm trying to take on more responsibility so there will be less for him to have to cope with."

Shaking his head, Rafe looked at her with narrowed

eyes. "Now I see why you were afraid to assist him when he asked you to. You're both obsessive-compulsives. How can you police his actions when you're just like him?"

Kate walked off in a huff. "That's not fair, Rafe."

"What's not fair is the amount of time we get to spend together," Rafe told her. Then, "Come on, I'll run you a bath. You need to work some kinks out of your muscles."

They were an unusual couple, they had the ability to argue while simultaneously showing concern for one another. Kate always felt comfortable saying exactly what was on her mind with Rafe because she knew he'd take it with a grain of salt. Just as she always tried to do with him.

She looked at him now. His golden brown eyes were full of impatience at the moment. She could understand that. Their love was new. At this stage, all you wanted to do was be with the one you loved, revel in him, get lost in him. She was not giving him the attention he deserved.

She let him remove her sweater. "This won't last forever." She reached up and gently rubbed his bottom lip with the pad of her thumb. "We have the rest of our lives, Rafe. Please try to be patient a little longer."

"How about a shower instead?" Rafe asked.

Kate's lips curved in a sensuous smile. "Okay."

Being the practical man that he was, Rafe asked, "Are you hungry?"

"Famished, but I can wait awhile."

"I'll order takeout while you're in the shower," Rafe said. He kissed her chin. "Mexican? Italian? Chinese? Soul food?"

"Nothing heavy, you decide," Kate said, and hurried to start her shower.

About five minutes later she heard Rafe entering the bathroom. He opened the shower stall door and stepped inside. "I ordered Chinese since you wanted light. I should have time for a quick shower before they get here."

Kate was not yet blasé about his male beauty. Each time she saw his nude body, she inhaled sharply and exhaled slowly. Her heart would race for a few seconds and then resume its normal pace. Her eyes would sweep over him with greedy thoughts of possession. Hers. He was all hers. She never got tired of thinking that.

Rafe reached for her washcloth and the soap. Kate handed them to him. He soaped the cloth well and put the soap in the shower caddy. He began by turning her around and washing her back for her. Making sure to spend a bit of time massaging her tight shoulders. The tension she'd felt earlier that evening melted away. Rafe then abandoned the washcloth altogether and soaped his big hands. He ran them all over her body. Her breasts. Her thighs. Her buttocks. Between her legs. Kate shut her eyes and let him awaken her body.

After he'd soaped her entire body, he finished by rinsing her with the dial on the shower massage set exactly where she liked it, pulsating. She was tingling nicely from top to bottom when he was done.

"Kate, open your eyes."

He held a clean towel in his hand. "I'll join you in a few minutes," he said, thrusting it into her hands. "You're dead tired, go rest until the food gets here."

"If I fall asleep, wake me," Kate admonished him.

"Okay," he said, knowing that's what she wanted to hear.

Two and a half hours later, Kate opened her eyes and found him lying in bed beside her wide awake, watching her.

"You didn't wake me."

"You needed to sleep."

"I could have slept afterward."

"You still can," he told her.

Kate's stomach growled.

"Feed the hungry beast first," Rafe said.

The both of them went into the kitchen, Rafe in a pair of pajamas and Kate in his robe that was much too big but smelled like him, so she was satisfied.

"You waited for me," Kate said, seeing the Chinese food containers unopened in the fridge. Rafe was busy getting plates. "I wasn't hungry then, I am now. Besides, I like eating with you."

"You mean you like watching me eat."

"Yes. You eat like you make love, passionately. Watching you eat is a definite turn-on for me."

"You're weird, Grant."

"Thank you."

"The way you described what you and your dad are doing makes me think of something out of science fiction," Rafe said once they had nuked their food and were sitting across from one another at the kitchen table. "I'm a *Star Trek* fan. You're talking about beaming atoms 'out there.'" He gestured toward the heavens.

"Nah," Kate said. "It won't work quite that well, especially not in the beginning."

She put a forkful of shrimp-fried rice in her mouth and chewed. After swallowing, she continued. "It'll work on the quantum-entanglement principle, which allows two particles to behave as one, no matter how far apart they are. What teleportation will do is transfer properties instantly from one place to another."

"That's beaming me up, Scotty," Rafe insisted. He laughed. "I'd have to agree with Bones, you won't get me in one of those contraptions, beaming *my* molecules all over creation."

Kate laughed, too. "Wait and see, one day our great-grandchildren will be teleporting all over the world in an instant. Flying on an airplane will be comparable to a horse and buggy."

They ate in silence for a while, both deep in thought.

Rafe looked at her. "I suppose you believe aliens have visited Earth, too?"

Kate smiled at him.

"You're kidding!" Rafe exclaimed, assuming her silence meant she did.

"I think it would be presumptuous of us to assume that we're the only intelligent beings in the known universe when there are countless other planets in countless other galaxies. Besides, I've seen something I couldn't explain several times in the Arizona night skies. I belong to a group that tracks them."

Rafe sat and simply looked at her. Kate was smiling as she continued to enjoy her meal. "You're sitting there telling me you've seen a UFO?" he said.

"Several UFOs," Kate confirmed. "The next time I get the call, usually in the middle of the night, I'll phone you and you can go out with us."

"On a UFO run?"

"We call it documenting sightings."

"Uh-huh," said Rafe. "Is there anything else I need to know about you?"

"Any other weird inclinations, you mean?"

"Well, yeah."

"Only if you can describe my singing as a weird inclination. I love to sing, but I sound like a croaking frog and a cat in heat trying to outdo each other on karaoke night. What about you?"

"I'm your average guy. Nothing that comes to mind." Then he asked her another question. "Do you believe in God?"

"Yes, of course."

"Oh, I thought scientists only believe in things they can prove truly exists."

"That's ridiculous. My father is a Baptist, and my

mother is a Catholic. I'm somewhere in between. I learned tenets of both faiths. Wait until day after tomorrow. On Christmas Day, our house is a mishmash of Baptist and Catholic traditions. My dad insists on an African-American Christmas feast. My mom insists on decorating the house with every religious image pertaining to Christ's birth in existence. The Huertas and the Matthewses come together. There will undoubtedly be at least one knock-down, drag-out fight, but mostly we get along. Dad's brother and his family will be coming from Florida this year. And you'll get the chance to meet my grandma Bea. That's dad's seventy-five-year-old mother."

She reached across the table and grasped his hand, squeezing it. "God is the greatest mystery of all. Aldous Huxley once said, 'Science has explained nothing; the more we know the more fantastic the world becomes and the profounder the surrounding darkness.' I have to agree with him on that score. We are lost without God. We're groping in the darkness. Another quote I recall from my graduate school days is one by Martin Luther King. He said, 'We have genuflected before the god of science only to find that it has given us the atomic bomb, producing fears and anxieties that science can never mitigate.' And that's why neither my father nor I will ever be involved with a project that would cause harm to anyone."

"How can you ever be certain that what you invent won't be used for nefarious purposes?"

"You can't," Kate said. "But you can make every effort to prevent it."

"By building safeguards into the design?"

"Hopefully, yes," Kate confirmed.

"What do you mean, hopefully?"

"There will always be someone who will try their best to get around the safeguards. For every scientist who makes a breakthrough there is another scientist trying to go a step further. It's the nature of the beast."

Rafe sighed. "Let's change the subject, shall we? This is too scary for me."

"Gladly," Kate said. "How was your basketball game with Vance and the fellas?"

"Interesting," Rafe said with a short laugh. "I usually play with a bunch of brothers. But playing with Native Americans, Mexican-Americans, and African-Americans taught me something."

"What?"

"It's not just white men who can't jump," joked Rafe.

Laughing, Kate said, "Oh, now you're going to talk about my Indian and Mexican brothers behind their backs!"

"No," Rafe said. "I'd tell them to their faces that they have no game."

"You are just too egotistical," Kate said, still laughing.

"Don't get me wrong," Rafe said. "This is not a racial slur. By no means. It's just that in the black neighborhoods, black kids are weaned on basketball. So they have the advantage. I'm sure if Native American kids and Mexican kids played basketball from the time they could walk, they'd be good, too."

"So you're saying it's a cultural thing."

"That's what I'm saying."

"Okay," Kate said. "But be warned. Just like Tiger Woods taught the world of golf a lesson, one of my Indian brothers will come along and kick your butt on the b-ball court one day."

"Maybe when I'm old and gray," Rafe said. He composed himself. "Vance mentioned that your tenth high school reunion was coming up right after Christmas. He said you told Sophie you wouldn't be caught dead there. I was wondering why you said that."

Kate knew what was up. Sophie had told Vance to ask Rafe to try and get her to go to the class reunion. She'd already told Sophie she wasn't going, and Sophie had tried everything in her considerable repertoire, including guilt, to convince Kate to change her mind. Kate hadn't budged.

"Sophie knows the reason why," Kate said now.

"Sophie might know, but I don't," Rafe countered.

"Okay." Kate sighed. "The only real friend I had in high school was Sophie. I was shunned, picked on, and generally made to feel like I had a flesh-eating disease."

"You're exaggerating," Rafe accused her lightly.

Kate rolled her eyes. "Maybe a little. But not much. Why would I want to revisit memories that were not, on the whole, pleasant for me? It makes no sense."

"It makes perfect sense," said Rafe. "You think you were a geek? Take a look at the head cheerleader ten years hence. She's probably not as lovely as you remembered her. And if she is, maybe she's undergone a personality change. People do change, you know. There was this guy in my class who used to try to beat my butt every chance he got. Some days I'd win, some days he'd win. Do you know what he'd become when I met him at our tenth-year reunion?"

"What?" Kate asked, imagining the guy had had a sex-change operation.

"A ballet dancer," Rafe said with a laugh.

"All the time he was fighting with you, he was fighting his attraction to you?"

"No, he wasn't gay. Not all male ballet dancers are gay, Kate. The thing is, he told me the reason he was always picking fights with me was that someone had told him I'd said I'd seen him doing pirouettes at a dance studio with the other 'ballerinas.' Of course I'd said no such thing. All the times he was trying to bloody my nose he never mentioned the reason why he was doing it. I could have told him his friend had lied to him. Turns out his friend was the boyfriend of a girl I had a crush on. That was his way of exacting revenge on me."

"Without getting his hands dirty," Kate said. She pushed her plate away. She'd had the chance to finish eating while he was talking. "That was good, thank you. Now, tell me, Rafe, do you really want to go to my class reunion? Because I'm not going unless you take me."

"I think it would be fun," Rafe said without hesitation. "All right. I'll go."

She sent in her check and registration form the very next day.

David's mother, Beatrice, his brother, Matthias, and his wife, Shirley, along with their two children, Anise and Matthias Jr., arrived shortly after noon on Christmas Eve. Kate moved in with Davida so they could have the guest house, which had two bedrooms and a couch in the living room that converted into a queen-size bed.

Kate, who had been in the kitchen with Carolina baking Christmas cookies, went to answer the door. David and Davida were in the living room hanging festive garlands that Carolina wanted at every corner of the large room. On Christmas night, the room would be transformed into a ballroom where friends and relatives alike would enjoy a lavish buffet after which they would dance the night away and, if the eggnog was flowing, get up and sing Christmas carols accompanied by a karaoke machine.

Kate peered through the peephole, but someone was covering the hole with his hand. She knew, then, that it was Uncle Matt. He always did that.

She swung the door open and screamed, their usual greeting. Kate was enveloped in her uncle's beefy arms.

He kissed her cheek, she kissed his. "Hello, pretty girl, how is my favorite niece?"

"Don't let Little David hear you say that," Kate said, laughing.

She turned and yelled behind her so that the whole house could hear, "They're here!"

Then she was being hugged by Grandma Bea, who nearly smothered her in her ample bosom. Beatrice was five-two and what she considered pleasantly plump. In spite of the extra pounds, she was healthy and vital. She attributed her good health to staying active and having a nice glass of wine before bed every night. Her medium brown skin was practically unlined. She was a walking advertisement for the saying "Black doesn't crack." And she wore her iron-gray relaxed hair in a very short, tapered cut. She reminded Kate a lot of Camille Cosby. The same type of classic beauty.

"Where is that boy of mine?" she asked excitedly.

More screams could be heard behind Kate. She knew to get out of the way. Her father, her mother, and Davida came into the room and another round of hugging commenced.

Afterward, everyone gathered in the kitchen, where David insisted on hearing about their trip. Matt, who took two weeks off from his job as a hospital administrator every year this time, loved to take long trips in the car. They'd rented a large late-model Dodge Caravan for this trip. In the middle of his speech about how pleasurable the van was to drive, Matt insisted on showing it to David. All three of the males got up and left the room. As soon as they were out of earshot, Grandma Bea said, "Now we can talk!"

Kate, Davida, Shirley, and Anise all sat on stools around the nook. Carolina was pulling a pan of chocolate chip cookies from the oven. The enticing aroma filled the room. "Are you seeing anyone special, Davida?" Bea joked.

"Grandma, you know I'm only fifteen," Davida said. "They won't even let me date."

"That's a travesty," Bea said. "A real travesty. How about you, Kate? Are you seeing anyone special?"

"That's who you really wanted to ask all along," said Anise, who was twenty-two and in her second year of law school. She had her grandmother's chestnut skin and auburn hair, with highlights, that she wore shoulder-length and very curly. She and Kate had always gotten along well together.

"True, that," said Grandma Bea, using an expression she'd heard from some youngster or other several years ago. Who knew that it was now considered passé?

The others laughed.

"Yes, Grandma, I *am* seeing someone special."

"Someone who's very hot!" Davida chimed in.

Anise's eyebrows shot up. "Really? Go, Kate!"

"Will we get to meet him over the holidays?" Shirley wanted to know. Shirley was what some African-Americans called a redbone. She had skin that was very light brown with a red tinge to it. Her long hair was naturally auburn-colored. She wore it long and usually in a French twist that gave her slim neck a swanlike appearance.

Laughing, Kate said, "Yes, you'll meet him tonight. He'll be bringing his sister, Jenny, with him."

"That's wonderful, sweetie," Bea said.

"What does he do?" asked Shirley.

"Is he in your field?" Anise asked. "Don't tell me you finally met a fine physicist? I didn't think, except for Uncle David, that they existed."

"He's not a scientist, he's a U.S. Marshal," Kate said, getting a word in edgewise.

"Like Arnold Schwarzenegger in that movie he did

with Vanessa Williams?" Anise asked. She grinned her approval.

"Yeah," said Davida excitedly. "And like Wesley Snipes in that film with Tommy Lee Jones."

"Will you two stop using movies as points of reference?" Bea, the retired teacher, vehemently asked. "Popular culture is responsible for the dumbing-down of America. The U.S. Marshals were established by the first Congress more than two hundred years ago. They support our courts and they run the Witness Protection Program. Read your history, granddaughters." She turned to Kate. "Now, Kate, I only want to know one thing about your young man, does he respect you?"

"Yes, he does," Kate replied. "We respect each other."

"That's good enough for me," said Bea.

Carolina put a plate of cookies on the counter in front of them. "Who wants coffee, and who wants milk?"

Bea looked up at her daughter-in-law, a woman whose ability to make her son happy she'd questioned thirty years ago, but had grown to love very much. "How is your gram, Carolina?"

Carolina smiled. "She's doing a lot better, thank you, Mother Matthews. She'll be here tomorrow night for dinner and dancing."

"I hope you're going to have some gentlemen here around my age," Bea said. "I can still cut a rug. On second thought, they'd better be younger than I am to keep up with me."

Everyone laughed and dug into the plate of cookies.

Every Easter the Pascua Yaqui put on a spring pageant that combines deer dances with the Crucifixion. Masked dancers move in the footsteps of their ancestors in thanking creation for its rich blessings.

Just like Easter is celebrated in their culture with a mixture of tribal traditions and Catholic teachings, so is Christmas. Carolina had decorated the house with traditional Pascua Yaqui artwork, plus poinsettias, miniature ceramic saguaros, and paper renditions of cactus flowers, courtesy of Davida and Josefina. It all worked to put the guests in the mood for a desert Christmas.

The outside of the house was bordered by icicle lights that winked golden in the night. Carolina and David greeted the guests at the door in their finest holiday attire, David in a black tuxedo, and Carolina in a red velvet dress whose hem fell a couple of inches above her knees. With her brown complexion and dark hair, falling down her back, the dress's color was very complementary.

Everyone wore their holiday finery, the men in tuxedos or dark suits, the women in dresses that spanned the colors of the rainbow and glittered like stars in the firmament.

Kate wore a short, sleeveless velvet sheath in royal blue. A bit of cleavage showed, which she covered up on occasion with a sheer wrap in the same shade. She'd put her hair up off her neck tonight, the better, she hoped, for Rafe to kiss her there at every opportunity.

She was nervous. For weeks now they'd kept their decision to wed a secret. Rafe was bringing the ring that they'd picked out together with him tonight, and he was going to slip it onto her finger just before they called for quiet and made the announcement sometime after dinner, but before the guests got too tipsy off of her father's eggnog. He was a bit heavy-handed when adding the rum to the mixture.

While her father and mother were manning the door, Kate and Davida were passing among the guests, friends, relatives, and her father's peers from the university, welcoming them and thanking them for coming.

Kate looked over at Davida, who was in her element tonight. She loved being in a roomful of people. She could hold her own with the best of conversationalists. Kate imagined she would one day be a journalist who interviewed heads of state. She was equally comfortable with her father's professor friends as she was with her school friends.

"Good evening, beautiful," said a voice behind Kate.

She turned and her breath caught in her throat. Rafe was resplendent in a black tuxedo, highly polished black slippers, and a red rosebud in his lapel. He flashed white teeth at her as he slowly walked toward her. "I thought you were at your most beautiful au naturel. But, I have to admit, this is a very close second."

He gently rubbed her cheek with the back of his fingers. Kate relished his touch, moving her face slightly against his fingers and fairly purring. She'd momentarily forgotten they were surrounded by a roomful of people. "Damn, you're fine," she said.

Rafe smiled, bent his head, and gave her a very brief buss on the lips. "I'm glad you think so."

He straightened up. Several pairs of eyes were on them.

Kate pulled herself together. "Where's Jenny?"

"Oh, you'll never guess who showed up on my doorstep this afternoon, looking bedraggled and every bit the contrite ex-lover boy."

"Zeke?"

"None other. He begged, he cajoled. He got down on his knees with a rock the size of a golf ball and proposed."

Shaking her head, Kate cracked up. "That's priceless! So, Jenny accepted and rode off with him on his white charger?"

"It was a black Jag but, yes, she did."

"Ah," said Kate. "Romance!"

"All I know is, he'd better take good care of her."

"Jenny knows what she's doing, Rafe. That's one smart woman."

"Yeah, I guess you're right," Rafe said thoughtfully. He ran his finger along her upper arm and leaned in. "I'd really like to kiss you, Kate. Can we go someplace less populated?"

"The only place where there aren't any humans tonight is in the stables," Kate told him regretfully. They wouldn't have gotten very far anyway.

"Kate, who is this handsome stranger?" her cousin Gerda asked as she walked up. In her mid-thirties and married nearly fifteen years, Gerda was the mother of four boys ranging in age from five to fourteen. All of them were running around someplace.

Kate put a welcoming arm about her cousin's shoulders. "Rafe, meet my cousin, Gerda Huerta Mendez. Gerda, this is my boyfriend, Rafael Grant."

Gerda vigorously shook his hand. "Pleased to meet you, Rafael."

Rafe smiled at the petite woman. "The pleasure's all mine," he said.

"Whew!" said Gerda. "Handsome *and* charming." She regarded Kate. "Good going, little cousin. I guess I should rethink introducing you to that software salesman I was saving for New Year's. Kate used to always be alone on New Year's," Gerda explained to Kate's embarrassment.

Kate had forgotten about the "blab factor." It was that frequently occurring phenomenon when relatives spilled little embarrassing moments about you to anyone you brought as a date to family functions.

"I can't believe Kate was ever alone for any New Year's Eve unless she *wanted* to be alone," Rafe said. He looked into Kate's eyes with such adoration that Gerda nearly swooned right alongside Kate. "What man in his right mind wouldn't want to spend the most romantic night of the year with her?"

"Excuse me, I could use a cold drink," Gerda said, fanning her face. "*Really* nice meeting you, Rafael." She hurried off.

Kate took Rafe by the hand, pulling him toward the closest exit. "In less than five minutes, everybody in this room is going to know your name. Let's go to the stables and scare the horses with loud kissing noises."

"Hi, Kate."

"Hey, Kate."

"Kate, what's up?"

"*Que pasa, prima chiquita?*" What's happening, little cousin?

Kate smile warmly at everyone but did not stop to chat. She paused only long enough to grab someone's coat from the foyer closet and put it on. She thought it was her cousin Anise's, but wasn't certain.

At the stables, Kate turned on a light at the entrance but did not light up the entire structure. Rafe had never been in the stables before. He hadn't yet taken her up on her offer to teach him to ride.

"I thought it would be colder out here," he said as Kate closed the door behind them.

"It has central heat and air," Kate said. "Controlled temps help keep them healthy."

The air smelled of hay and, faintly, of horse manure. Figuring a city boy like Rafe wouldn't be used to that aroma, Kate said, "The stalls are cleaned daily, but the horses go between cleanings. If you'd rather not stay . . ."

"Oh, please, Kate, I've been in barracks with men who think washing their socks is bad luck. I can stand a little horse manure." Then, he kissed her.

His talented tongue teased, pleased, appeased. Kate could not get enough of him.

Somewhere in the back of her sex-crazed mind, she remembered the office and the big leather couch right there on the premises. She turned her head, breaking off the kiss. "We can go into the office. There's a couch."

Rafe had become tumescent and he would have liked nothing better than to make love to her right there. But he thought about all the eyes that would be on them in a few minutes when he and Kate announced their engagement, and he knew he couldn't go through with making love to her only moments before such a sacred occasion. Call him old-fashioned, but that's how he felt.

"No, baby, I want to take you back to my place after I put that ring on your finger and make love to you in our bed."

Kate was, frankly, disappointed but she agreed. Besides, she could stand to practice a bit of self-control. She'd been a steaming caldron of sensuality ever since the night Rafe had given her her first lesson in manual orgasms. Greedy in the bedroom, that's what she'd become. But very satisfied.

She smiled up at Rafe. "It's those kisses of yours. If they could be bottled you'd put the company that makes Viagra out of business in no time."

Rafe pointed her toward the exit and patted her behind. "Out. Get out of here, girl, before I change my mind."

They got back to the house in time to get in line at the buffet table. Kate looked around them as they filled their plates with turkey, ham, corn bread dressing and giblet gravy, candied yams, and collard greens. She saw that Vance, Sophie, and Renata had made it. She was glad. In spite of the fact that Sophie kept insisting that she and Vance were just friends, she'd noticed positive changes in Sophie since Vance had shown up with flowers on her front porch. Sophie was calmer. She didn't speak negatively anymore about never loving another man. She was accepting social invitations again. Wanting them all to attend their class reunion together was evidence of that. Kate was pleased she'd let Rafe talk her into going tomorrow night. Ah, the holidays. It was one party after another.

Twelve

An eclectic group of artists entertained the guests over the sound system as they ate Christmas dinner: Johnny Mathis, Nat King Cole, Los Lobos, Ella Fitzgerald, and Aretha Franklin. Tables had been assigned, although Kate noticed that many of the younger guests were choosing to stand in groups while they ate, carrying on lively conversations highlighted by fits of raucous laughter. Everyone seemed to be having a good time.

She and Rafe were sharing a table with Sophie, Vance, and Renata. Sophie and Renata looked lovely tonight in red and white satin dresses that Sophie had designed and sewn herself. Vance wore a dark blue suit with a crisp white button-down shirt and a blue silk tie with yellow stripes. Kate thought her cousin looked very handsome, and she told him so.

"Sophie picked out the suit," Vance said, smiling at Sophie, who blushed. "She has great taste."

"Stop it," said Sophie, embarrassed and eager to change the subject. Looking around the room, she said, "Your mom outdid herself with the decorations this year. I'm tempted to steal this centerpiece when I get ready to go home."

"Please do," said Kate of the bouquet of paper cactus flowers in red, green, and white. "Gram and Little David would take it as quite a compliment if you did."

Sophie was busy cutting up a slice of ham into smaller pieces for Renata. "Then, I will. They would look good on my mantelpiece."

Renata speared a chunk of ham with her fork and brought it to her lips, touched it with her tongue to sample it before committing to putting it in her mouth, and, grinning at her mother, popped it in and chewed.

"Good?" asked Sophie.

Renata nodded vigorously. Though at two she could talk, she was shy when in public.

"Great," said her mother. "Try to get some of those greens down, too, okay?" To the rest of the table, she said, "She's definitely a carnivore. All she wants to eat is meat. I have to practically bribe her to get her to eat fruits and vegetables."

"Small kids can be finicky," Kate said. "I remember when Little David was around Renata's age, she only wanted to eat hot dogs. She would throw a tantrum if you didn't give them to her. That didn't last long, though, because Mama told her she could starve if she didn't want to eat what the rest of us ate. Two days, tops, she was putting away everything Mama set before her."

"That seems kind of cruel," Sophie said. "I don't think I could let Renata go without."

"I know what you mean," agreed Kate. "When you have one child you do tend to treat him with kid gloves. But Mama had four running around here and she'd seen that the rest of us had survived her tactics, so she felt free to use the same ones on the baby of the family. They always say raising the first child is the hardest. The more children you have, the more lax you become when it comes to handling them as if they are delicate creatures. You know, they're tougher than they look."

"That's so true," Sophie said. "I noticed how strictly my parents raised my older sister, Joyce, and myself, but by the time our kid brother came along they just didn't care anymore. They spoiled him rotten. Now, it's coming back to haunt them because he's twenty-two and still living at home. No college degree, no job, no prospects. He thinks he's gonna live off of them the rest of his life."

"Can we get off the subject of freeloading relatives?" Vance asked. "I want to know more about the class reunion. Do I have to wear a suit two nights in a row? This thing is cutting off my circulation." He loosened his tie a bit to make his point.

"No, tomorrow night's casual dress," Sophie told him. "They're gonna have a live band, and we're all supposed to get down and get funky with our bad selves."

"Sophie, we graduated in the nineties, not the seventies," Kate said with a laugh.

"The seventies was a much more interesting decade," Sophie said. "Can you name one artist from the nineties that you simply loved and still play his or her CDs?"

Kate thought hard. "To be honest, I'm either into artists from bygone eras or the really new artists. I really can't think of one artist from the nineties that I still listen to on a regular basis."

"That's what I'm talking about. It's like the artists who were popular when we were in high school like Prince, Mariah Carey, Whitney Houston have all sort of faded away."

"Good evening, everybody, I hope you're all enjoying the food," Carolina said into the karaoke machine's microphone. The buzz of voices died down. "Those of you who have come to celebrate Christmas with us know we have a tradition in the Matthews home. Every Christmas we invite friends and family to get up and embarrass themselves by warbling Christmas carols. Joe of Joe's Bar fame was kind enough to lend us his karaoke machine tonight, so we have hooked it up to a big-screen TV. No one can use the excuse that they can't read the words, like some did last year." She peered into the crowd and spotted Joe Montgomery, a tall, husky African-American man in his late fifties with a huge bushy black moustache. "Thanks, Joe!"

Joe grinned from his corner of the room and gave her a thumps-up sign.

"Okay," Carolina said. "Do I have any volunteers? Don't be shy. Just come up here, tell me which song you want to sing, and I'll punch it in and you're a star!"

Kent stood and came up to the podium. The youngest Matthews son at twenty-four, Kent wore his curly hair in a ponytail and was rarely seen wearing anything but jeans and denim shirts. He was an avid horseman, too, and had made many a lady sigh when she saw him coming astride a stallion. Tall and rangy, he had the easy gait of a cowboy. After accepting the mike from his mother he bent to kiss her satiny cheek.

"This one's for you, Mama. 'Silent Night.'"

The ladies in the room sat up expectantly, watching him with admiration.

"Silent night, holy night . . ." He had a solid baritone that was rich and soulful. Carolina looked on with pride. Josefina, sitting down front, applauded enthusiastically. "That's my grandbaby!"

The young ladies who weren't relatives wondered if he was unattached. The older ladies just dreamed.

After Kent came a succession of friends and relatives brave enough to risk sour notes and ridicule. Sophie got up and sang "Rudolf the Red-nosed Reindeer" for the youngsters.

Vance did a pretty decent rendition of "Hark! The Herald Angels Sing!"

As the evening wore on, folks started noticing the fact

that Kate, who loved to get up and sing at these parties, had not moved from her seat next to Rafe. Sophie elbowed her. "Kate, aren't you going to sing your favorite, 'O Holy Night?'"

"Not tonight," Kate said.

"What's wrong?" Sophie whispered. "Sore throat?"

"Rafe has never heard me sing," Kate whispered back.

Sophie couldn't help herself, she laughed. Then she rose and started chanting, "Kate, Kate, Kate!"

Soon everyone had joined in. Kate knew the younger cousins just wanted the opportunity to rib her relentlessly, like they always did. While her aunties and uncles and grandmothers simply loved her so much they turned a deaf ear to her screeching.

With moist palms, Kate rose. But before she took the stage, she bent and said to Rafe, "If you still love me after this, then you must *really* love me."

She walked up to the raised platform and took the microphone from her mother.

Carolina smiled at her. "You show 'em, Kate."

"All right, you asked for it," Kate joked. "'O Holy Night.'"

The intro began and Kate opened her mouth and started singing the words: "O holy night, the stars are brightly shining . . ." She dipped when she should have risen. Though she tried her level best, her throat was not the conduit through which angelic sounds were meant to be communicated. She felt the words in her soul. She wanted with all her heart to be able to deliver them with the purity and beauty they deserved. All the previous years she'd gotten up and sung, she'd done it with gusto, laughing at herself before others could, but this year was different. This year Rafe was in the room. She could not bear to look at him and see the undoubtedly horrified expression on his face. Instead, she rushed on through the song.

"Fall on your knees. O . . ." Then, a clear, beautiful bass voice began singing with her. ". . . hear the angels voices. O night divine. O night when Christ was born!"

Everyone sat rapt as Rafe joined her onstage, placed his arm about her waist, and they finished the song together. There was thunderous applause. Tears were streaming down Kate's cheeks as she smiled up at the man she loved.

After the applause died down, Rafe got down on one knee and said, "Kate, would you do me the honor of becoming my wife?"

Everyone waited. The room was so silent, Kate could hear the thumping of her heart.

Blubbering now, she answered, "Yes!"

More applause, this time accompanied by cheers and whoops of joy.

Rafe stood, and Kate threw her arms around his neck. No one was more surprised than she. They'd planned to get up and simply announce their decision to marry. She hadn't expected him to propose in front of friends and family.

Rafe retrieved the ring from his pocket and slipped it onto her finger.

"Ring, ring!" a female voice cried.

They wanted to see the ring. Kate held up her hand with the two-karat solitaire on it.

More cheers. Then, some smart-mouthed cousin said, "Kate, you just may have a child in your future who can carry a tune!"

Everyone laughed, Kate included. At that moment she was too happy not to.

She and Rafe gave each other chaste kisses; then her parents were standing next to them, each taking a turn hugging both her and Rafe and offering sincere congratulations.

"Welcome to the family, Rafael," said David.

"I *knew* I liked you the moment I met you," Carolina said with tears shining in her eyes.

After many, many more congratulations, Kate and Rafe managed to slip away.

Once outside in the crisp winter air, they hustled, hurrying to his car. "I can't believe you," Kate said, nearly running. "You have a *beautiful* singing voice! Why haven't I ever heard you sing before?"

"The opportunity never presented itself," Rafe said modestly.

At the Expedition he quickly unlocked the doors and handed Kate in. "You don't know what you did to me when you started singing," Kate went on as soon as he was inside. She was tearing up again. Wiping the tears away with her fingers, she continued, "I know it's foolish but I was so nervous about getting up and singing in front of you. You're always telling me how perfect I am. God knows, I know I'm not perfect. But singing is something I'm *really* bad at and I just didn't want you to know how bad."

Rafe had started the car and switched on the heater. He turned on the seat to face her. Clasping her cold hands in his warm ones, he said, "Kate, you sang as if you were a member of God's choir. You sang from the heart and, according to my daddy, who was a minister, that's all God cares about. You do everything with passion. And that's one of the reasons why I love you so much."

Kate went into his arms and kissed him. She pulled back from the kiss long enough to say against his luscious lips, "Merry Christmas, baby."

* * *

There had been more than five hundred in Kate's graduating class at Tucson High. It seemed to her that every last one of them and their significant others had shown up tonight. The high school gym was packed.

Kate, Rafe, Sophie, and Vance were asked to stop and sign in before entering. Three former classmates, two women and one man, sat behind a long table covered with stick-on name tags. Behind them was a huge bulletin board upon which were old yearbook photos of each classmate secured with push pins. Next to each yearbook photo was a Polaroid of the classmate as he/she arrived tonight.

One of the women stood with a Polaroid camera in her hands. "Sophie Peterson, right?" she asked, recognizing Sophie.

"That's right!" said Sophie, delighted. "And you are?" she asked, scrutinizing the tall, brown-eyed brunette.

"Jamie Westwood. We were on the yearbook staff together, senior year, remember?"

"I do!" Sophie cried and gave Jamie an enthusiastic hug.

Parting, the two laughed. "It's so good to see you, Sophie." Jamie turned her eyes on Kate. "Katharine Matthews!"

"Hi, Jamie," Kate said. Kate had no trouble remembering Jamie Westwood. Kate had beaten her out for class valedictorian by only a few points. Jamie had been the salutatorian.

"You both look great," Jamie said.

"So do you," said Kate. In fact Jamie hadn't changed much at all. She was still slim and attractive and outgoing.

"Mind if I take your photos, with your dates of course, to add to our Then and Now bulletin board?"

"Snap away!" said Sophie.

She grabbed Vance by the arm and they struck a pose.

Jamie took their photo and waited for it to slide out of the camera's body.

Then Kate and Rafe smiled for the camera.

"Wonderful," said Jamie. "Thanks, guys. Now, please fill out your name tags, put them on, and go have a good time."

"See you later?" Kate asked. She was curious as to what Jamie had been doing the past ten years. Sophie had been right, she *did* want to know how everyone was getting along in life.

"Sure will," Jamie said, glad Kate had asked. "I'll bring my husband, Tad, by later so we can catch up."

The foursome entered the gymnasium. The hum of live voices drowned out the background recording of Mariah Carey singing "Vision of Love."

"Okay, ground rules," Vance joked. "No dancing with former boyfriends. I'm your date, you should dance every dance with me. And no disappearing into the ladies' room for hours on end."

Sophie tossed her head back in a deep laugh. "I'll dance every dance with you as long as you can keep up with me, but the moment you poop out, all bets are off. And as for the ladies' room, the lines are usually so long at these get-togethers that I'll probably not see the inside of the ladies' room tonight. So, not to worry, dear."

Kate's ears perked up at the mention of the endearment. Sophie calling Vance "dear." Now, that was something to pay attention to and bring up the next time Sophie told her that she and Vance were "just friends."

Rafe caught her smiling. "It's nice to see you're having a good time so far."

"I haven't run into any of the poodle brigade yet," Kate said, still skeptical.

"The poodle brigade?"

"The cheerleaders who used to gang up on me and call me names like half-breed. That's what Sophie and I started calling them because they would preen so much they reminded us of pampered French poodles."

They were making their way through the crowd toward the back of the room where tables had been set up for sitting, and also where rows of tables were laden with food and drink. Rafe kept his arm about Kate's waist, which she found very reassuring.

What a wuss she was, nervous about a class reunion!

What was the worst they could do to her?

Take back her Most Likely to Succeed senior class superlative? As far as she was concerned, they could have it back if they wanted it.

Someone bumped into her from behind.

She turned and came face-to-face with Trudy Rodriguez. Trudy wasn't alone. Sheila Davis, Juanita Espinoza, and Hailey Cochran was with her. Kate suddenly had a flashback to her senior year when all four of them had cornered her at her locker, called her a half-breed and, in parting, spat on her shoes. She'd never even told Sophie about the shoes. It had been too humiliating.

"Kate," said Trudy, "glad you could make it."

Then, Trudy noticed Vance with Sophie on his arm. Her dark eyes flashed with pique. "I see you brought your friend, Sophia, with you. You two were inseparable back in the day. Some things never change."

Sophie stepped in front of Vance and smiled at the four women. "Girls," she said in greeting, "don't all of you look lovely tonight!"

"Thanks," came the wooden responses. Not one of them returned the compliment.

Kate was watching the manner in which Trudy was looking at Vance, and how her chest had begun heaving as though she could barely contain her anger.

Trudy's disturbance at seeing Vance with Sophie made Kate wonder just how clear Vance had been when he'd broken up with Trudy. Men were notoriously inept when it came to ending a relationship. "I'll call," they would say. Or, "I'd like to take things slower," all vague excuses that some women interpreted as "he's still interested." When he was actually moving on.

"Ladies," Kate said, "I'd like to introduce you to my fiancé, Rafael Grant. Rafe, you've already met Trudy. This is Sheila, Juanita, and Hailey."

Anything to dispel the evil spirits that were floating in the air.

Rafe smiled at them. "Good evening, ladies."

Sheila, Juanita, and Hailey, who had formerly been standing behind Trudy, "having her back," now abandoned her to admire Rafe.

"Fiancé?" said Hailey, a tall blonde with dark brown eyes, as she sidled up to him. "When did this happen?"

"Just last night," Kate said, grasping Rafe's hand with one hand to show she was protecting her territory, and flashing the ring on her other hand.

"That's gorgeous!" cried Sheila, a tall redhead with green eyes. She took Kate's hand and brought it closer so she could get a better look at the ring. "That's a white diamond, isn't it?"

"How did you know?" asked Kate in complimentary tones.

"My husband owns a jewelry store," said Sheila. "Diamano's?"

"Ah, yes," said Kate. "It's in the new mall."

"Yes," said Sheila, smiling warmly. She met Kate's eyes now. "Congratulations to you both, Kate."

"Thank you," said Kate sincerely.

The other two women took turns admiring the ring.

Off to the side, however, things were not so congenial.

"So, she's why you haven't called me?" Kate heard Trudy say a bit too loudly.

"I'm sorry, Trudy. But I told you I couldn't see you anymore," Vance tried to explain in a much lower voice.

"No, what you told me was, you needed a little space," Trudy corrected him, again in a loud voice.

Soon people around them had stopped talking in order to catch what was brewing right under their noses.

"Can we take this outside?" Sophie suggested evenly.

Trudy regarded Sophie with her hands on her hips and with her neck working. "Didn't nobody say nothin' to you! This is between me and him!"

"Come on, Trudy, don't make a scene," cajoled Sheila. "We're here to have fun, not fight."

"Shut up, Sheila!" said Trudy. "This," she said, pointing at Vance, "*man* was supposed to bring me tonight, not her!"

"I never said I was going to take you," Vance denied.

"You never said you weren't," Trudy said, sounding hurt. "You knew how much this meant to me. What were you doing, humoring me?"

"Yes," said Vance. "Because I didn't want to hurt your feelings."

"Well, I would rather you had hurt my feelings," Trudy said.

"Amen!" said Sophie, shocking everyone by agreeing with Trudy. She turned in a huff and began walking toward the exit. "You can have him, sister."

"I don't want him, you keep him!" shouted Trudy, also turning to leave.

Vance looked lost. He looked at Rafe for some clue. Rafe shrugged. He didn't know what Vance could do to get out of this one. Vance ran after Sophie.

The crowd that had gathered dispersed and the volume of human voices in conversation grew louder again, like the buzzing of bees.

Kate sighed and turned to Rafe. "Can we just go? This was supposed to be Sophie's night, and I don't think she's having much fun."

In the parking lot, Vance was trying to convince Sophie to get in his car so he could drive her home. "At least let me take you home, Sophie. I can explain everything on the way. I love you. *Please.*"

Sophie's plan was to go to Rafe's car and wait for him and Kate to show up. Knowing Kate, and she did, it wouldn't be a very long wait. Kate hadn't wanted to come tonight anyway. Now, she wished she hadn't either.

She paused in her tracks and looked up at Vance. "I'm not angry at you, Vance, I'm angry at myself for letting my guard down. I knew I wasn't ready to let anyone into my life. To let myself believe I could find happiness without Jessie. I'm just not ready yet. If I had been thinking clearly, I would have told you to leave that day you came to the house. I was just grasping at something. Seeing how you made Renata smile again, like she used to do with her daddy. How you made me feel. Don't you see? You were bringing back the good times I'd had with Jessie. You offered a break from my grieving, and I took it when I shouldn't have."

"That's not it," Vance said. "What you're feeling is embarrassment, Sophie! I did a foolish thing, I was not honest with a woman who cared about me more than I cared about her. Because I didn't want to hurt her feelings I didn't say the right words the last time we spoke. I was never very good at hurting a woman's feelings. I only want to make her feel good, so I tell her what I think she wants to hear. Does that make me a bad person?"

"Honesty can hurt, but it's better than being led on, and that's what you did with Trudy," Sophie said. "I know you're not a bad person, Vance. But you can't go through life being ambiguous with people. Just like you came to me and told me you loved me and you were taking a chance on telling me, you should have told her you were not interested in her. Even if it hurt her. Even if it made you uncomfortable. Now, I'm going to tell you something that's going to make us both uncomfortable. I'm scared, Vance, of risking my heart on a man who may someday tell me he needs space, when he means it's over."

Vance looked stunned. He opened his mouth to say something, decided against it, and closed it again.

By that time, Rafe and Kate were walking up.

"Kate, Rafe, would you please take me home?" Sophie asked.

Kate went to Sophie and put her arm about her shoulders. "Sure, sweetie."

Sophie looked at Vance with sadness mirrored in her brown eyes. "Good night, Vance."

"Good night," Vance said, his voice breaking. He cleared his throat to disguise the fact.

He turned in the opposite direction and walked away.

Later that night, after Kate and Rafe had taken Sophie home and stayed awhile to make certain she was all right, they went back to his house and simply sat on the sofa holding each other while a fire crackled in the grate.

"They'll work it out," Rafe said, choosing to be positive.

"I don't know," said Kate. "Sophie and Jessie were a phenomenon. There was such depth and meaning to their relationship. They dated for ten years before they ever married. From the tenth grade. It was like they were a part of each other. I think Sophie's right, she's not ready for another relationship yet."

"But Vance loves her."

"Vance might love her, but he has a lot of growing up to do. Look at how he handled the breakup with Trudy. You heard him, he didn't tell her it was over because he didn't want to hurt her!"

"Sophie's angry right now because she *does* feel something for Vance," Rafe said.

"I agree," Kate said. "Now she's going to have to figure out exactly what it is, and if it's worth fighting for."

The phone rang but Rafe didn't budge. "Let the machine get it."

A few seconds later, they heard the beeps and then Jenny's voice say, "We're married, bruh!"

"Damn!" Rafe said, and jumped up to go answer the phone on the desk a few feet away. "Jenny, what? When? Where? How?"

"We're married," Jenny said again. From the sounds in the background, Rafe would guess the *where* was Las Vegas. He knew the sound of slot machines when he heard it. "And we're in Vegas," Jenny said, confirming his suspicions. "It was chintzy and mushy, and an Elvis impersonator sang 'Love Me Tender.'"

What could Rafe do except say, "Congratulations, sis. I hope you'll be very happy."

"I will be," Jenny said, her voice so excited, Rafe had to smile. "I mean, I am! Talk to you later, bruh. We just wanted you to know. Give Kate my love."

"Okay, take care of yourself," Rafe said. "I love you."

"I love you, too!" Jenny said.

They rang off and Rafe started back across the room to reclaim his seat beside Kate.

Kate was on her knees on the sofa, looking expectantly at him. "Jenny and Zeke got married?"

Grinning and nodding, Rafe said, "Yes, in Vegas with Elvis serenading them."

Kate burst into tears.

Rafe went and pulled her into his arms. "Why the waterworks?"

Kate smiled through her tears. "I always cry at weddings."

"You weren't there, silly girl," Rafe said, kissing her moist cheeks one after the other. "But there is somewhere I'd like to take you tonight."

Kate languidly lay back on the sofa, her head supported by the arm. "Where?" she asked, looking at him with smoldering eyes.

"Heaven," Rafe said, rubbing his palms across both nipples and feeling them harden. "Ah, Kate, you're so responsive these days, all I have to do is look at you and your body reacts."

"How do you know I'm not thinking of some other man?" Kate joked.

Rafe was busy running his hands beneath her blouse and freeing her breasts from her bra that, thank goodness, hooked in the front. This done, he ran his tongue across both dark brown buds, making her squirm with pleasure. "I don't have to worry about that, Kate. We're in each other's blood."

In his blood. In his heart. In his soul. He could not imagine life without this incredible woman.

Kate's hands were on his belt, loosening it, then dispensing with the top button of his jeans and carefully unzipping them. She slipped her hand inside his jeans and rubbed his engorged penis through the cotton cloth of his briefs.

Rafe had worked his way down to her flat belly, his tongue leaving a hot, wet trail.

Kate was wearing a short skirt. Underneath she wore sexy bikini panties, a garter belt, and stockings. The garter belt and stockings were more of an effort to put on than panty hose, but Rafe enjoyed taking them off her, so she felt the benefits outweighed the drawbacks.

Rafe's hands were beneath her hips, lifting them so he could push the skirt up around her waist. Kate happily assisted him. Once he had her skirt up, the garter belt was next to go and with it, the stockings. Rafe bent and kissed the area below her belly button, just above the waist of her hip-hugger panties.

Rafe moved back upward, leaving kisses on her belly, between her breasts, until he reached her mouth, where he entered it and sucked on her tongue. Kate moaned, and the sound made Rafe's libido increase in spades. He loved that sound.

Breaking off the kiss, he said, his voice husky, "Bedroom?"

"Here," Kate said urgently.

"The condoms are in the bedroom," he reminded her.

"I want you now," Kate said.

Rafe laughed softly and briefly kissed her mouth. "And have you turn up pregnant at the wedding? Get real, sweetie."

He rose, picked her up, and carried her to the bedroom.

Dropping Kate onto the bed, he said, "Be careful what you say to me in the heat of passion, Kate. Don't think that because I'm a nice guy, the dog can't come out every now and then. I started to take you then and there."

He walked over to the nightstand, got a condom, and tossed it to Kate, who began tearing it open while he stripped. "You had my permission to do it," Kate told him.

"I don't care how high your IQ is, Kate, you cannot be taken seriously when you're in heat."

"In heat! You make me sound like a pussy cat."

Rafe laughed as he stepped out of his underwear. His

fully erect penis saluted Kate. She got up and went to him, the unwrapped condom in her hand. "I am never so turned-on that I don't know what I'm doing."

"Oh, really?"

He took her hand and put it on his penis. Kate's insides quivered as she felt him move in her hands. He was hot, and so hard that it seemed his skin was covering steel instead of flesh and blood.

Her female center throbbed. Her nipples hardened even more than they already were. She started to pant. Rafe bent his head and kissed her, his tongue entering her mouth immediately and taking no prisoners. Soon, she was at the point of having an orgasm on her feet.

Rafe raised his head and peered into her lust-glazed eyes. "You were saying?"

"Oh, shut up, and make love to me," Kate breathed as she backed up, making her way toward the bed with his penis still in her hand.

Rafe stood while she sat on the edge of the bed, placed the condom on the tip, and rolled it onto him. She lay back on the bed then. Rafe bent and removed her panties.

"Very pretty, little pussy cat," he said.

Kate laughed and pulled him down for another kiss. "If you're not inside me in two seconds, I'm gonna scream."

"Baby, you're gonna scream anyway," Rafe said, and entered her.

Slick, wet, and throbbing, Kate took all of him easily. Gone were the days when she felt timid or uncertain of her sensuality. She knew she had the power to make his eyes roll back in his head and she loved doing it.

Thirteen

Kate tried to talk Sophie into coming out to the ranch to spend New Year's Eve with her, Rafe, and the rest of the Matthews clan. Sophie opted to drive to Phoenix and see the new year in with her parents. Sophie told her she'd spoken with Vance since the night of the class reunion. He'd told her he had formally apologized to Trudy for his behavior, and now the ball was in Sophie's court. Either she would forgive him and let him back in her life, or she could completely shut him out. He could not bear to be just a friend any longer.

Sophie told him she needed time to think.

With the new year came added work and responsibility for Kate. Her father seemed to return to the lab with added vigor, and his enthusiasm was contagious. Kate and the research assistants felt the energy coming off of him, and returned it in kind.

One morning in February, she and her father were making minute adjustments to one of the pods, which was approximately the size of a large microwave oven. The pod was well insulated so that when turned on, gamma rays could not escape.

They had the device atop one of the work counters and she was on one side of it while her father stood on the other. They'd been having trouble with the lock that sealed the door when it was shut. Both were in long white lab coats and wore opaque goggles. Kate was welding the lock in place while her father held the door steady.

Finished, she turned off the small butane torch.

She and her father were alone in the lab because the assistants hadn't arrived yet. They usually got there at around nine in the morning.

"Kate, do you remember the first time you took apart an appliance?" her father asked suddenly. He removed his goggles and smiled at her.

Kate reached over and turned off the gas on the torch for safety's sake, and then looked at him with a wistful smile on her face. "Two years old?"

"No, you were sixteen months old, and it was an old transistor radio I had in my office. You used to love being in my office. You'd steal things from all corners of it, take them underneath my desk, and stay there for hours fiddling with them. I never did get that radio together again. But I knew, watching you, that you had an inquisitive mind and that you were good with your hands. From then on no appliance in the house was safe from you. Thank goodness, when you were five or six, you started actually putting them back together again."

"I don't know why I was so fascinated with knowing what was inside things," Kate said, remembering. "I guess if a radio made a sound, I wanted to know why. It seemed like magic to me back then."

"Don't you feel that magic again?"

Kate thought he had a point. Working with him the past two months had been the hardest labor she'd ever done, without a doubt, but it was also very satisfying. She felt as though she was finally where she should be. And she supposed she felt that way because her life was in balance. She and her father were intent on making teleportation a household word, but she wasn't obsessed about it. She divided her time among work in the lab, Rafe, and her family. Her father had kept his word to her mother and he didn't work after nine-thirty P.M. So, his health wasn't suffering, and his mind was sharper than ever.

"I am pretty happy," Kate admitted.

"That's because you've found that happy medium, Kate," her father said. "You're using your God-given talents, *and* you're in love with Rafe."

"Good morning!" The lab assistants had arrived, bringing with them aromas of coffee and fresh-baked muffins.

Unwilling to let go of the private moment she and her father were sharing, Kate met his eyes. "You were right, Dad, I *can* do this!"

"I never had a doubt," said her father.

Sandra Abongane, a graduate student from South Africa, walked up to them. "I brought coffee and muffins for both of you," she said, smiling warmly.

"Thank you, Sandra," David said graciously.

From the adoring expression on Sandra's pretty brown face, it was easy to see she held him in high esteem.

"Thanks, Sandy," Kate said, accepting a cup of black coffee and a blueberry muffin.

The first day of Jason's trial arrived.

Kate had been called to testify. She had ambivalent feelings about testifying against Jason. Her father, not indecisive in the least, was leaning toward forgiving Jason for what he'd done.

Since his arrest, Jason had staunchly maintained that he hadn't stolen anything.

It had all been a ruse designed, he said, to get David back into the laboratory. And it had worked! He pointed out that had he chosen less criminal-minded associates who tried to extort money from the Matthewses after the practical joke had been pulled, none of them would be in this predicament.

He said the two men who had broken into the house had somehow destroyed the disks and the hard drive. He didn't know what they'd done with them. He certainly hadn't sold the information to a technologies company as it was rumored he had done.

So it was, as Kate and her father sat in the courtroom, that she began to wonder why Jason hadn't simply pleaded guilty because of insanity. His reasoning was definitely insane. He'd confessed to her that he'd sold the information to a company for two million dollars. Had he forgotten he'd told her that?

"I can't perjure myself, I have to tell the truth," she whispered to her father.

Both of them were dressed conservatively in dark suits, Kate in a skirt suit and her father in a three-piece suit complete with a vest. Kate wore her hair in a wavy chignon and tiny pearl studs in her ears.

"Tell the truth, Kate. Tell the truth as you see it. Remember him for what he was to you for many years, a loving godfather who doted on you. Isn't it possible that he momentarily lost his mind?"

Her father's words were rewinding in her mind after she was called to the stand.

Reporters and photographers were present because this was the most sensational story to hit the college community in some time. Plus, it had international undertones due to the nature of Dr. David Matthews's work. The courtroom was packed with spectators.

Kate sat down after she was sworn in.

The judge gestured to the prosecutor to begin his questioning.

The prosecutor was dark-haired and intense. Trim, with angular features, his eyes held very little warmth, not even for Kate, who could help him win his case with her testimony.

"Would you state your name and occupation for the record?" he asked.

"Katharine Matthews. I'm a physicist, and I'm currently working with my father, Dr. David Matthews, on a project at the University of Arizona."

"Dr. Matthews, what is your relationship with the defendant?"

"Dr. Edmonton is my godfather."

"Your godfather. And your father's best friend, am I correct?"

"Yes."

The prosecutor turned to regard the jury and said dramatically, "Making his crime that much more heinous!"

He turned back around to look Kate in the eyes. "Dr. Matthews, in a statement you gave the police following your abduction by Dr. Edmonton, you said he'd told you that he'd sold your father's notes to an unnamed company for two million dollars, did you not?"

"Yes, I did," said Kate. "But I'd like to add that Jason was not himself when he said it."

"I move that the witness's last comments be struck from the record, Your Honor," said the prosecutor.

"I'm interested in Dr. Matthews's opinion of Dr. Edmonton's state of mind when he committed these crimes, Mr. Prosecutor; therefore I will allow her freedom to speak."

"I must protest, Your Honor. Dr. Matthews doesn't hold a degree in psychology. She is a physicist."

"Nevertheless, I'd like to hear what Dr. Matthews has to say, so please allow the witness to continue," the judge suggested with quiet authority. "Go ahead, Dr. Matthews."

"I've known Dr. Jason Edmonton all my life, Your Honor. He was open, charming, gregarious. All of the

Matthews children loved him when we were growing up. His work relationship with my father was reciprocal in nature. He supported my father in every way conceivable, making the way clear for my dad to work without needless red tape. You could say they were a team. When my father got sick and the future of that team ever working together again was at risk, I think Dr. Edmonton suffered a nervous breakdown, and he went to extreme lengths because of his diminished thinking. My father also believes that's what happened. We're not asking that everything be forgiven. The meting out of justice is not up to us, it's up to the court, but we ask that you be lenient because of his state of mind during the execution of his misdeeds."

"Very well said," the judge commented after some consideration. He looked at the prosecutor. "You may resume your questioning now."

When the prosecutor was finished questioning Kate, he called her father to the stand. However, before David could get out of his seat, the defense attorney rose and cleared her throat. "Your Honor, my client would like to change his plea."

Excited murmuring sprang up in the courtroom.

"Silence in my courtroom!" bellowed the judge.

Everyone quieted down.

"Go ahead, counselor. Exactly what would your client like to change his plea to?"

The defense attorney, a young African-American woman with her black hair in dreadlocks, said, "Your Honor, in light of what has been said by the prosecutor's first witness, my client would like to change his plea to guilty."

The spectators once again raised their voices in agitated speculation.

"Silence!" the judge ordered. "The next person who says a word will be held in contempt of court and jailed."

Only the sound of papers being shuffled by the prosecutor could be heard in the courtroom.

The judge directed his comments to the defendant's attorney. "Would your client like to explain why he has chosen to change his plea at this late date?"

"Your Honor, my client feels regret for what he has done. And to prove his sincerity, he would like to reveal the name of the company that purchased Dr. Matthews's notes from him."

"This is outrageous!" cried the prosecutor. "If Dr. Edmonton thinks he can plea-bargain his way out of this, he is sadly mistaken!"

"Perhaps," the judge said, "you have forgotten that this is my courtroom, Mr. Prosecutor, and you are not to speak unless I tell you to. Please sit down or I will hold you in contempt of court!"

Eyes narrowed, nostrils flaring, pulse thundering in his ears, the prosecutor sat. He didn't relish spending any time in the lockup, possibly with criminals he'd personally sent to jail.

"Now, counselor," the judge said, satisfied that he wouldn't be interrupted by the prosecutor, "this is a most unusual request. Has your client thought of the consequences of changing his plea to guilty?"

"He has, Your Honor. If it would please the court, my client would like to make a statement."

"Go right ahead," the judge said, his interest level high.

Kate squeezed her father's hand reassuringly as Jason stood. He had grasped her hand when Jason's attorney announced he was changing his plea. Kate, too, felt anxious. Nearly two months in jail seemed to have changed Jason both physically and emotionally. He'd lost weight, and he looked haggard. Despite one of his best suits, he was disheveled. Kate thought perhaps it was his de-

meanor that made him appear so. Gone was his bound-
less self-confidence.

He rose slowly and faced the judge. "Your Honor, I
willfully, and with malicious intent, stole research from
Dr. David Matthews. I did it for the money. I did it because I'm a middle-aged paper pusher who had no
prospects whatsoever of achieving the kind of greatness
Dr. David Matthews is capable of. I did it because I ulti-
mately valued an easy life over my friendship with Dr.
Matthews and his family. I can't honestly say whether I
would have or would not have done what I did if Dr.
Matthews had not fallen ill. I would like to think it
wouldn't have occurred to me if I hadn't become afraid
that my plans for fame through the achievements of Dr.
Matthews and my department had fallen through. It ap-
pears that that was what precipitated my actions, but, like
I said, I can't state emphatically that that's the case. At
any rate, I deserve whatever punishment is coming to
me."

He looked at Kate and David. "I would also like to say
I'm sorry to Dr. Matthews and his family, especially Dr.
Katharine Matthews, whom I took hostage in an attempt
to escape."

His eyes were glassy as he held David's gaze across the
courtroom. Kate, still holding her father's hand, placed
her other one atop it. Her father had tears in his eyes.

"Thank you, Dr. Edmonton, you may sit down," the
judge said curtly.

Everyone sat in silence for at least a minute during
which time the judge twirled his gavel in his hand and
looked out over the courtroom. Then he cleared his
throat and spoke: "After more than thirty years on the
bench, I am still amazed by human avarice. Of course
avarice is solely a human desire. No dog ever turned on
another for a quick buck. However, what I was dumb-

founded by this morning is the ability of the human spirit to run the gamut from avarice to altruism. Dr. Matthews's decision to forgive his former best friend speaks well of humankind."

He looked at Jason. "Dr. Edmonton, because the people you wronged are willing to forgive you, and you have changed your plea to guilty, I have decided that you will spend five years in prison for taking Dr. Matthews against her will, and two years for stealing the senior Dr. Matthews's notes. I'm only giving you two years on that count because you've agreed to disclose to whom you sold Dr. Matthews's work. That is my judgment. Court is dismissed!"

Kate noticed a young woman and then two other people pop out of their seats and leave the courtroom. She figured they were reporters rushing to beat their competitors to a front-page story.

Her father rose. "I want to say something to him," he said, moving purposely down the row. Kate followed him, saying, "Excuse us, please" to people as they stepped around them to get to Jason before he could be taken away by the bailiffs.

At last, David and Jason stood in front of each other.

David held out his hand. "Good luck, old man."

Jason gratefully grasped David's hand. "Thank you, David."

And that was all. The bailiff, a young Native American, led Jason away.

Kate did the same with her father.

She was glad it was over, and even happier that the other two defendants, Stephen Erwin and Martin Penichiero, had pleaded guilty. There would be no testifying in courtrooms in the foreseeable future.

* * *

March blew in like a lamb rather than the proverbial lion. Temperatures got up to seventy-two during the day and plummeted to the lower forties at night. One Saturday night, Kate and Rafe were sleeping in each other's arms when Kate's phone rang.

She'd started leaving it on the nightstand on her side of the bed. She barely opened her eyes as she picked it up and answered, "Kate."

"There are triangles moving toward Tucson. Right now they're over Mount Lemmon; soon they'll be over the Catalinas if they continue in their present trajectory."

"Clive?"

"You know it. How've you been, sugar?"

Rafe sat up in bed and rubbed his eyes. Kate imagined that her saying another man's name had awakened him.

"I've been great, and you?" Kate said.

"Good, good," Clive King, an astronomer from Phoenix and a longtime friend of Kate's, said. "So, are you coming out? We could all meet up in the desert and wait for them."

"Jody still with you, or have you broken up again?" Kate asked. Now, she really had Rafe's attention.

"She's still with me. She'll be coming. She can't wait to see you. Someone told her you were engaged. Is it true?"

"Yeah, it's true."

"Bring him with you."

Kate paused.

"Oh," said Clive. "You haven't told him about this part of your life."

"I've told him. I don't think he believed me, though. Look, if I can make it, what are the coordinates?"

Clive hurriedly gave her the coordinates. Kate memorized them and said, "Thanks, Clive, give Jody a big hug for me."

"Come and give it to her yourself," Clive said good-naturedly, and hung up.

Kate pressed the off button on the cell phone and smiled at Rafe. "Remember that time I told you I belonged to a group that tracked UFOs?"

Rafe sat up farther in bed. His chest was bare, as they'd taken to wearing one pair of pajamas between them. Kate thought he was at his absolute sexiest when he was awakened out of a sound sleep. She wanted to put her arms around his neck, pull him on top of her, and make love to him, but she also wanted to check out what Clive had just told her. It had been nearly two years since she had been part of a tracking party. She missed the sense of wonder and excitement at seeing those bright lights in the night sky.

"That was your call in the middle of the night?" Rafe asked, remembering that she'd said the calls usually came in the middle of the night.

"That was it," Kate confirmed. "Wanna come with me?"

"You're going?"

"If I can borrow your truck. Otherwise I'd have to go home first and get Mom's. The Camry is not suited for desert detail."

"Sure, I'll come," Rafe said, not sounding very enthusiastic.

"It'll be fun, really," Kate said as she climbed out of bed and went into the bathroom for a quick shower. "Come on, join me in the shower. It'll wake us up."

Yawning, Rafe asked, "What time is it anyway?"

"Three-thirty!" Kate called over her shoulder.

After a very quick shower, they dressed and hurried out the door. "I'll drive," said Kate. She knew exactly where the others would be, and with traffic on I-10 at a minimum, she could get there in about twenty-five minutes.

There wasn't any moon to speak of tonight, but the sky was blanketed by stars.

"March is a very active month for them for some reason," Kate said as she backed the truck out of the driveway and put it in drive.

"Are you all sure they're not experimental aircraft the air force doesn't want you to know about?"

"Could be," Kate admitted. "However, the air force seems to be as clueless as we are as to the identity of the craft. I once saw several A-10 fighter aircraft trying their best to keep up with a triangle; that's what we call the newer craft that started appearing around 1998. To be honest they move so fast sometimes we can't really tell what shape they are, but they have lights underneath at points that form a triangle, so we call them triangles. I've also seen a teardrop-shaped craft that flew so low over us, we could practically read the numbers on it, if it had had any. It was completely silent, which freaked me out more than anything else. Something that big, that can move that fast, but can hang suspended in the air too, made no sound. How did it propel itself? What kind of engine did it have?"

"Kate, you're going eighty in a fifty-five-mile-per-hour zone."

Kate eased up on the accelerator.

"Okay, sweetness, I'm going along with you on this but, believe me, there is a perfectly reasonable explanation for these sightings."

"Well," Kate said, "I wish someone would explain them to me."

As they were nearing the coordinates Clive had given her they heard several aircraft flying overhead. Rafe got the first inkling that there might be something to what Kate had been telling him.

"They've come to investigate," Kate told him, not surprised by the aircraft's presence. "They've taken to listening in on our radio transmissions. We're kooks to them, but still they monitor our communications."

"Gotta know what you kooks are up to," Rafe said cynically.

Kate didn't say anything. She used to be a cynic, too. There was nothing like your first sighting to make you a true believer. Then, it didn't matter what anyone said, you knew what you'd seen, and no one could talk you out of it.

"The good thing about the military aircraft being in the sky is that if something more alien shows up, you'll be able to compare the way they both move relative to each other."

Kate slowed the truck and turned off onto a desert road. Two miles later, she turned again. Going slower than before, she put on her bright lights. The deeper they went in the desert, the darker it became. There were no city lights or even lights from nearby houses to help illuminate the deep blackness of the desert.

In the distance, Rafe saw several other vehicles parked in a huge circle. In the center of the circle someone had built a fire, and around the fire stood or sat about thirty people. One of the vehicles was a large white RV. It had a satellite dish on top that was slowly repositioning itself.

"We're here," Kate announced. She parked the Expedition in a space in the circle that appeared to have been left for her. She smiled at the notion. Clive must have known she wouldn't be able to resist coming.

"Hullo, Kate!" It was Clive, as big and boisterous as he'd always been.

Clive was in his sixties. He was descended from Viking ancestors, and he looked it. His long, thick hair was still more blond than gray and he wore it in a single braid down his back. Six feet three and thick around the middle, he usually wore jeans, western shirts, and keen-toed boots. His girlfriend, Jody, was African-American. She was in her late forties. A statuesque beauty with doe-eyes and skin the color of caramel. She wore her black hair in braids. She was right beside her man.

Clive lifted Kate in a bear hug. "It's been too long!"

"Nearly two years," Kate said. She gave him a kiss on his cheek. Then she was hugging Jody. Jody squeezed her tightly. "How are you, baby girl?" she asked in her southern-accented voice.

"Really good," Kate said. She gestured to Rafe. "I want you two to meet my fiancé, Rafael Grant. Rafe, this is Clive King and Jody Stovall. They're very good people with whom I've been sky-watching since I was eighteen."

"Hello, Rafe," Clive said, vigorously shaking Rafe's hand. "It's a pleasure to meet you. Glad you let Kate twist your arm into coming out. Maybe your presence will bring us good luck."

"Good to meet you, Rafe," Jody said, giving his hand a firm shake. "And congrats on your upcoming marriage. We're partial to her, but we don't think you could have chosen better."

"Thank you," said Rafe, liking both of them immediately. "I couldn't agree more."

Kate and Rafe accepted the lawn chairs Clive had gone to his RV to get for them, and they joined the rest of the group around the campfire in the center of their makeshift "circling of the wagons," a western tradition.

As was their custom on these nights, as they waited for their alien brothers to put in an appearance they told stories of previous sightings. After everyone had welcomed Kate and Rafe, they continued telling stories. Rafe looked around at the group. There were mostly Caucasians present, but there were also a few African-

Americans, Mexican-Americans, Native Americans, and one Asian-American.

The woman speaking now was Caucasian and in her mid-thirties. A man was standing next to her with his hand on her shoulder. He was Native American. "The first time I saw one was in 1998 when I was living in Phoenix. We've all heard about the Phoenix Lights that they're now saying were flares. Anyway, George"—she affectionately touched the Native American man's hand that was on her shoulder—"and I were driving from Prescott and we saw them fly overhead and disappear in the southwest. Then, when we got to Phoenix, we saw them again coming from the north, fly over Phoenix, and go southeast. Twice in one night. Both at times when Davis-Monthan Air Force Base claimed the flares had not even been dropped. So, I never believed their flare story."

"But," she continued, "that wasn't the first time I'd ever heard of them. My grandparents saw them over Tucson back in 1949. Hundreds of people saw crafts then, not just lights. They kept the newspaper article from the *Daily Press* documenting the sighting. Both my grandparents are gone now, but they're the reason I believe in the phenomenon. If craft were behaving as they described back in 1949, then there must be something otherworldly to this. We didn't have that kind of technology back then."

"We don't have it now," Clive said, and they all laughed.

Suddenly a loud beep began issuing from somewhere inside the RV. "Get ready, children," Clive said, running toward the RV, climbing the steps, and disappearing inside.

Rafe watched in amazement as everyone returned to their individual trucks. Then he saw what they were doing. They were getting their cameras, video cameras, and microphones ready. That beeping sound must have meant they'd gotten a bite on their detecting equipment.

Kate took his hand. "Come on, we're gonna sit atop Clive's RV with him and Jody. I don't have any equipment with me tonight. If I'd been at home when I'd gotten the call I would have had my video camera with me, too."

Jody and Clive were already on the top of the RV, which had a steel boundary built all around the roof. It was like sitting on your deck.

"Lights to the east," Jody yelled.

She handed Rafe and Kate spare pairs of binoculars. The two immediately looked in the direction she'd indicated.

The lights in the sky were only more fighter aircraft, though. Three of them, flying in a triangle formation, heading west.

"That's not them," Kate said.

Rafe could see that for himself. He'd seen aircraft like these many times before.

He kept looking at the sky. Out of the corner of his eye, he saw a faintly glowing green light. Light green; he, at first, assumed it was a spot on the binoculars. Then he saw another light aft the green light. It was red and very bright, no dimness whatsoever. "What is that?" he asked.

Kate trained her binoculars on the sight. "I think we may have something," she said. Clive pointed his video camera and started shooting. "It's one of them, all right! And look behind it: three more!"

Rafe could not pull his eyes away from the sight. He now knew why these people believed these craft were from elsewhere in the universe. They moved so smoothly it was as if they were gliding in the air. They had to be huge. How large, he couldn't tell, but the scale had to be significant for him to be able to see them so clearly. All of them seemed to glow in the dark with a green-white light. Multicolored lights ran along the perimeter of each craft. They appeared to be in no hurry. Where the fighter aircraft had zoomed past in no time, these craft moseyed along at a much slower pace.

It was as if they were aware they were being watched and were putting on a show. Rafe gasped when the lead craft doubled in size. It had happened so quickly he thought he might be experiencing an optical illusion, but soon the other three craft grew in size too.

"Have you ever seen any of our aircraft do that?" Kate asked.

"No, can't say that I have," Rafe said, really impressed. "But they could still be experimental aircraft that the air force does not want us to know about. Maybe they take advantage of the fact that there are people out here looking for UFOs, and whenever you all report a sighting, no one believes you. It's a sneaky but effective way to keep their secrets."

"You could be right," Kate said. "But, on the other hand, you could be wrong."

The strange aircraft reverted to their smaller sizes, turned until the red light that had been aft each of them was now pointed upward. Then, in a flash, they were gone from sight.

"Damn!" said Rafe. "Where'd they go?"

Kate lowered her binoculars. "Back to the air force base?"

She knew she had him. He could not believe that mankind had the technology to move that fast.

"That was really freaky," said Rafe, his voice awe-filled.

"We've got another one!" exclaimed Clive, welcoming Rafe to the fold.

* * *

Later, on the drive back to Rafe's house, Kate was quieter than usual. Rafe drove this time and he was staying within the speed limit. Kate sat close to him with her head on his shoulder. "You're not asleep, are you?" he asked.

"No, just thinking."

"About what?"

"About how much we've shared in the short time we've been together. I'm so happy, it makes me nervous that something bad is going to happen."

Rafe laughed. "I never thought you could have a fatalistic bone in your body. Not you, the lady who believes we're being visited by benign aliens with very fast ships."

Kate laughed too. "They kick butt, don't they?"

"Lots of butt kicking was going on tonight."

"Then you believe?"

"I'm keeping an open mind," said Rafe.

"That's the way I feel about it," Kate said. "If it's our technology, I want to know about it. If it's not ours, I want to know about it, too."

"Look at those stars," Rafe said. "I guess you're right, Kate. It would be presumptuous of us to assume we're the only intelligent life in the universe."

Kate snuggled even closer to him and sighed with contentment. Yet another reason to love this man. He didn't just have thighs that could crush walnuts between them, he was *deep*, too.

Fourteen

"You cannot get married at the courthouse!" Carolina said, aghast. "Do you know how long I've been saving for your wedding, young lady? Twenty-nine years! Ever since you were born. You have over thirty thousand dollars sitting in the bank right now."

"What?" Kate said, her turn to be taken aback.

It was a Sunday morning in April and she, her parents, and Davida were having a leisurely breakfast.

Kate sipped her coffee and met her mother's eyes across the table. "Put it in Little David's wedding fund, Mama. Rafe and I want a simple wedding. The simpler, the better. Family and a few friends. I don't want the expensive dress and all the frills."

Frowning, Carolina appealed to her husband. "David, talk some sense into your daughter. Explain to her that a wedding is a once-in-a-lifetime event. Explain to her that when she's old and gray she's going to regret not having her big day when she had the chance!"

"We didn't have a big wedding and we turned out just fine," David said.

Carolina angrily blew air between her lips. "Little David, help me out here."

"I agree with Kate," Davida said, disappointing her mother. "I'm never getting married. I'm going to live in the forest and study the behavior of chimpanzees."

"You do that, Little David," Carolina said, knowing Davida changed her dreams and aspirations as often as she changed her clothes. "If you're still intent on becoming a primate-watcher when you turn eighteen and you go to college and get your degree in anthropology or zoology, upon your graduation I will buy you a ticket to any jungle in the world."

"Africa," Davida said. "I want to study the chimpanzees of equatorial Africa."

"Wonderful," David said. "I'm glad to see you've done your research."

"So am I," Carolina said. "But we're discussing Kate at the moment."

Kate, for her part, was glad Davida had taken the heat off of her. "Mama, you know the wedding date Rafe and I have chosen: Saturday, May twenty-second. That gives us six weeks to pull our plans together. You can't plan a big wedding in that length of time."

"Never say never, sweetie," Carolina said. "We can plan a fabulous wedding in two weeks, let alone six weeks. Come on, Kate. Let's try to reach a happy compromise. Is it Rafe who doesn't want anything lavish, or is it you?"

"Neither of us wants all the fuss," Kate answered sincerely. "The only thing that's important to us is that we become husband and wife as soon as possible."

"Why can't we do both?" Carolina said. Her eyes held a determined glint. "How about a wedding here at the ranch? I'll have a gazebo built. The backyard will look festive but understated, since you and Rafe want things kept simple. We'll invite a hundred guests instead of the three hundred I was hoping for. And I'll hire a photographer to chronicle your special day. Don't tell me you were thinking of not having pictures taken!"

Kate had to admit, her mother made a good case for

not getting married at the courthouse. She *would* regret not having pictures commemorating their wedding day.

"All right," she said at last. "I'll talk to Rafe about it."

Carolina got up, came around the table, and threw her arms around Kate's neck. "Splendid! I'll get on it today, right after breakfast. Believe me, sweetie, you won't regret it."

"A backyard wedding?" Rafe said that night over dinner at his place. "The temps can reach the low nineties in May. Hopefully, this will be a morning wedding."

"Definitely," Kate said.

"I have no objections," Rafe said. "It would be nice to see you in a wedding gown."

This was new to Kate. "I thought you wanted things kept simple."

"I thought that's what *you* wanted, darlin'. I can go either way," Rafe told her.

"Well, okay," Kate said. "I'll get a gown, a short gown, and you'll wear a suit."

"And a minister will marry us," Rafe insisted.

"Yes, a minister. Baptist? Catholic?"

"Doesn't matter."

Kate had no preference either. "I'll let Mama choose. She'll love that." Rafe smiled at her. They were sitting in the dining room. Kate wore a short, sleeveless sheath in sky blue. Her hair was up. Rafe wore black dress slacks, and a gray polo shirt. Kate loved to watch his biceps move in his arm each time he brought the fork to his mouth.

"It's her first daughter's wedding. She's excited about it," Rafe said reasonably.

"Thanks for being so understanding," Kate said.

"I like your family, Kate. It's a good thing because I'm not just marrying you, I'm marrying into the family. I know what that means, and I welcome it. Jenny and I haven't had much of a family for a long time. Now, she's a wife and going to be a mother. I'm soon to be a husband. I'm ready for the changes to come."

They'd finished their meal and had pushed their plates aside, enjoying conversation and being together at the end of the day. Kate now stood and walked around to his side of the table, sat on his lap, and wrapped her arms around his neck.

Rafe inhaled the light, flowery scent of her cologne and placed his arm about her waist. Kate had kicked off her shoes. She wasn't wearing panty hose, and her coppery brown expanse of shapely legs and thighs drew his gaze. "Did I ever tell you how much I like looking at your big legs?"

"Big?" Kate said, pretending hurt. She knew what he meant. Southern men, especially, had this thing about a shapely pair of legs. They liked fleshy legs with feminine curves, not legs that were shaped straight up and down. No stick legs for them. Give them a little meat on the bones.

"Throw your big leg over me, Mama, I might not feel this good again." Rafe sang a verse from "Cakewalk Into Town" by Taj Mahal.

"You know I can't resist you when you sing to me," Kate said. "You'll have me naked in no time."

"That's the plan," said Rafe, his hand up her dress. Kate smiled when he discovered she wasn't wearing any underwear.

"Young lady, where are your panties?" Rafe asked sternly.

"On your bed," Kate told him, kissing his chin, his cheeks, and the tip of his nose, which showed no signs of her attack in October of last year. "I put them there when I went into your bedroom for this." She reached inside her cleavage and produced a condom.

"Ah, Kate, my ever-inventive student. You're full of surprises."

"And the crotch of your pants is full of something else," Kate said saucily.

Rafe reached up, grabbed her behind the neck, and drew her down for a long, wet kiss. During the kiss, Kate straddled him.

Breaking off the kiss, Rafe unzipped his pants. "I'm gonna have to get up for a second, babe," he said of his desire to pull his pants down.

Kate got off his lap. He rose, pulled down his pants, and stepped out of them, kicking them aside. Kate took it from there, going to him, pressing the full length of her body to his, and grabbing his buns through his boxer-briefs. "As long as I live, I'll never get enough of you."

She felt his penis against her crotch straining to be released from his briefs. Reaching down, she lowered the front of his briefs and took him in her hand. He was long, hard, thick, and throbbing. Kate felt weak with desire.

Rafe sighed, her hands felt so good on him.

Kate sat on the chair and rolled the condom onto him. Rafe removed his briefs and switched places with Kate. She stood and slowly guided his penis deep inside her.

Rafe held her naked hips in his big hands. Kate reached behind her and unzipped her dress. Rafe pulled it over her head, and she took it and tossed it onto one of the dining room chairs. Then she twisted a bit and Rafe undid the clasps on her bra. She let that fall to the floor.

"I'll never be able to eat in here again without blushing," Kate said as his mouth descended upon her nipple.

* * *

In early May the plans for the wedding were in full swing. Jenny phoned to say baby, Victoria Rose, had been born at one twenty-one A.M. on Monday, May 3. Rafe noted that she'd named her new daughter after their mother and their maternal grandmother, respectively.

Kate had lunch with Sophie one Saturday and Sophie told her Vance was going to escort her and Renata to the wedding. "I had to start being brutally honest with myself, Kate," she'd said. "I like Vance. He isn't perfect. I'm not perfect, either. Do you know how many imperfect people have established perfectly happy lives together?"

"Every happy couple I've ever known," Kate had replied.

As for her work with her father, things couldn't have been better on that front.

She would never forget the morning of Friday, May 14. The morning of the sighting of a special *flying saucer*.

The time had come for the fourth trial run of the pods. They'd gone through three previous trials that had left them puzzled but still optimistic that they must be close to something, and that the "something" was within their ability to discover it, integrate it into the mix, and finally make the experiment work.

For this particular trial run, the head of the physics department, Dr. Teresa Andrews, asked to be present. Like everyone in the department, she was pulling for Dr. Matthews and thought being there for his next trial run would bring him good luck.

So there were six people standing behind the glass partition wearing shaded goggles when David threw the switch. In the next room, the two pods sat on a counter six feet apart and connected by cables. Spherical, the pods had a circumference of forty-six inches. Black, they resembled two very large bowling balls when the doors on them were closed. Built in the center of each pod was a tray. Inside one pod sat a clay saucer. Although baked in an oven until hard, it was unglazed and, therefore, more porous.

The object of the experiment was to transfer the molecules of the clay saucer from one pod to the other one.

"Here we go," David said, and threw the switch.

Kate stood beside him, her eyes trained on the saucer sitting in the first pod. Nothing happened. Then, the red clay saucer began to float apart. As if magically lifted on air, the parts looked to Kate like the molecules of blood as seen through a microscope. Soon, the parts broke even farther apart and blue-white light appeared from nowhere, saturating the molecules until they became an explosion of light. An instant later, the lights, the molecules, the saucer all disappeared. Kate moved her gaze to the second pod. Inside it, the light appeared, and gradually turned into the red clay molecules, which congealed into the saucer. The saucer had teleported over to the other pod!

Pandemonium erupted in the laboratory. Everyone was jumping up and down, hugging each other, yelling, dancing, laughing, and crying simultaneously.

Kate hugged her father tightly. "You did it, Dad, you did it!"

"*We* did it, Kate," he said and hugged her again.

Carolina had hired a wedding planner to take care of all the little details she might have forgotten. She had not broken her promise to Kate, however. Everything from the decorations to the menu of the dinner at the reception to be held at the Hyatt Regency in town was a study in simple elegance.

The backyard's lawn was so well kept it resembled a thick, green carpet. The large gazebo was painted white and on either sides of it chairs, also white, were lined up ten chairs across, and ten chairs deep. Therefore the number of guests had been kept at one hundred. A red carpet ran between the chairs, all the way up the steps of the gazebo.

Father Alfonso Ballesteros stood behind the podium in the gazebo, now, in his full priestly raiment. Next to him Rafe stood in a beautiful black tuxedo. His best friend, and fellow deputy marshal, Ethan Brooks, was standing up for him. Ethan had flown in from Philadelphia the night before and he, Kent, and David Jr. had joined Rafe and some of the Tucson marshals in an impromptu bachelor party. Some of them had fuzzy heads this morning. Rafe, however, was clearheaded and eager to see his bride-to-be.

The Huerta women had kept her away from him for the past three days with dress fittings, a wedding shower, and myriad other excuses. At this point, he was nervous with anticipation.

Music floated on the still-cool morning air. Rafe looked up and saw Renata walking down the aisle, an angel in pale pink, leaving rose petals in her wake. Behind her was Sophie, lovely in pale blue, a bouquet of flowers held in her hands. Next came Davida, radiant in pale yellow, also holding a bouquet of pastel flowers. Jenny bought up the rear, attired in lavender, still carrying a few extra pregnancy pounds but radiant nonetheless.

The wedding march began.

Rafe's eyes never left their spot. When Kate appeared on her father's arm, resplendent in off-white, he sucked in air. She was a vision out of his wildest dreams. Her mounds of hair fell in soft curls down her back. The dress's hem fell about two inches above her knees. It was tight enough to embrace her flaring hips and show off her small waist. Sleeveless, the dress had a scoop neck that dipped modestly, revealing a hint of cleavage. The train was slightly longer than the dress itself.

She was definitely worth waiting for. He didn't feel so irritated at the Huerta women for keeping her from him anymore.

The minister began the ceremony: "We are gathered here today to unite these two people in holy matrimony . . ."

". . . I now pronounce you husband and wife. You may kiss the bride."

When you've kept the bride-to-be and the groom-to-be apart for three days you should not expect a chaste kiss after the ceremony. That was the lesson the Huerta women learned on that fine May day. Because Rafe and Kate kissed, and kissed, and kissed some more.

Laughing uproariously, Carolina thought, seriously, of turning the hose on them.

Dear Reader,

I hope you've enjoyed Kate and Rafe's story. As some of you know, I've been known to delve into science fiction. *Desert Heat* can be classified as a science fiction romance due to its subject matter, quantum physics. Teleportation is not possible today, but it's in our not-too-distant future. For more information on black physicists, please check out Physicists of the African Diaspora on-line at http://www.math.buffalo.edu/mad/physics/physics-timeline.html. I think you'll be pleasantly surprised.

If you like the science fiction aspects of my writing, please check out my 1998 book, *Out of the Blue*.

You may write me at P.O. Box 811, Mascotte, FL 34753-0811. Or leave a message for me on my Web site at http://www.janicesims.com.

Until next time, keep turning those pages!

Janice Sims